DUCK THE HALLS

A MEG LANGSLOW MYSTERY

DUCK THE HALLS

DONNA ANDREWS

THORNDIKE PRESS
A part of Gale, Cengage Learning

GALE
CENGAGE Learning®

Detroit • New York • San Francisco • New Haven, Conn • Waterville, Maine • London

GALE
CENGAGE Learning®

Thorndike Press® Large Print Mystery.
The text of this Large Print edition is unabridged.
Other aspects of the book may vary from the original edition.
Set in 16 pt. Plantin.

LIBRARY OF CONGRESS CATALOGING-IN-PUBLICATION DATA

Andrews, Donna.
 Duck the halls : a Meg Langslow mystery / by Donna Andrews. — Large print edition.
  pages ; cm. — (Thorndike Press large print mystery)
  ISBN 978-1-4104-6428-6 (hardcover) — ISBN 1-4104-6428-8 (hardcover)
 1. Langslow, Meg (Fictitious character)—Fiction.
 2. Murder—Investigation—Fiction. 3. Large type books. I. Title.
 PS3551.N4165D83 2013b
 813'.54—dc23   2013030307

Published in 2013 by arrangement with St. Martin's Press, LLC.

ACKNOWLEDGMENTS

Thanks, as always, to everyone at St. Martins/Minotaur including (but not limited to) Matt Baldacci, Anne Brewer, Hector DeJean, Kymberlee Giacoppe, Lauren Hesse, Andrew Martin, Sarah Melnyk, Matthew Shear, and my editor, Pete Wolverton. And thanks again to the Art Department for yet another fabulous (and very Christmassy) cover.

More thanks to my agent, Ellen Geiger, and the staff at the Frances Goldin Literary Agency for handling the boring (to me) practical stuff so I can focus on writing, and to Dave Barbor at Curtis Brown for taking Meg abroad.

Many thanks to the friends — writers and readers alike — who brainstorm and critique with me, give me good ideas, or help keep me sane while I'm writing: Stuart, Elke, Aidan, and Liam Andrews, Renee Brown, Erin Bush, Carla Coupe, Meriah

Crawford, Ellen Crosby, Kathy Deligianis, Laura Durham, Suzanne Frisbee, John Gilstrap, Barb Goffman, Peggy Hansen, C. Ellett Logan, David Niemi, Alan Orloff, Valerie Patterson, Shelley Shearer, Art Taylor, Robin Templeton, Dina Willner, and Sandi Wilson. Thanks for all kinds of moral support and practical help to my blog sisters and brother at the Femmes Fatales: Dana Cameron, Charlaine Harris, Dean James, Toni L.P. Kelner, Catriona McPherson, Kris Neri, Hank Phillippi Ryan, Mary Saums, Marcia Talley, and Elaine Viets. And thanks to all the TeaBuds for years of friendship.

Three characters in the book were named in honor of real people. Charlie Gardner's sister, B. G. Ritts, made a generous donation to benefit literacy at the Bouchercon auction to win the right to have her brother in the book. Robyn Smith, the Episcopalian rector, is named after a longtime reader who could recite plots, characters, and dialogues from the Meg books. About the time I was starting this book, Robyn died after a long illness, and her friend and fellow reader Ginnie Schoepf asked if there was any possibility I could mention Robyn in a future book. As luck would have it, I was just looking around for a name to give Caerphilly's new Episcopalian rector. And my friend Joni Langevoort answered all my questions about things Episcopalian — I still wish I could have seen the look on Father Rick's face when she asked him what he'd do if they found a dead body in the basement of Holy Comforter. In return for all her help, and at Joni's suggestion, I named the retired rector of Trinity Episcopal Dr. Rufus J. Womble in honor of the priest who baptized her. As always, any resemblance between the characters and the real people after whom they were named is purely coincidental.

CHAPTER 1

The buzzing noise woke me from an already restless sleep. In my dream, it was Christmas morning. We were opening presents and all the boxes I'd wrapped so neatly had suddenly become empty. Or worse, they contained odd, inappropriate objects, like bottles of vodka for my four-year-old twin sons and a subscription to *Guns & Ammo* for my cousin Rose Noire, who couldn't even stand to see anyone use a flyswatter for its intended purpose.

"What interesting choices," Mother was murmuring, holding up the power drill that had been in her box. Where had the drill come from? And why did she keep turning it on and off, on and off, making that irritating noise?

Just then I woke up. I fumbled on my bedside table for my phone. It was a little past 4:00 A.M. December twenty-first, not the twenty-fifth.

"Only a dream," I murmured.

The buzzing wasn't coming from my phone and I could still hear it. Not a power drill. It appeared to be coming from Michael's side of the bed, from under the pillow. Some battery-operated toy, perhaps, that the boys had dropped while Michael had been reading them *How the Grinch Stole Christmas* before bedtime?

Michael stirred.

"Blast." His voice was sleepy and annoyed. Then he sat bolt upright and began searching frantically under his pillow.

"What is it?" I asked.

"My pager." He found the offending object, pressed something, and the buzzing stopped. A female voice took its place.

"Box fourteen oh four for the structure fire. One thirteen Clay County Road. Engine companies fourteen and two, truck twelve, rescue squad two, ambulance fourteen respond. Oh four fourteen."

I recognized the voice of Debbie Ann, the local police and emergency dispatcher. And the "oh four fourteen" part must be the time. As for the rest —

"We have a call!" Michael sounded excited and leaped out of bed.

My stomach clenched. Ever since Michael, in a burst of civic zeal, had joined the

10

Caerphilly Volunteer Firefighters, I'd been dreading this moment. The pager had been his constant companion since he'd finished his training a week ago. And now here it was: His first fire.

The address sounded familiar, too. I had the feeling if I were a little more awake, I'd remember exactly what was located at 113 Clay County Road.

Michael dove into the walk-in closet.

"Maybe you should wake Rob," he called over his shoulder.

"Doesn't he have a pager, too?"

"You know Rob."

Yes. My brother — also a newly fledged firefighter — was capable of sleeping with a brass band rehearsing at the foot of his bed. I got up and winced when my feet hit the cold floor. It was in the twenties outside, and didn't seem much warmer inside. Not a night for running around barefoot or in pajamas. I threw on my clothes, then raced out into the hall, and headed up the stairs to the third floor of our overlarge Victorian farmhouse, where my brother lived in one of our many spare rooms.

On my way upstairs I passed my cousin Rose Noire who occupied yet another third-floor spare room.

"Rob's awake," she said. "His pager woke

me from across the hall, so I woke him. I'll make them some coffee."

I could hear thuds and exclamations from down the hall. Rob was in motion. Had the noise awakened my twin sons? They'd only recently moved to separate bedrooms. Although it had been their own request and they were vastly proud of their new solo lairs, they were both still a little anxious when awakened in the middle of the night and prone to creeping into our room or each other's.

I went back down and peeked into Josh's room first. A few less beloved stuffed animals were scattered across the royal blue sheets and blankets on his bed. Both boys were fast asleep in Jamie's room, curled up together beneath the bright red bedding. I pulled the door closed to make sure they didn't wake when Rob came thundering down the stairs in full gear, including the world's noisiest boots. He'd probably have tried sliding down the banister for greater speed if the polished oak hadn't been completely swathed in evergreen and tinsel. Then when the noise died down, I slipped out again. Rob was standing in the hallway outside Michael's and my bedroom door.

"Where's Michael?" he stage-whispered.

"Here." Michael stepped out of our room,

still fastening bits of gear. "I'll drive."

"Right," Rob said. "Meet you out front."

I pitched in to help Michael with his gear. Rob clattered the rest of the way down to the front hall, where Rose Noire was standing beside the Christmas tree, holding two travel coffee mugs.

"It's only instant," she said as she handed one to Rob. "So I added just a hint of nutmeg."

"But it's caffeinated, right?" he asked as he grabbed the mug and opened the door.

"Of course." Rose Noire looked mildly affronted that he'd doubted her, but given her fondness for trying to reform everyone else's caffeine habits with odd-tasting herbal concoctions, I could understand why he'd asked.

Rob ran out. I finished fastening the last buckle holding bits of gear to Michael's belt.

"Thanks," he said, giving me a kiss. "And yes, I'll be careful."

"Where's the fire?" Rose Noire asked.

"At one thirteen Clay County Road," I said. "Whatever that is."

"The New Life Baptist Church." Michael frowned. "At least I think. It would help if they just came out and said it."

"Sounds right to me," I said. "Somewhere in town — you can have Rob look it up on

13

his cell phone well before you need to make any turns."

"Good idea." Michael took the second travel mug, murmured his thanks, and followed Rob.

Rose Noire and I looked at each other. We knew many of the New Life congregation — particularly Henry Burke, our local police chief, and his wife, Minerva. And I'd been over at the church last night when a friend who had to work the night shift asked me to take her daughter to choir rehearsal.

We heard Michael's car start up and race off.

"It's four twenty — a.m.," Rose Noire added, as if she thought I might not have noticed the darkness. "I doubt if there would be anyone there now."

If she was trying to make me feel better, it wasn't working.

"Which could mean the fire would have plenty of time to become big and dangerous before anyone reported it," I said. "Watch the boys, will you? I'm heading over there."

I grabbed my coat from the enormous Victorian hat rack and my purse and keys from the hall table and dashed out into the bitter cold night.

Then I dashed in again, and upstairs to

14

add another layer of clothes.

Even though I prided myself on how quickly I could get dressed and ready in the morning, I was at least five minutes behind Michael and Rob when I set out. Maybe ten.

A good thing this hadn't happened two nights ago, when we'd had near-blizzard conditions. Or last night, when the plows still hadn't finished moving the foot of snow off our roads. All we had tonight was the bitter cold, which meant the huge mounds of snow lining the roads weren't going away any time soon.

I was relieved when I drew near the New Life Church and could still see its enormous steeple rising proudly into the air, illuminated by floodlights below — and with no flames or smoke.

By the time I pulled into the parking lot, I was not just relieved but downright puzzled. The church looked unharmed. All three of Caerphilly County's fire vehicles were there, along with four police cruisers. All their lights were flashing. The firefighters and deputies were all standing around in clumps, staring at the church, except for one larger group that seemed to be staring at something at the back of the ambulance.

I scanned the scene. No, the church was

fine. Not just the church but the entire sprawling complex, including two wings and a small outbuilding, all filled with class-rooms, meeting rooms, and the multiple rehearsal rooms for New Life's nationally renowned gospel choir. The floodlit façade was serene and unmarred by any signs of a conflagration.

I pulled into a parking space toward the side of the lot, about twenty feet from the ambulance, and close to where Michael and the other firefighters had parked. I was aiming to be far enough away that I wouldn't be underfoot, but close enough that I might overhear what was going on. And my chosen spot was partly behind one of the mountains of snow that the snowplows had piled up, so maybe the firefighters wouldn't notice me quite as easily.

As I turned the engine off, I saw a particularly tall fireman detach himself from the group around the ambulance and stride over toward my car. So much for my attempt to stay unnoticed. I braced myself to defend my right to rubberneck, and then relaxed. It was Michael. I opened the door and stepped out.

"The good news is there's no fire," he said.

"What's the bad — Oh, gross!"

The wind had shifted, bringing with it an

16

unmistakable odor, like garlic, rotten eggs, and burned rubber all mixed together.

"Is that what I think it is?" I asked.

"Yes. The church has been skunked."

CHAPTER 2

"Skunked?" came a voice from nearby. I glanced over to see that I wasn't the only spectator. I'd assumed the other cars in the lot belonged to the firefighters, but in several of them I could see people huddled, with their motors still running, trying to keep warm. Other spectators who were more hardy — or perhaps, like me, had taken the time to dress for the weather before coming out — stood by their cars, talking in twos or threes as they stared at the church. It was one of those groups that had overheard Michael's words.

"It appears so," Michael said. "No fire, and no apparent damage to the church, but the stench is awful."

The group passed his words down to the next group, and soon the entire crowd was buzzing.

Just who were these spectators? Members of the New Life Baptist congregation? Worried relatives of other new firefighters? Surely not just curious bystanders drawn by the sirens — not at four thirty on a cold morning like this.

I could see another car turning into the parking lot, and more headlights farther down the road.

"What's happening over there?" I pointed to the crowd around the ambulance.

"The guy who found the skunks," Michael said. "Apparently one of them sprayed him right in the eyes and — oh, here's your father. Good — the EMTs don't have a lot of experience with skunk attacks."

Dad's familiar blue minivan zoomed past us to park near the ambulance. The sleigh bells he'd fastened to the bumpers and the door handles to amuse Josh and Jamie were jingling madly.

"Did they call him?" I asked. "Or do you suppose he's been having insomnia again and whiling away the time by listening to the police and fire department bands on his radio?"

"No idea," Michael said. "But thank goodness he's here."

We both headed toward the ambulance.

By the time we joined the cluster of firefighters and police officers at the back of the ambulance, Dad's familiar black doctor's bag was sitting nearby and he was bent over his patient, an elderly black man wearing a bulky down jacket over striped pajama pants and fleece-lined bedroom slippers. I recognized him as Nelson Dandridge, the church's caretaker.

The two EMTs had stepped back, apparently happy to let Dad take over. They stood nearby, holding wads of white gauze over their noses. Some of the other bystanders were doing likewise, while the rest merely wore pained expressions. I didn't need to ask why — I could smell the reason. Apparently poor Mr. Dandridge had taken a direct hit from the skunk.

"Try not to move your head," Dad was saying. He was holding one of Mr. Dandridge's eyes open and peering in with a small flashlight. Mr. Dandridge moaned and stopped trying to toss his head, but he began twitching his feet slightly as if some kind of motion would ease the pain.

"You'll be fine." Dad was peering into the other eye.

"But I can't see!" Mr. Dandridge whispered. "And it burns."

"Perfectly normal," Dad said. "And you'll probably feel some discomfort for the next few hours."

"Discomfort?" From his tone it was obvious that Mr. Dandridge thought the word wholly inadequate for what he was feeling.

"Let's continue the ocular irrigation for a little bit before we take him down to the hospital." Dad turned to the EMTs who, to their credit, only hesitated for a few moments before returning to their patient's side.

" 'Hospital,' " Mr. Dandridge repeated. He sounded unsure whether to feel happy that his condition was being taken seriously or worried that it might be more serious than Dad was telling him. The medics had taken up posts on either side of his head and were squirting saline into his eyes.

"There's always a chance of complications," Dad said. "Skunk spray is very caustic. Occasionally you see corneal ulceration, or uveitis, or conjunctivitis. And occasionally —"

"Dad," I said. "I think you're alarming Mr. Dandridge."

Mr. Dandridge had begun moaning again and moving his head back and forth, impeding the medics' efforts.

"But all those are very unusual," Dad hastened to add. "And the best way to prevent them is for us to do a very thorough irrigation here at the scene. Try not to thrash around quite so much."

With a visible effort, Mr. Dandridge stilled his head, but his feet began twitching again.

"I'll see if I can arrange for an ophthalmologist to meet us at the hospital, just in case." Dad stepped aside and pulled out his iPhone.

"That would be Dr. Garza," I said. "Unless Caerphilly has recently acquired a second ophthalmologist."

"Doc, can we scrub him with the tomato juice now?" one of the medics asked.

"Please do," Dad said.

"Tomato juice?" Chief Burke asked.

"We actually carry it in the ambulance just in case," one of the EMTs said. "Can't say I've ever seen it used before."

"Do we have an ETA on that change of clothes for him?" one of the medics asked.

"I'll go check," Michael said. He ran off — away from the church, I noted with relief.

Two more firefighters stepped forward to help the medics by swabbing Mr. Dandridge's hands and face with rags dripping with thick red liquid. Mr. Dandridge opened one eye slightly and then closed it again tightly. I wasn't sure if he couldn't see or didn't like what he saw.

"Does that tomato juice wash out?" Mr. Dandridge asked.

"A darn sight better than the skunk odor,"

a medic replied.

"May we ask Mr. Dandridge a few questions while the medics are working?" Chief Burke. Standing at his side was Jim Featherstone, Caerphilly's new volunteer fire chief.

The medics nodded. With visible effort the chief came closer and squatted down at Mr. Dandridge's side.

"Nelson, it's Henry Burke," he said. "I'm sorry to bother you, but we need to know a few things."

Mr. Dandridge nodded slightly and assumed a stoic expression.

"Like why the devil did you call the fire department?" Chief Featherstone demanded.

"Because the county doesn't have a skunk department," Mr. Dandridge said. "Anyway, I didn't ask for the fire department. I just called 911."

"But you said the church was burning."

"I never said the *church* was burning." Mr. Dandridge tried to sit up and was prevented by the EMTs. "I said that I was *in* the church and that I'd been sprayed by skunks, and my *eyes* were burning. But perhaps I wasn't speaking too clearly. Those miserable skunks were still trying to spray me."

"Skunks?" Chief Burke asked. "Plural? How many? And where were they?"

"In the choir loft," Mr. Dandridge said. "And I have no idea how many of them there were. I thought it was cats at first, and I went closer to see why someone had left a whole cage of cats in the church —"

"Cage?" Chief Burke and Chief Featherstone said in unison.

"Yes, cage. And I have no idea how many of them there were in the cage. A whole swarm of them."

"Actually, the traditional term is a 'surfeit of skunks,' " Dad put in. "I was just talking to Debbie Ann — she's arranging for the ophthalmologist — and it's pretty obvious what happened. Mr. Dandridge called her to say that he thought there were intruders in the church —"

"I saw the lights on from my house," Mr. Dandridge put in. "I live just across the road."

"And as Debbie Ann was urging him to leave the building and wait for the arrival of a deputy, he began shouting 'It's burning! It's burning!' Which was a perfectly natural reaction to being sprayed in the eyes by a skunk."

"Skunks," Mr. Dandridge corrected. "Could be dozens of them."

"And of course Debbie Ann made the logical assumption that he was talking about

24

the church," Dad concluded.

The chiefs looked mollified.

"I've sent in two of my men wearing SCBAs to check out the church thoroughly, to make sure there's definitely no fire and no other hazards," Chief Featherstone said.

"SCBAs?" Chief Burke repeated.

"Self-contained breathing apparatus. I can lend you some if you want your men to investigate."

"Thanks," Chief Burke said. "I'd appreciate the gear — I plan to go in myself. I'm pretty familiar with the layout of the church."

"I told my men to stay away from the choir loft as much as possible," Chief Featherstone said. "At least until Eli Slattery from animal control gets here to remove the skunks."

"Did he say how soon he'd get here?" Chief Burke asked.

"No idea." The fire chief was frowning. "I left a message on his voice mail."

"Eli's a sound sleeper," one of the firefighters put in.

Chief Featherstone's frown deepened.

"Chief," another firefighter said. "We could just call Osgood Shiffley down at the service station. He's open all night, and only a few blocks from Eli's house. He could probably pop over and pound on Eli's door."

Chief Featherstone blinked in surprise. He had retired after twenty years in a big-city fire department and moved to Caerphilly to take over leadership of our volunteer force. He was still getting used to life in Caerphilly, and looked as if he wasn't sure whether to be pleased or horrified by this kind of small-town solution to the problem.

"Let's give Eli a chance to respond," he said finally. "But I'll keep the idea in mind if the delay becomes too inconvenient."

"Maybe someone should just try to take the skunks out," one of the firefighters said. "I always heard that after they spray they can't do it again immediately."

"Not what I've heard," another firefighter said.

"Besides," Chief Featherstone said. "Mr. Dandridge says there are multiple skunks. We have no idea if they all sprayed him or if some of them didn't and are just waiting to go after the next person to stick his nose in the choir loft. Anyone want to take that chance?"

The firefighters fell silent.

"So we wait for animal control," Chief Burke said.

"Do you have any more questions?" Dad

asked. "Because I'd like to transport him to the hospital." Dad looked at his watch. "The ophthalmologist will be meeting us there within the half hour."

Both chiefs nodded their approval. Dad packed his bag and hopped into the back of the ambulance. The two medics helped Mr. Dandridge in. Then they conferred briefly, and one stepped into the back of the ambulance with the patient. The other almost skipped on his way to the less odorous driver's seat. Michael and another firefighter came running up.

"Wait a sec," Michael called. "We've got his change of clothes."

The back door of the ambulance opened. Dad leaned out to take the clothes, and looked around until he spotted me.

"Meg," he said. "Your grandfather's in my car. Could you see that he gets home safely?"

"Why in the world did you bring him along?" I asked. While Grandfather was hale and hearty for someone in his nineties, I didn't think either the weather or the hour were suitable for dragging him out of his comfortable bed in my parents' guest room.

"I didn't exactly bring him," Dad said. "He heard the sirens. And when I got out to the car, he was already sitting there, ready to go. No use even trying to talk him out of coming. And once we figured out there was no fire, he decided to stay in the car and sulk."

He sounded uncharacteristically exasperated — with me, or with his headstrong father? No telling. He slammed the door and the ambulance set out, steering a careful course through the growing throng of onlookers.

"Well, that might solve the skunk removal problem," I said to the chiefs.

Chief Featherstone looked puzzled and glanced at Chief Burke as if seeking enlightenment.

"Meg's grandfather is Dr. Montgomery Blake," Chief Burke explained. "A very distinguished zoologist."

"Blake?" Chief Featherstone frowned slightly, no doubt puzzled that Dad and his father had different surnames. Since he was new in town, presumably he hadn't already heard about how Dad had been abandoned at birth, adopted, and only recently reunited with his long-lost father. Then he spoke again.

"The one you always see on Animal Planet?" he asked. "Getting bitten and peed on by exotic animals?"

"That's him," I said. "And I happen to

28

know he's particularly fond of skunks. He likes their attitude."

"I'm glad someone does," Chief Burke said. "Could you ask him if he'll help, please?"

CHAPTER 3

I took my time approaching Dad's van. I had misgivings about the whole idea of involving Grandfather in the skunk removal. Yes, he was a seasoned zoologist, but he'd also spent years filming nature documentaries. No documentary about skunks would be complete without showing how they sprayed their would-be attackers. And that was precisely what we wanted to avoid. What if Grandfather forgot, even momentarily, that there weren't any cameras rolling?

Dad had left the van running, obviously so the heat would stay on. Grandfather had reclined the front passenger seat as far as it would go and was fast asleep and snoring vigorously.

"Grandfather?" I touched his shoulder gently.

He started upright.

"What the hell is going on?" he asked.

"Where's James?"

"Dad went to the hospital with his patient," I said.

"Well, take me home, then," he said. "Nothing to see here. So much for your big exciting fire. Should have stayed in bed and taken care of my cold."

"I can take you right away," I said. "Unless you feel up to helping us with a wildlife problem."

"Ah! What's the problem?" He unfastened his seatbelt and buttoned up his coat.

"Skunks. There are skunks in the church."

"Impossible."

"Impossible?" Couldn't he smell them? Oh — the head cold. I wasn't sure whether to order him back into bed or envy him his apparent immunity to the prevailing stench.

"Or at least highly unlikely," he continued, as he reached over and pulled the seatbelt back across his body. "They'd all be asleep."

"You mean skunks hibernate?"

"No, but they sleep a lot more in the winter. Especially when it's cold. And with this much snow on the ground, they'd probably be snowed in their dens. Sleeping the weather out. Someone probably just saw a black-and-white cat." He closed his eyes and appeared to be settling back to continue his nap.

"Well, then we've got a whole cage of black-and-white cats, and at least one of them did a pretty good imitation of a skunk. Good enough to fool Mr. Dandridge into thinking he'd been sprayed in the eyes."

Grandfather opened one eye.

"Good enough to fool Dad into taking Mr. Dandridge down to the hospital to see an ophthalmologist."

Grandfather made a growling noise.

"Well, that could be, then," he said. "And they wouldn't like it if someone dragged them out of their dens in weather like this. And if you woke them up, they'd be downright peeved."

Apparently they weren't the only ones.

"So do you want to see the peeved skunks or do you want to go back to your den and sleep the weather out?"

He reached over, pulled a tissue from a box on the floor, and blew his nose. Then his eyes lit up.

"Ah, yes!" He sniffed appreciatively a few times, like a wine connoisseur assessing the bouquet of a rare vintage. "You could be right. Help me out of this wretched seat," he added, as he unfastened the seatbelt again.

I brought the seat back to its upright position and helped him down from the van.

Then I turned off the engine, took the keys, locked the van, and scrambled to catch up with Grandfather, who had apparently regained his energy and was striding over to the two chiefs. I hoped he didn't hit an ice patch on the way.

"I hear you have a skunk problem," Grandfather said.

"Indeed," Chief Burke said. "I don't think you've met our new fire chief."

After a round of introductions, Chief Featherstone held up a piece of headgear that looked like a cross between an astronaut's helmet and a praying mantis's head.

"You can put this on to go inside," he said. "Can someone help Dr. Blake with the air tank?"

" 'Air tank'? Nonsense," Grandfather boomed. "What do we need that for? I thought there wasn't a fire."

"There isn't, but the skunk smell's pretty overwhelming," Chief Burke said. "We thought —"

"Nonsense," Grandfather said. "I've smelled a few skunks in my time. Hasn't killed me yet. Come on; let's get inside. It's damned cold out here."

With that he began striding toward the front doors of the church.

"I should go with him," I said to Chief

Burke, and took off in Grandfather's wake.

The two chiefs followed more slowly, probably because they stopped to put on their own helmets and strap oxygen tanks on their backs. Another firefighter followed in their wake with an armload of some kind of gear. The half dozen gleaming white steps leading up to the church slowed Grandfather down and we all stepped together into the vestibule. It was a large entryway decorated from floor to ceiling with evergreens, gold tinsel, and red velvet bows. Along the walls were brightly colored felt appliquéd banners that looked to be the work of the Sunday school classes, each illustrating a different beloved Christmas carol. The contrast between the beautiful Christmas decorations and the overpowering skunk odor would have been funny if I wasn't having so much trouble breathing.

Even Grandfather halted with a surprised look on his face. Evidently his head cold wasn't giving him total immunity.

"Where did you say the spraying happened?" he asked.

"In the choir loft." Chief Featherstone's voice was muffled by the breathing apparatus. He and Chief Burke looked rather insectoid, and the mechanical sound of their breathing was curiously unnerving, like sharing space with a pair of Darth Vaders.

Chief Featherstone marched across the vestibule and flung open the broad double doors into the sanctuary. As he was silhouetted in the doorway, I realized that even without the mask he was rather an odd figure, with a stout, barrel-shaped body perched on the thinnest legs I'd ever seen.

We followed him and stood just inside the doorway. I was beginning to regret hastily scampering after Grandfather without demanding that the fire chief lend me my own breathing apparatus.

The New Life sanctuary always overwhelmed me when I first walked in. Not so much because of its beauty, although the soaring expanses of light oak and whitewashed walls looked particularly elegant with all the evergreen, tinsel, and ribbon. No, it was the size that always got me — the place was so incredibly huge. The stained-glass windows wouldn't have been out of place in a medieval cathedral. And at the back of the church the choir loft, looming high over the altar, could probably fit almost as many people as the entire sanctuary of Trinity Episcopal, where Michael, the boys, and I had begun going a lot more regularly now that Mother had been elected to the vestry.

The sanctuary was also lined with the Christmas carol banners whose bright, cheerful colors contrasted strangely with the rank odor that was assaulting our noses. I wondered if the felt was absorbing the odor, and whether it would be possible to fumigate the banners.

"Up there." Chief Featherstone pointed at the choir loft, which was top-heavy with great looping ropes of ribbon-trimmed greenery.

"Pretty powerful odor to be coming from way up there." Grandfather sounded dubious.

"Unfortunately, it's not just coming from up there," Chief Featherstone said. "One of my men reported that in spraying Mr. Dandridge, the skunk or skunks also appear to have scored a direct hit on an intake duct for the air circulation system."

"That's going to be a challenge for the church, isn't it?" Grandfather said. "Well, how do we get up there?"

He struck a familiar pose: shoulders back, chin high, mouth firmly set, visibly determined to push through all obstacles. If we were filming one of his nature specials, this would be the signal that he was about to jump in the tank with the sharks, crawl into the lion's den, step out into the path of the charging elephant, grasp the rattlesnake's head, or whatever other foolhardy and camera-worthy stunt he'd come up with.

It would have looked more dramatic if he hadn't chosen to pose in front of a banner filled with several dozen cotton-ball sheep with broad black pipe-cleaner grins.

"I don't think there are enough handholds to do a free climb up there," I said. "But we could get some ropes and rappel up. Or — Wait! There's no camera crew. Why don't we just take the stairs?"

"Better yet, there's an elevator," Chief Burke said. "We installed it to make sure the less spry members of the choir could save their breath for singing."

"I'm perfectly able to climb a few steps," Grandfather began.

"And so am I," Chief Burke replied. "But since it doesn't look as if we'll be finished here any time soon, I think we should save our energy. Follow me."

He set off at a brisk pace toward the back of the church and to my relief, Grandfather followed.

The elevator was so small it could only fit two people at a time, so the fire chief and I waited below while Chief Burke and Grandfather went up. As soon as the elevator door closed, Chief Featherstone beckoned to the firefighter who had been trailing us. The firefighter handed me something. Another insectoid helmet.

"In case you change your mind when we get up there," Chief Featherstone said.

"I already have." With his help, I donned the helmet. The firefighter strapped on the attached oxygen tank and I sucked greedily at air that was gloriously free of skunk odor.

"Thanks," I said.

"I'm having another brought up," he said. "Maybe we can shove your grandfather into it before he pukes."

The elevator returned and we rode up in anxious silence. My heart was beating a little fast when the door opened to reveal ground zero of the skunk smell.

CHAPTER 4

Luckily we peered out before exiting. The skunk cage — a huge thing, six feet square and nearly as tall — was perilously close to the elevator door. Easy to see how Mr. Dandridge had stumbled into it. Several of the skunks turned when the elevator door opened and were hissing at us. One of them appeared to be pounding his front feet on the ground. Several others were doing the same thing in the other direction, where Grandfather and Chief Burke were. Apparently they'd managed to make their way to the other side of the choir loft, where there was room to stand a lot farther from the cage.

"How far can those things spray?" I called over to Grandfather.

"Maybe twenty-five or thirty feet," he said. "But they're only accurate to about ten feet."

Since the cage was only about twelve or

fifteen feet from the open elevator door, I didn't find that reassuring.

"Come out of the elevator very slowly," Grandfather said. "And hug the wall all the way to the back of the loft. Then you can work your way across to here. And if one of them turns around and lifts his tail really high, run like hell."

Chief Featherstone and I looked at each other.

"Well, let's get this over with," I said.

I went first. The skunks seemed to hiss a lot more, and two of them hurled themselves against the side of the cage, as if trying to charge me. They became even more agitated when the fire chief followed me, but seemed to calm down in direct proportion to how far we were from the cage. Eventually, we joined the others, who were studying the cage from the safer distance of about thirty feet.

I also found myself studying the choir loft with amusement. The top half — everything that could be seen from the main body of the church below — was pristine and festooned, like the rest of the church, with evergreen, gold tinsel, and red velvet. Red velvet cushions softened the pews at the back and the sturdy wooden folding chairs in the remaining space. But at floor level, where the congregation couldn't see, I could see untidy stacks of music books and loose sheet music, trash cans overflowing with water bottles and candy wrappers, odd misplaced garments — the same sort of homely clutter that I'd seen accumulate backstage at the shows Michael directed or acted in at the college.

And how much of it, decorations and personal clutter, had been ruined by skunk spray and would have to be thrown out. I glanced back at the skunk cage.

"Someone has a sense of humor." I pointed to one corner of the cage, which was decorated with a single, bright-red stick-on bow.

"There's no way that cage came up in the elevator," Chief Featherstone said.

"I suspect it's also too big for the stairs," Chief Burke said. "Which means either the perpetrators brought up the pieces and assembled it here before putting in the skunks or, more likely, they winched it up over the front of the choir loft."

"Probably the only feasible way for us to get it down." Chief Featherstone was leaning out over the edge of the balcony and studying the beams.

"Agreed," Chief Burke said. "But I want my crime scene specialist to examine those

41

beams first, for any trace evidence."

"You have a full-time crime scene specialist?" Chief Featherstone sounded surprised.

"Officially he's a deputy," Chief Burke said. "But he was a full-time crime scene specialist for York County before joining my staff, so when we do need forensic work, he's available."

I felt sorry for the crime scene specialist, who happened to be my cousin Horace Hollingsworth. He wasn't keen on heights, and I was pretty sure he'd be spooked at having to do forensics in close proximity to so many skunks. And if I got the chance, I'd warn him not to pass up the offer of breathing apparatus.

Just then the firefighter who'd trailed us into the church emerged from a doorway behind us. Evidently there was a stairwell on this side of the loft. I wasn't sure whether to feel relieved that I didn't have to go near the skunks on the way out or annoyed that no one had properly explained the geography before we'd come up to the loft. The firefighter began outfitting Grandfather with his own helmet and oxygen tank. Grandfather made surprisingly little protest.

"How many of the blasted things are there?" Chief Burke asked.

"I count twelve." My grandfather had

pulled out the pocket binoculars he always carried and was studying the skunks through them. "Nine full grown and three half grown."

"Definitely a surfeit of skunks," Chief Featherstone said, with a chuckle.

"If you ask me, one skunk's a surfeit when it's someplace you don't want it," Chief Burke said.

"More interesting is the fact that at least one of them isn't a common striped skunk." Grandfather pointed toward the cage. "See that one that's gray and white instead of black and white? That would appear to be a domesticated skunk — possibly gone feral."

"Pet skunks aren't legal in Virginia," Chief Burke said.

"Then you'll have one more thing to charge the perpetrators with when we find them," I said.

"Which shouldn't be too hard." Chief Featherstone was becoming almost jovial, perhaps because this call was turning out to be everyone's problem but his. "Look for the guys who reek like polecats."

"Actually, they might have managed to avoid being sprayed," Grandfather said. "If they knew something about safely handling skunks."

"There's a safe way to handle skunks?"

Chief Featherstone asked.

"If I wanted to move that cage without getting skunked," Grandfather said. "First thing I'd do is make a cover for it."

"What kind of cover?" Chief Burke asked.

"Opaque," Grandfather said. "Something that covers all four sides and the top. If you look close, you'll see the bottom is solid." He handed the Chief Burke his binoculars.

"So they're less likely to spray if they can't see us?" Chief Burke was peering intently at the cage. "Why is that?"

"They're smart," Grandfather said. "They know they have a finite amount of spray before they run out, and if they use it all up, it could take a day or two to replenish. And if a predator figures out they can't spray, they're dead ducks. So they're much less likely to spray if they don't see a good target. That's why they do all that hissing and foot stomping we saw. Usually they can scare off predators without having to spray."

"So we put a cover on the cage and they won't spray us?" Chief Burke said.

"Probably won't spray us," Grandfather corrected. "I'd still keep my distance. The adolescents might be a little trigger-happy."

Chief Burke nodded.

"I think I'll call Randall Shiffley about this," he said. And then, turning to Chief

Featherstone he added, "Mayor Shiffley's family owns both a construction company and a moving company. Between the two of them, they should be able to figure out how to get this confounded cage out of the choir loft."

He turned back to Grandfather.

"So who, apart from zoologists, would know about how to handle a caged skunk safely?" he asked.

"Hmmm." Grandfather looked thoughtful. "Animal control officers. Veterinarians, as long as they've worked at a zoo or wildlife shelter. Maybe hunters. Domestic skunk breeders. Maybe someone who works at a pest control company, one that includes wild animal relocation in its services."

"Great," I said. "We're in a county full of hunters, where wild animals regularly stray into people's yards and houses, near a college with a graduate zoology program, and just down the street from a small but world-famous private zoo. Isn't there anything we can think of to narrow the chief's pool of suspects?"

Everyone fell silent for a few moments. We were all frowning and thinking — except for Grandfather, who had returned to studying the skunks through his binoculars. Then Chief Featherstone spoke up.

"We saw no signs of a break-in," he offered. "So it would have to be someone who knows something about skunks and has access to the church."

Chief Burke frowned, no doubt because that meant the prankster was more than likely a fellow member of the New Life congregation.

"Not necessarily," I said. "There were a lot of people at the choir rehearsal last night."

"Weren't they mostly family of choir members?" Chief Burke asked.

"Not entirely." I shook my head. "I was there. Aida Butler was on patrol last night, so I brought her daughter to the rehearsal."

"One of my deputies," Chief Burke said to Chief Featherstone.

"And I saw Abe and Rivka Sass." I was ticking off the non-Baptists in attendance on my fingers. "They're taking off on a cruise tomorrow and won't get to see tonight's concert so I assume they got permission to come to the dress rehearsal. And they weren't the only ones. There's pretty much an open door for rehearsals."

Chief Burke winced and nodded.

"What's all this about a concert?" Chief Featherstone asked.

"Everyone wants to hear the New Life

choir's Christmas performance," I said. "But most people also want to attend Christmas services at their own church, and on top of that on Christmas the New Life Church is full to overflowing with just the congregation. So they always give a concert on the last Saturday before Christmas. This year, it's tonight."

"You may have to reschedule the concert, then," Chief Featherstone said. " 'Cause there's no way this church is going to be fit for human habitation by tonight."

I winced. I didn't look forward to breaking the news to Jamie and Josh if the concert were canceled.

A deputy popped in from the stairwell just behind us.

"Chief," the deputy said. "Reverend Wilson's downstairs. Wants to know what's happening with his church."

From the chief's pained expression, I deduced that he did not relish breaking the bad news to his pastor.

"Want me to go along and help?" Chief Featherstone said.

"I appreciate the offer, but maybe I should be the one," Chief Burke said.

With that we all trooped down the stairs. Even Grandfather, who looked preoccupied.

CHAPTER 5

When we exited the church we spotted Reverend Wilson's small, stooped frame at the bottom of the building's front steps. He looked every one of his eighty-some years, and the expression on his round dark face was one of profound anxiety — almost pain. Michael was standing just behind him, breathing apparatus pushed back on top of his head. He appeared to be hovering, as if worried about the elderly minister.

"How bad is it, Henry?" Reverend Wilson called out when we appeared in the doorway.

"Pretty bad, Ambrose," Chief Burke said.

Chief Burke pushed back his mask and went down the steps and stood talking to Reverend Wilson in a low tone. Someone had turned on all the outside illumination, including all the strings of holiday lights, which twinkled with incongruous gaiety behind them.

Chief Featherstone strolled back inside the vestibule to confer with some of his men. Grandfather and I stood on the steps of the church. I realized I was feeling a little claustrophobic in the breathing apparatus, so I pushed the mask back and took a few deep breaths. Grandfather followed suit. The air might have smelled pretty bad to anyone who hadn't been inside the church, but I found it refreshing. Grandfather seemed to feel the same, so we stood side by side for a few moments, breathing and surveying the scene below.

The church looked almost festive now, with the holiday lights twinkling and spotlights illuminating the larger-than-life plaster Nativity scene on the front lawn. You could almost imagine that the small groups of people dotting the parking lot had come to carol. Even the flashing red and blue lights of the fire engines and police cruisers seemed to add a curiously festive note.

"So tell me," Grandfather said. "Did I sleep through the part where we found out who did this stupid prank and why?"

"No," I said. "Still a mystery." Although I wondered if it was necessarily a complete mystery to Chief Burke. Quite apart from the knowledge of Caerphilly and its inhabitants he'd picked up in his years as police chief and deputy sheriff, he was a member of the New Life Baptist congregation. If the church had enemies outside or malcontents within, he probably already knew all about it.

And fat chance getting him to say anything before he was ready.

"Well, time's a-wasting," Grandfather said. "We need to get Caroline over here." His old friend and frequent partner in mischief, Caroline Willner, ran a wildlife sanctuary about an hour's drive from Caerphilly. "We could use her help with these skunks."

"I thought you were the skunk expert," I said.

"Yes, but she's had a lot more hands-on experience with skunk removals," he said. "I suppose it's a little too early to call her."

"It's a lot too early to call her." I pulled out my cell phone and checked the time. "It's only a little past five. Let me take you home where it's warm."

"I should wait till six," he said.

"You should wait till nine, at least," I said. "She needs her sleep, especially if you want her to drive all the way up here to —"

"Ah," he said. "There she is now. She must have heard the sirens, too."

He hurried down the steps to where he

had spotted the short, plump figure of Caroline Willner. Beside her was Mother, looking as tall and willowy as ever in spite of the heavy winter coat she was wearing.

"No one tells me anything," I muttered as I fell in step beside Grandfather. "I gather she came up for the holidays?"

"And to see my new marmots," Grandfather said. "We're having a special exhibit to raise funds for the Vancouver Island marmot. Fascinating creatures."

"I should have known a mere human holiday wouldn't be enough to drag her up here," I replied.

"Merry Christmas, Meg!" Caroline enveloped me in a hug as we joined them.

Mother leaned over to give me a kiss on the cheek.

"Such a relief that it's not actually a fire," she murmured. "What are Michael and Rob thinking, volunteering for something so dangerous? You'd think they were still in their twenties."

I shook my head. If she was expecting an explanation, she'd have to get it from Michael and Rob — I agreed with her.

"We need to help the fire and police departments," Grandfather was saying to Caroline. "Someone brought a cage into the

51

church that contains twelve *Mephitis mephitis.*"

"Twelve!" Caroline looked startled. "Oh, my. That's a very large family group."

"From what I've observed of their behavior, I don't think they're all related," Grandfather said. "Are you missing any skunks?"

"No." Caroline shook her head firmly. "It's been an unusually slow season for skunks, ever since about September. Normally this time of year, between nearby county animal control officers and the private companies that specialize in wild animal removals, we'd have gotten a few injured ones to rehabilitate and a couple dozen to rehome, but we've only had three all season."

The two of them immediately drew aside and fell into an intense discussion about whether rabies, distemper, canine hepatitis, leptospirosis, or several other polysyllabic diseases were affecting the local skunk population enough to reduce the number of rescues she was seeing. I focused on whether I should tell the chief about Caroline's skunk shortage, since it seemed to give a potentially useful clue to finding out where the skunks had come from. If there were any animal control officers or pest removal experts nearby with a grudge against the

New Life Baptist Church —

"Meg, dear." Mother was looking stern. "How bad is it?"

"The church, you mean?" I asked. "It reeks. They have a hideous cleanup ahead of them, and for all I know, they might have to replace some of the wood and fabric that got sprayed. I'm not sure you can ever get the smell out of something organic."

Mother nodded grimly.

"I'm glad I got to hear the dress rehearsal last night," I added. "Because there's no way they're going to be able to give a concert in there tonight. And the boys will be inconsolable. What a pity."

"We must do something!" Mother was using her Joan of Arc voice.

I felt a sudden wave of tiredness wash over me and yawned, hoping against hope that I wasn't going to be included in her "we."

"They will need a great deal of help for the cleanup," Mother said. "And the concert must go on! I will speak to the rector. And the ladies of St. Clotilda's Guild."

I was relieved. So far I'd managed to resist Mother's attempts to enlist me in the guild, which was Trinity Episcopal's chief women's organization for church and community good works. So while I probably couldn't escape being sucked into the cleanup and whatever Mother had in mind for finding the concert a new venue, at least her organizing talents would be spread across the entire membership of the guild, and not focused solely on me.

"And look!" Mother's voice held a note of warm approval. "There's the dear rector now."

I still did a double take when Mother used "dear rector" to refer to the new pastor of Trinity Episcopal. Most people just called her Robyn. Sometimes Reverend Smith if they didn't know her that well, and in a few cases "that new girl" if they were traditionalists and disapproved of her gender and relative youth. Mother had fallen initially into the "new girl" camp until she figured out that Robyn's theological stance corresponded almost exactly to her own: liberal social views and a very traditional high-church liturgy. And when Mother had discovered that Robyn shared her fascination with interior decorating, she skipped over the "Robyn" and "Reverend Smith" phases entirely.

"This is terrible!" Robyn was exclaiming. "I hear their church will be unusable for days. What a sore trial at any time, but at Christmas! We must do something!"

"Several somethings," Mother agreed.

"What did you have in mind?"

"As soon as it's decent, we should start calling people," Robyn went on. "We can get together a work detail to help with the cleanup."

"I doubt if they'll have the skunks removed and the crime scene processed for several hours," I said. "You'll have plenty of time to organize the work detail."

I didn't add that given the enormous size of the New Life congregation, they might not be all that short of helping hands. Why rain on an impulse that was both neighborly and ecumenical?

"I think the bigger problem may be finding a space for their concert," I went on. "It could be a day or two before the church is habitable."

"They're welcome to use our sanctuary," Robyn said. "I'm not sure we could fit in half the people who want to come. But we'll work out something."

"Reverend Wilson!" Mother called.

Reverend Wilson, who was still talking to Chief Burke and Michael, looked up. He returned Mother's wave and the three of them headed over to join us.

"What a trial for you and your congregation!" Robyn said, taking both of Reverend Wilson's hands in hers. "All our prayers are with you, of course. And we're going to bring in some hands to help with cleanup. Have you thought of another space for the concert yet?"

"Sadly, no." Reverend Wilson looked uncharacteristically doleful. "Nor for all our other Christmas worship and fellowship events."

"I'm going to see if the college can offer some space," Michael said. "Normally at this time of year there would be any number of classrooms and auditoriums standing empty. But since the college is hosting those big basketball and debate tournaments this weekend, I'm not optimistic."

"The college has even borrowed some of the larger spaces in the county office buildings," Chief Burke added. "So that option's out."

"And apart from the college and the county, I'm not sure anyone has a space large enough for our concert," Reverend Wilson said.

"Could you have two concerts?" Mother asked. "One tonight and one Sunday night?"

"Trinity Episcopal could host one," Robyn said. "Possibly both — let me check our calendar. And we can contact all the other local churches. I'm sure among us we can find sufficient spaces for everything."

"That would be wonderful," Reverend Wilson said. "Take quite a bit of work to arrange, though."

I'd already figured that out. And since the last few weeks of nonstop holiday preparations had left me feeling stretched a little thin, I began trying to think of a tactful way to leave before a big chunk of that work landed on my plate. Luckily, Grandfather helped me out.

"Meg!" He appeared at my side, looking his usual impatient self. "Caroline's going to stay here to supervise the skunk removal. Can you take me over to the zoo? We've got to get a temporary habitat ready for these skunks."

CHAPTER 6

Perfect. Even if readying the skunk habitat took hours, I decided that chauffeuring Grandfather offered the best chance of seeing my bed sometime before nightfall.

"I'll be happy to take you out to the zoo," I said. And then, before Mother could protest that she needed me here, I added, "The sooner we have a place to put them, the sooner the cleanup can begin."

Mother nodded her approval and returned her attention to the two ministers. Robyn had already taken out her Day-Timer and was scribbling notes. A woman after my own heart, although my notebook-that-tells-me-when-to-breathe, as I called my giant to-do list, was currently housed not in a Day-Timer but a small well-worn, tooled-leather ring binder made by a fellow craft show artist.

Reverend Wilson was looking less glum. The situation was in hand; I could sneak off with a clear conscience.

Grandfather brooded quietly on the way over to the zoo, only breaking his silence occasionally to favor me with some tidbit of information about skunks. I'm not sure why he felt obliged to tell me that the Great Horned Owl, due to its nearly nonexistent sense of smell, was the skunk's only serious predator. And while I found it interesting that the Native Americans used skunk oil as a mild liniment or healing balm, I hoped he wouldn't repeat this information in front of Rose Noire. Given her fascination with natural remedies, I could easily see her collecting skunk spray and smearing it all over any family member who seemed in need of healing.

The zoo's night-shift head keeper met us at the gate. He looked pale and anxious as he swung open one half of the enormous wreath-laden metal front gate. I pulled my car into the small gravel circle that served as a loading zone when the zoo was open and Grandfather's private parking when it was not. A dozen live potted evergreens edged the circle, each decked with ribbon-trimmed seed balls and chunks of suet. Was this Grandfather's idea or one of Caroline's suggestions?

"Morning, Victor," Grandfather called out

as he climbed out of my car. "Have you finished checking on the animals the way I asked?"

"Oh, yes," he said. "Both of our skunks are there. All of the animals are there except . . . except . . ."

"Out with it, man!"

"Cleopatra's missing."

"Missing?" Grandfather exclaimed. "How? Did someone leave her cage unlocked?"

"Who or what is Cleopatra?" I asked.

"The emerald tree boa," Grandfather said. "Unusually large specimen. Nearly seven feet long."

"Wouldn't she be hibernating this time of year?" I suggested. "That's what snakes do in the winter, right? Maybe she's just burrowed under whatever bedding's in her cage."

"It's called brumating in a snake," Grandfather said. "And yes, she'd be doing it now — she might wake up if the weather became unseasonably warm, but with the air this cold, she'd be asleep. We keep the snake house cold enough that they'll sleep, but not so cold as to be dangerous. Victor, I assume you checked the bedding thoroughly."

"Thoroughly!" Victor nodded vigorously. "And every corner of the snake house, from drains to rafters. She's not there. And there are no cracks or crevices she could have used to escape."

"And no Cleopatra-sized bulges in any of the other large snakes, I assume," I added.

"Of course not," Victor snapped. "I'd have noticed. And we only have one or two snakes anywhere near her size."

"She couldn't get far, surely, on a night like this?" I asked.

"In the unlikely event that she got outside, she'd go dormant almost immediately," Grandfather said. "And likely die if she wasn't found soon enough."

"She wasn't lying dormant anywhere within ten feet of the snake house," Victor said. "We checked even though it was obvious she didn't leave on her own."

"You think she was stolen?" Grandfather frowned.

"It's the only reasonable explanation," Victor said. "I checked her cage last night, the way I always do when I make my rounds. She was there and the padlock was in place. And I closed the snake house door after me and made sure it was secure — I know how dangerous a draft could be. When I went 'round just now, the padlock was gone and the cage door was wide open. Someone must have cut off the padlock and taken her."

Grandfather looked grim.

"I do not like the direction these pranks are taking," he said. "First someone puts a surfeit of skunks in a highly unsuitable environment, where they are in serious danger of being harmed by hysterical people —"

How like Grandfather to side with the skunks.

"— and now someone has quite irresponsibly removed an innocent reptile from its habitat and exposed it to weather that could be injurious to its health. When will people learn —"

"Let's tell the chief." I pulled out my cell phone and dialed 911. "I have no idea if this is in any way related to the skunk thing, but he will want to know. Hello, Debbie Ann? I'd like report a missing snake."

I wouldn't have thought the words "snake" and "skunk" were that easily confused, but it took us a while to sort out the mix-up. Debbie Ann relayed the stolen snake report to the chief, along with a warning to keep an eye open for Cleopatra in the church.

"She wouldn't be the least bit bothered by the skunks' spray," Grandfather said. "And it's been a while since she was fed, so one of those smaller, adolescent skunks might look rather tempting to her. Have the chief put out an APB."

I relayed this suggestion — though coming from Grandfather, it sounded more like an order.

"I'll see what I can do," Debbie Ann said. "After all, it wouldn't be the strangest APB we've put out here in Caerphilly. But is there any particular reason to think it's in the church?"

"No," I said. "Except that it seems a little far-fetched to think that there would be two people — or groups of people — pulling animal-related pranks on the same night. What if whoever put the skunks in the church also turned Cleopatra loose there?"

"Oh, my."

Debbie Ann hung up, presumably to put out a snake alert to those working in the church.

"We must go down there and look for her," Grandfather said.

"What about the skunk habitat?"

Grandfather hesitated.

"It will only take me a little while to show Victor what I have in mind," he said finally. "You wait here."

He and Victor bustled off. I called home to make sure the boys were okay and after Rose Noire assured me all was well, I stretched out on the couch in Grandfather's office and closed my eyes. If my luck held, once they got started, Grandfather would insist on supervising every detail of the skunk habitat, and I could get a nap.

I managed an hour before Grandfather stormed back in, intent on returning to the church.

He entertained me on the way back to town with amusing trivia about emerald tree boas, including the fact that they gave birth to live young in litters of six to fourteen, and that the newborns were not emerald green like their parents but a distinctive brick red or orange color — information I fervently hoped would never be of any practical use to me.

It was past dawn when we arrived back at the New Life Church, although the sky was still gray and overcast with the threat of more snow. Its parking lot was now half full and the crowd had swelled — although I was relieved to see that most of the newcomers appeared to be men and women carrying buckets, mops, and totes full of cleaning supplies. They were all staring at the church doors, which were flung wide open to the cold.

A gasp ran through the crowd when four men emerged from the front door, carrying what appeared to be one end of a telephone pole. They held the pole above their heads as if in triumph, and the crowd cheered in response. Then they began picking their way carefully down the front steps. The rest of the pole was slowly emerging from the church door until suddenly a large black object appeared — the skunk cage, thoroughly swathed with black tarps and supported by a huge net suspended from the pole. The men had to lift the front of the pole very high indeed to drag the cage over the top of the steps and they were moving very slowly, to avoid jarring the skunks any more than they could help. After the cage, the other end of the pole lengthened until finally four more men emerged, holding their end of the pole high over their heads.

When the black-clad cage finally reached the bottom of the steps, the crowd fell back to a respectful distance as the men carried it to a waiting flatbed truck, incongruously decorated with evergreen garlands and red ribbons. No doubt it had recently been used as the platform for one of the floats in the town's annual holiday parade. The men lifted the cage onto the bed of the truck. More cheers from the crowd. Then another half dozen men raced over to assist with sliding the pole out of the loops at the top of the net while others threw tie-down ropes over the cage, darted forward to secure them to the bed of the truck and raced back to a safe distance.

"Take me over there," Grandfather said, pointing to the truck. I pulled up as close as I could without interfering with the crew.

Another cheer went up when the crew finally stepped back, presumably to declare the loading operation complete. The men began slapping each other on the back in celebration — I assumed because this phase of the skunk removal had been accomplished without additional spraying. Caroline Willner's diminutive figure appeared in the midst of the men, patting them on the arm or the back.

"Time to get this show on the road," Grandfather said. He scrambled out of my car and trotted over to the truck. Once there, he had a hasty conference with Caroline and some of the firefighters. I deduced that he was sharing the news about Cleopatra, which seemed to break up the celebration. Several firefighters dashed back into the church with serious expressions. Two of the remaining crew hopped into the cab of the flatbed truck while Grandfather and Caroline and the rest of them boarded a nearby van. The truck set off at a slow pace, probably to keep the skunks from being annoyed or dislodged, and the van followed.

As I watched the truck's stately progression out of the parking lot, Michael came up to stand at my side.

"Almost looks like another parade," he said.

"We could be seeing the formation of another holiday tradition," I said. "The annual procession of the skunks."

"Good grief — I hope not." Michael shuddered at the thought. "Please don't mention that idea to Randall Shiffley — it's just the kind of thing that would strike our mayor as a unique tourist attraction."

"My lips are sealed," I said. "How close are you to going home to get some sleep?"

"Not sure," he said. "But I don't think it can be that much longer. I should head back in. I've been helping Horace with the forensics. Now that the skunks are gone, he's got to finish up the last part of the choir loft."

He gave me a quick kiss, took a few deep breaths, and strode back toward the church.

"Meg, dear." I turned to find Mother and Minerva Burke, the chief's wife standing nearby. Minerva headed up the Ladies' Auxiliary, the New Life Baptist Church's equivalent of the St. Clotilda's Guild that Mother now ran at Trinity Episcopal. From the way they were both beaming at me, I deduced they were about to draft me for some chore. Probably scrubbing down the choir loft when Horace had finished with it. I braced myself.

"The dear rector has already contacted all the local clergy," Mother said. "And everyone is simply delighted to offer what space they can to help out the New Life congregation."

"Fabulous," I said.

"She's a wonder, that Robyn," Minerva said. "But it's starting to get dreadfully complicated — everyone's got their own program of holiday events."

"Except for the temple," Mother put in. "Thank goodness Hanukkah came early this year, so they only have their usual activities."

"And somebody's got to figure out a schedule that works everything in, and then manage it," Minerva said.

"And you're so good at that sort of thing," Mother said.

I cringed. It sounded like a tedious, time-consuming task, one that would probably require every bit of diplomacy and negotiating skill I possessed. The last thing I needed to take on in the busy holiday season. And from what I could see, Robyn was very good at organizing herself.

Of course, this was already Robyn's busiest season, and I'd already begun to worry about her. She was looking tired. Not just tired, but frayed around the edges. And Caerphilly College's winter break had begun, which meant that Michael would be not only free to take care of the boys as much as needed but eager to spend more time with them.

Most important of all, the organizing tasks would probably last at least as long as the cleanup operation and give me a perfect excuse not to go back into the New Life choir loft.

"I'll do it," I said. "Provided Robyn can get everyone to send me their calendars."

"She's already working on that," Mother said. "And she has a room you can use as a small temporary office over at Trinity."

An office? I wasn't sure why I would need an office at the church — surely this was something that could be solved in a few hours with a telephone and a computer, or even just a good supply of paper and ink. But Trinity was several miles from the stench of the choir loft, so although the office was clearly overkill, I didn't mind the idea.

"Can you give us a ride over there?"

Minerva asked.

"We're going to start getting things ready for tonight's concert," Mother added.

"Which is the one nonnegotiable item on that schedule of yours," Minerva said. "The first concert will go on at eight o'clock tonight at Trinity Episcopal."

"Your carriage awaits." I opened the front and rear passenger doors of my car and Mother and Minerva climbed in.

Chapter 7

"It's small, but I think it will work," Robyn said as she opened the door to my new temporary office.

The room itself wasn't actually that small — it might have been a little larger than her own comfortable study. But it was filled almost literally to the ceiling with boxes and pieces of furniture, all of them either old, broken, shabby, ugly, or all of the above.

"Unfortunately, we're using it right now as a kind of storage room," Robyn said as she showed me in. "For stuff that doesn't fit into the undercroft."

It took me a moment to remember that what Robyn — and Mother — referred to as the church's undercroft was what plebian souls like me called the basement.

"Most of these old relics used to be in my study," Robyn went on. "I'd have exiled them to the undercroft until this spring's rummage sale, but the undercroft's already packed tight with Mrs. Thornefield's belongings."

"Mrs. Thornefield?" The name sounded familiar. "Oh — the lady who left her entire estate to the church."

"God rest her soul," Robyn said. "Yes, and we got a very good offer a few weeks ago for the house — well above its real value, if you ask me."

Clearly she wasn't yet familiar with Caerphilly's chronic housing shortage.

"But the offer was contingent on the buyer being able to move in by Thanksgiving," she went on. "So we had to empty the house, and rather than spend money on storage, we just brought all the stuff here and stowed it in the undercroft. Where frankly it's driving me bonkers."

I could understand why — Robyn clearly shared my preference for clean, uncluttered surroundings. I still couldn't get over how she'd transformed the previous rector's dark, claustrophobic study into a bright, inviting, airy space.

"But that's a problem for another day," she said, in her brisk, businesslike tone. "Here you go." She pointed to the sturdy, battered desk that turned the space just inside the door into a cramped but usable work space. The top of the desk was empty except for a telephone, a legal pad, and a few pens and pencils stuck into a cracked coffee mug with the red, white, and blue Episcopal shield on it.

"The other churches are either dropping off their schedules or e-mailing them to you," she went on. "Here's the password for our wireless router. Dial nine to get an outside line. And if you need anything, I'll be out in the sanctuary, helping with the setup. And Riddick will be in his office next door. I'm sure he'd be happy to help as well if you need anything."

I nodded, though I doubted I'd want to ask for help from Riddick Hedges, Trinity Episcopal's office manager, bookkeeper, and general factotum. Apart from the sexton he was Trinity's one paid staff member. I had no idea whether he was genuinely over-worked or merely bad at multitasking and constantly feeling overwhelmed as a result, but he could generally be seen darting about the church in a state of high anxiety, wringing his hands and getting in the way of anyone who was performing actual useful work.

Robyn hurried out. I sat down at the desk and looked at the papers she had left me. First was a photocopy of the St. Byblig's schedule for the holy season. They had a lot going on, but I noted some possible empty spaces that the Baptists might use. Next up was a schedule from Temple Beth-El of Caerphilly — obviously printed out from a computer file. Seeing it made me realize that I needed more information from St. Byblig's — the temple schedule didn't just tell me the times and locations of each event, it had a column for each available space, and included the duration, the name of the event's leader or other responsible person, the anticipated number of attendees, and any special needs, like a projector or a coffee setup. I was about to give Rabbi Grossman top marks for thoroughness until I found the Trinity schedule Robyn had prepared. It was a printout similar to the Temple Beth-El's, but Robyn had also given the capacity of each room, attached a list of the people I might need to call about rescheduling their events, and penciled in useful if offbeat suggestions of where some of the Trinity events could be located to free up space for the Baptists.

And she noted that she'd sent me an electronic copy as well. Fabulous. There was no need to reinvent the wheel — I could just take her file and add another column for each room available in the county's un-skunked churches and whatever other venues we could find. Sorting the events into the available spaces would be easy.

Okay, not easy. Doable.

But to do that I'd need to run home to get my laptop. And speaking of home — I pulled out my cell phone. Nine o'clock. Not too early to call Rose Noire and check on the boys.

I called home. Michael answered.

"Jamie and Josh's residence." I could hear peals of childish laughter in the background.

"Good," I said. "Chief Featherstone finally sent you home."

"I feel guilty," he said. "Some of the guys are still there helping with the cleanup. But I got a reprieve because I spent so much time helping Horace in the choir loft. The chief assigned someone else to stay with him till the bitter end. And I do mean bitter."

"You're going to get some rest now, right?"

"I'm going to take the boys to town this morning to shop for your Christmas present."

"Hamsters!" piped up a small voice in the background.

"Sshh! Want surprise Mommy," said another small voice.

"Please convince them that I don't need any hamsters," I said. "I know the boys think they're cute and cuddly, but they're

75

just rodents to me. And if you ask me, we have more than enough pets already."

"I've told them," he said. "Hang on a sec." I heard footsteps, and then a door closing. "Back," he said. "Out in the hall, so they can't hear me. I completely agree with you about the hamster thing. I have no intention of taking them anywhere near the pet store or any other establishment where rodents of any kind can be acquired."

"Just make sure they don't talk Rob into taking them," I said. "Or Dad."

"Or your grandfather, or my mother," Michael said. "Understood. I've spoken to the owner of the pet shop and the manager of the animal shelter. If anyone from either of our families shows up attempting to buy or adopt hamsters, guinea pigs, gerbils, rats, or mice, they'll be told that all the available rodents are already bought or adopted and are waiting for their new families to pick them up. There will be no rodents on the Waterston-Langslow homestead, apart from those the barn cats are supposed to be dealing with."

"Thanks," I said. "I wish you'd just stay home and rest, but if you're coming into town anyway, could you drop my laptop off at Trinity Episcopal? I'm helping out with the effort to find places to relocate all the

New Life concerts, services, classes, and social events."

"Can do," he said. "And don't worry. As soon as I talk the boys into some kind of sensible presents for you, I'll bring them home so we can all nap in preparation for tonight's concert."

"Good plan."

We signed off and I returned to my task. I discovered that in addition to her very detailed schedule, Robyn had given me a list of the other clergymen in town, with their e-mails, office, and cell phones.

I had been fond of Father Rufus, our previous rector, a genial soul who habitually walked about so deep in thought that he bumped into walls and had been known to get lost while traveling from his study to the pulpit. Not everyone liked the tidal wave of energy and efficiency Robyn brought to the parish, but if you asked me, they were exactly what it needed.

And it looked as if she'd already done a good half of the job I'd been assigned.

I couldn't do much more until Michael arrived with my laptop, so I decided to see how the concert preparations were going.

CHAPTER 8

I stepped outside my temporary office and walked up the small hallway, past Robyn's study and toward the archway that opened into the vestibule. I stopped in the archway and stared in amazement at the frantic activity taking place. I recognized several Shiffleys — relatives of the mayor and probably employees of his family's construction company — hauling lumber and tools into the main body of the church, from which sounds of sawing and hammering emerged. Matrons from the Ladies' Auxiliary and St. Clotilda's Guild were scurrying back and forth carrying stacks of prayer books and hymnals; music stands; bundles of red satin and gold lamé choir robes; armloads of holly, ivy, and evergreen; real and battery-operated candles; and the several dozen near life-sized figures from the enormous Nativity scene that for the last few weeks had occupied the space between the communion rail and the first row of pews.

I could see why they were moving the Nativity scene — no doubt they needed the space to fit in all the New Life choir members. And having it there had made navigation difficult. But it had been fun watching several of the more curmudgeonly parishioners who habitually sat in the front row either propping their feet up on the outlying sheep or hanging their canes over the wise men's outstretched arms.

Since I had no pressing reason to go out in the vestibule and didn't want to risk getting trampled by the busy masses of volunteers, I was about to pop back into my temporary office to await Michael's arrival. Then I overheard two women having a conversation that caught my interest.

"It's racial, I tell you," the first one said. "An attack like that on an African-American church?"

"Historically African-American," the second corrected. "These days they're getting pretty diverse. But I think if it was racially motivated they'd do something really nasty."

"You don't think the skunks are really nasty?"

"Only silly nasty. If you ask me, it's those Pruitts."

The other woman pondered that for a while. As did I. At one time, the Pruitts had been the self-proclaimed leading citizens of Caerphilly County, but in the last few years they'd lost most of their money and all their political power. The ones not in jail for various sorts of embezzlement had retreated to neighboring Clay County to lick their wounds and, no doubt, plot their comeback. They certainly had it in for Caerphilly. But why would they choose the New Life church as their target? And besides, however much I disapproved of the skunking, I had to admit that executing it required a degree of organization, ingenuity, and boldness that I had a hard time imagining any Pruitt displaying.

"Too clever for a Pruitt," the first woman said, echoing my thoughts. "And not nearly nasty enough."

I hoped they were wrong about that, and about the possible racial motivation as well. But of course the chief had to keep that in mind in doing his investigation. In fact, that possibility, even more than his own membership in the New Life church, probably accounted for how seriously he was taking the prank. I wasn't sure he'd normally have had Horace do forensics on what would otherwise amount to a misdemeanor.

The two women strolled off, still arguing.

As soon as they were out of earshot, I heard muffled snickers from just outside the doorway.

"Oh, man," a young male voice said.

"Yeah," said another.

"At least they have no idea," the first voice said.

"Have you heard anything about old man Dandridge?"

"He'll be fine." The voice didn't sound that confident. "Let's go look useful."

I realized that they probably had no idea I was there. The hallway was dimly lit while the vestibule blazed with light. So I crept forward a little — just far enough to see who had been speaking.

Two teenagers. I recognized one — he was short and compact, with a café au lait complexion and large, slightly almond eyes. My friend Aida Butler's nephew, Ronnie. I couldn't put a name to the other, who was tall, lanky, pale, and freckled, but if he wasn't a Shiffley, he was one of their first cousins. And I recognized the look on their faces — the eager, smiling, "Who, me?" look of someone who has something to hide and thinks he's getting away with it. If I found one of my sons wearing that look, I'd search the immediate area for broken objects and scraps of forbidden treats.

Was I looking at the perpetrators of the skunking?

But what reason could they have for doing it? I knew of no grudge that any of the Shiffleys had against the New Life Baptist Church, and Ronnie Butler was a member of the congregation.

But still. I kept my eyes on them. One of the older Shiffleys called out "Caleb!" and the Shiffley boy hurried to help him carry some lumber. I didn't recall where Caleb fit into the Shiffley family tree, but it wouldn't be hard to find out. Ronnie was standing at attention in front of Minerva Burke, as if eager to receive an assignment. Both boys' faces looked innocent — ostentatiously innocent.

I made a mental note to tell Chief Burke what I'd overheard as soon as I was someplace where I couldn't easily be overheard.

"This is impossible!"

Jerome Lightfoot, the New Life choir director, was standing in the middle of the vestibule, hands raised to the ceiling in a theatrical gesture. Since he was even taller than Michael — probably about six foot six — he'd have stood out even if the bustling crowd hadn't fallen back respectfully to give him room.

"What are these people thinking?" Lightfoot wailed. He had now grasped his hair with both hands, as if about to tear it out in despair, although I noticed that he wasn't really gripping it hard enough to muss it up, much less yank any out.

I'd seen him carry on like this last night, at the rehearsal, when one of the soloists had made some mistake undetectable to me. He'd berated the poor girl for a good five minutes, and she'd been visibly on the verge of tears. Afterward, when I was dropping off Aida's daughter Kayla I asked her if this was typical.

"Yeah," she'd said. "Especially on the eve of a concert. The worse his nerves get, the more he takes it out on us. I was up for that solo, you know. Really bummed me out when I didn't get it. But maybe losing it wasn't so bad after all. At least I don't get chewed out like that."

And Lightfoot was no better today. Everyone was giving him a wide berth, murmuring polite little apologies as they went past.

"Do I have to do everything myself?" As Lightfoot said this he glared at the people surrounding him. Clearly, since no one jumped to his side offering assistance, everyone assumed this was a rhetorical question. Lightfoot snorted with impatience and strode toward the archway where I was standing.

Given how dim the hall was compared to the brightly lit vestibule, perhaps it wasn't entirely his fault that he slammed into me, knocking me into the wall with a thud. But he could have been more polite about it.

"Watch it!" he said, as if I were the one who'd done something wrong.

The lack of sleep combined with the shooting pains through my shoulder did me in and I lost my temper.

" 'Watch it'?" I snapped. "You practically knock me down and all you say is 'watch it'? Where the hell did you learn your manners — a stable?"

"Well, why were you standing there blocking the hallway?" he shouted.

"I wasn't blocking the hallway," I snapped. "I was just standing in it. If you weren't so hell-bent on making sure everyone saw your little temper tantrum, maybe you'd have seen me."

His eyes narrowed, and he took a step toward me, fists clenched. Out in the vestibule, I heard several people gasp, and I found myself wondering if he'd ever been physically abusive to any of the choir members. I remembered how some of the younger ones almost flinched when he came near them.

But my temper was up, and I had no intention of letting him see me cower, so in spite of the throbbing waves of pain in my shoulder, I took a step forward, too, lifted my chin, and glared right back at him. I didn't really think he'd try to strike me, but if he tried, in spite of the shoulder and the eight-inch difference in our heights, I was betting I'd come out on top. Working as a blacksmith had made me a lot stronger than most women, and I still hadn't completely forgotten what I'd learned in several years of martial arts training. Lightfoot, on the other hand, had the weedy, hollow-chested, pasty look of someone who never bothered to exercise and was thin only because he didn't really care about food.

And just now he looked a little startled, as if not used to people standing up to him.

"Hmph!" he said. Then he turned and stalked down the hall. I watched him barge into Riddick Hedges's office. Then I turned and saw that everyone in the foyer was staring my way in stunned amazement. Or maybe in accusation — had I just spoiled everyone's holiday mood?

"I can't wait to find out," I said. "Which one of us gets the title role in *How the Grinch Stole Christmas*."

Not much of a joke, but it broke the tension. People laughed far more than it deserved, and a few even applauded.

Minerva Burke appeared at my side.

"You go, girl," she said. "I think he'll get the part, but you deserve a medal. Not many people stand up to old Bigfoot."

"Probably just as well, since that means he doesn't dislocate that many people's shoulders." I was trying to move my arm — fortunately, the left arm — and feeling a little faint from the resulting waves of pain.

"You're serious, aren't you?" Minerva said.

I was fumbling in my pocket for my cell phone.

"I'm calling Dad," I said.

CHAPTER 9

I pulled out my cell phone, but I didn't want to move my left arm, and trying to hold the cell phone and dial it with my one good hand wasn't working too well.

"Here," Minerva said, taking it out of my fingers. "Let me do that. Let's get you sitting down someplace. Ronnie! Virgil! Come help Ms. Meg!"

I had to admit, it was nice to be half carried into my temporary office and sit back with my eyes closed while Minerva called Dad and ordered him to come over and see to me.

Next door we could hear occasional bellows from Lightfoot, interspersed with the nasal whine of Riddick's voice.

With her phone call made, Minerva pulled over a convenient box for me to put my feet on and another to sit on herself. The two of us, by unspoken agreement, fell silent and tried to figure out what all the fuss next door was about.

"— very sorry," Riddick was saying. "But it's just not practical to remove the altar rail and the first few rows of pews just for the concert —"

"Then how am I to give a concert in this wretched little sty!" Lightfoot bellowed.

"Some of the choir will just have to stand in front of the communion rail," Riddick went on.

"I was told we'd get complete co-operation!" Lightfoot shrieked.

They went back and forth that way for several minutes.

"I confess," Minerva said. "I won't be sorry to see him go."

"Go? Lightfoot? You mean he's leaving?" The news was almost as good as a Percocet.

"Well, he doesn't know it yet," she said. "And I'd appreciate it if you'd keep this to yourself, but yes. We voted not to renew his contract. Unfortunately, it doesn't run out till the end of August, so that means we still have to suffer with him for another eight months. But at least we know there's an end in sight."

"You think maybe he knows?" I asked. "And that's why he's in such a bad mood?"

"I haven't noticed that he's been in a particularly bad mood — for him," she said.

"This is pretty much what he's like most of the time."

"Meg, dear." Mother. She swept in, visibly alarmed. "Are you all right?"

"Possible dislocated shoulder," I said. "And I doubt if I have a temperature," I added, as she put a hand to my forehead.

"You never know," she said. "Your father should be here very shortly."

Just then I saw another figure pass the open door, no doubt heading for Riddick's office.

"Who was that?" Mother asked, glancing over her shoulder.

"Barliman Vess," I answered.

Mother uttered a small sigh of exasperation.

"Mr. Vess is a member of our vestry," I added to Minerva. "An elderly retired banker, a lifelong Trinity parishioner, and Mother's particular bête noire."

"He's not my bête noire, dear," Mother murmured. "He has good intentions, even if he is sometimes a little trying."

"This is ridiculous!" Vess's high, cracked voice carried easily through the wall, and probably as far as the vestibule.

"I can handle it," Riddick said.

"We've already gone to considerable expense to accommodate your unreasonable demands," Vess said.

Mother sniffed dismissively.

"Likes to think he's the watchdog over all of Trinity's financial and administrative affairs," she murmured. "As if the rest of us were incapable of grasping it all."

Vess and Lightfoot began bellowing back and forth at each other. I spotted Riddick slipping down the hall, looking back over his shoulder with an angry look on his face. Then he stopped, closed his eyes, took a couple of deep breaths, moved his lips slightly — whether praying or cursing I couldn't tell — and resumed his customary calm if slightly anxious expression.

"That man!" Mother muttered.

I waited to hear whether she was talking about Vess, Riddick, or Lightfoot, any of whom could possibly have provoked her displeasure.

"I hate to speak ill of someone," she went on. "Especially at this time of year — but Ebenezer Scrooge has nothing on him."

That would be Vess.

" 'A tightfisted hand at the grindstone, Scrooge!' " I quoted. Thanks to Michael's annual one-man dramatic readings of *A Christmas Carol,* I could quote Dickens with the best of them. " 'A squeezing, wrenching, grasping, scraping, clutching, covetous, old sinner! Hard and sharp as flint, from which no steel had ever struck out generous fire; secret, and self-contained, and solitary as an oyster.' "

"Precisely," Mother said. "If he posts one more notice asking who used the church office phones to make an unauthorized ninety-cent long-distance call to California, I may have words with him! And to make it worse, he has the manners of a troll."

"What's he done?" Minerva asked.

"Just last week he tried to have the cleaning service fired for not doing a good enough job," Mother said. "And if you ask me, they were doing a perfectly adequate job."

Coming from Mother that was high praise indeed — her "perfectly adequate" was equivalent to someone else's "fabulous." From Minerva's nod, I could tell she understood this.

"What he really wanted," Mother went on, "was to get rid of the cleaning service altogether, to cut expenses, and have the ladies of St. Clotilda volunteer to do the cleaning. We straightened him out on that notion."

"I should think so," Minerva exclaimed.

"Wasn't it him who tried to get the twelve-step groups banned from using the church building?" I asked.

"Yes," Mother said. "He claimed they weren't leaving enough change to cover the number of coffee packets they used during their meetings. I realize that in these difficult times we all have to keep expenses down, but to begrudge a few pots of coffee to people who are struggling to rebuild their lives!"

"I completely agree," Minerva said. "If he keeps it up, tell him that the Baptist Ladies' Auxiliary would be happy to donate as much coffee as the twelve-step groups could possibly need."

"I think we've already squelched him on that one," Mother said. "But thank you. And perhaps if I could mention your offer, it would shame him into abandoning that particular crusade."

"Please do," Minerva said.

We listened for a few more moments as Vess and Lightfoot bellowed at each other. Vess, predictably, was complaining about the unnecessary expense and trouble the choir was causing, while Lightfoot was bellowing that Vess was a philistine with no appreciation of art. They weren't even arguing with each other, really, just venting.

"If Josh and Jamie were behaving like that, I'd put them both in a time-out," I said.

"One of us should go in and break it up," Minerva said, with a sigh.

"Or both of us," Mother said, with a matching sigh.

"Let's hold off for a few minutes," I said. "At the rate they're going, I think there's a good chance that they'll kill each other off, like the cats of Kilkenny."

Mother and Minerva burst out laughing.

"Besides," I added. "The choir can't begin rehearsing until the Shiffleys have finished whatever it is they're building, so maybe it's a good thing someone's keeping Mr. Lightfoot busy."

"True, dear," Mother said. "And it really isn't funny: You should have seen that wretched Mr. Lightfoot carrying on! He was actually throwing things around in the sanctuary!"

"The Shiffleys' tools and your vases and hymnals," Minerva said. "It's a disgrace!"

Then they looked at each other and burst out giggling again.

"Kilkenny cats!" Minerva spluttered.

"Well, obviously things can't be so bad." Dad appeared in the doorway, holding his trusty medical bag. "What seems to be the trouble?"

Dad agreed with my diagnosis of a possible dislocated shoulder, and he insisted on bustling me down to the Caerphilly Hospital. We nearly came to grief before we even left the parking lot. His van hit a patch of black ice and skidded to a stop against a mound of snow and his medical bag, which unlike us was not strapped in, launched itself out of the backseat into my shoulder, sending more waves of pain through my arm. By the time we reached the hospital, I was mutinous and refused to be taken down for X-rays until they gave me a painkiller of some kind.

Dad and the orthopedic surgeon whiled away the time waiting for the results by trading stories of dislocated joints they had seen in their careers. Since most of the stories involved ghastly complications rather than boringly successful outcomes, after the fourth or fifth story I told them what I thought of their bedside manner and shooed them out of my cubicle.

I was overjoyed when the X-rays finally showed that my shoulder wasn't dislocated. Very badly bruised, but either it hadn't been dislocated in the first place, or it was only partially dislocated and something had popped it back in. My money was on our close encounter with the snow mound in the parking lot.

Dad and the orthopedist were more restrained, cautioning me that there could still be muscle and tendon damage and insisting on an MRI. I found myself wondering, briefly, if they were disappointed that they weren't getting a chance to perform a reduction on me, which I had by now figured out was a euphemism for forcibly shoving my dislocated shoulder back into place. But I had to admit that it was a relief when the MRI showed no serious damage.

Of course, my shoulder still hurt. And I would still need to wear a sling until the abused muscles healed a bit. And even in a small hospital, with Dad urging everyone on, the whole thing took quite a long time. Luckily, while I was waiting my turn in the MRI machine, Michael and the boys dropped by with my laptop. The boys were a little worried until I demonstrated that I had no visible wounds, after which they relaxed and began to explore all the exciting new opportunities for mischief that the ER provided. When they began fighting over who got to ride in the wheelchair and who had to push, Michael and I decided it was time for him to whisk them away to resume their Christmas shopping mission. I whiled away the long wait by finishing up a provisional schedule for relocating all the various church services, classes, pageants, rehearsals, dinners, brunches, and other events. It was a little annoying, having to type one-handed, but still — without my laptop and my cell phone, this would have been an impossible feat.

Of course, in a world without laptops and cell phones, Robyn would have had to find someone else to do the organizing after I'd gone to the hospital. And I could have had whatever pain meds Dad was willing to prescribe, instead of asking him for something that wouldn't muddle my mind.

When I emerged from the MRI, I found that Dad and the orthopedist and several of the nurses had decided to go caroling up and down the halls of the hospital as soon as they finished treating me.

"You're welcome to join us," Dad said.

"I have a few things to do back at Trinity," I said. "And then I think I'll go home and rest."

So Dad took me back to the church, singing "Good King Wenceslas" with great enthusiasm, although he did interrupt himself after nearly every verse to see how I was feeling.

CHAPTER 10

I arrived back at Trinity with my left arm in a sling, feeling extraordinarily cheerful thanks to the tranquilizer Dad provided, which didn't do much to relieve the pain in my shoulder, but did make me feel curiously detached from it.

I continued to feel cheerful, mellow, and detached for two hours as everyone I talked to picked holes in my draft schedule. In short order I made not one but three complete revisions.

Along the way, I developed a whole new sense of how hard Robyn's job was. Her study saw a steady stream of visitors. Most of them, from the small bits I could overhear, were well-meaning volunteers who wanted her to make some decision that I'd have made myself. Her voice carried better than most of theirs, so I had a chance to appreciate her patient, gentle attempts to empower them to make their own decisions.

Me, I'd have been tempted to just shout "I don't care! Figure it out yourself!"

At least every ten minutes either Lightfoot or Vess would appear in her office. Sometimes both at once. I never had any trouble overhearing every word they said. Usually they were complaining about each other, although both occasionally took a few verbal jabs at the Shiffleys doing the construction. Randall Shiffley showed up a couple of times to repeat that if everyone would stop bothering him and his crew they could have the construction finished by three o'clock when the choir practice was due to start. And Minerva Burke showed up a few times to calm down Lightfoot, who kept declaring the concert off. I finally decided he was serious, and apparently so did Minerva. A few minutes later, Reverend Wilson arrived and told Lightfoot off in the tone of voice he usually reserved for his summer revival hellfire and damnation sermons.

"And if you still feel unable to continue," the reverend boomed, in tones people could probably hear in the next county. "I'm sure Sister Burke here would be happy to take your place. The concert must and will go on!"

After that Lightfoot made himself scarce for a while.

Although after both Reverend Wilson and Robyn left, he and Vess both showed up again and turned their wrath on poor Riddick. After his first encounter with them, the poor man actually ducked into my office to hide from Lightfoot, only to be so startled at finding me there that he jumped and hit his head on the corner of a broken-down five-drawer wooden file cabinet.

I jumped up to make sure he was all right, and closed my office door partway to conceal him.

"Why do they have to be here?" he whispered. He was holding the heel of his hand to the brow ridge just above his right eye, and I remembered Mother saying that he was a martyr to migraines.

"Well, Robyn did offer Reverend Wilson the use of Trinity for the concert," I said. "And it's a wonderful chance to show how well the church looks for the holiday. But I think you have a point. Mr. Lightfoot doesn't seem to appreciate our hospitality, so while I'm rearranging, I'll see if I can move any other events he's involved in to other churches. The Catholics have a big sanctuary. Maybe I could schedule him there."

Riddick gave a weak smile and closed his eyes. I went back to my work, and he stood there, motionless, until the hallway outside grew silent again. Then he slipped out without saying anything.

Would the church become more peaceful when the construction was finished and music took the place of hammering? Probably not. From what I'd seen at the last rehearsal, Lightfoot wouldn't let them sing more than a few bars without cursing at them. Although at least he'd be yelling from farther away, not next door.

And waiting for the chief to call me back was also wearing on my nerves. I'd called him shortly after arriving back at the church to tell him what I'd overheard. Of course I got his voice mail. Not knowing who might be around when he played it back, I'd made my message noncommittal.

"Hi. It's Meg Langslow. I overheard something this afternoon that might be relevant to the question of who pulled off that prank. Would be happy to fill you in at your convenience."

Was the investigation going so badly that he had no time to return my call? Or so well that my small clue was of no importance? Every time the phone rang, I had to remind myself not to sound cranky — it wasn't my callers' fault that they weren't the chief.

But it was their fault that they weren't all

being as organized and cooperative as they could be. Randall Shiffley strolled into my temporary office about the time my meds were wearing off, to hear me barking into the phone at the secretary of the Methodist church.

"I said I'll fix the problem!" I said. "But until further notice, the schedule stands!"

I hung up and looked at Randall, fully expecting him to make some unreasonable request or point out some aspect of my schedule that was less than perfect. He held up both hands as if surrendering.

"I just stopped in to see how you're feeling," he said.

"Cranky," I answered, with a sigh. "And rude. That was rude. I shall probably feel obliged to apologize to Mrs. Dahlgren later."

"What's the old biddy on about now?" Clearly Randall knew Mrs. Dahlgren. He crossed his arms and leaned against the massive Victorian breakfront that formed one boundary of my office space.

"She tells me they can't possibly host the Baptist Ladies' Auxiliary potluck dinner tonight because they don't have enough bathrooms."

"You could tell her that you'll ask all the Baptists to be patient while they wait in line," he said.

"I did," I said. "I also told her if the lines got really bad we could arrange for people to pee next door with the Unitarians."

"I reckon she wasn't too pleased with that idea." He was smothering a chuckle.

And he was holding a large hammer. Evidently he'd been helping out with whatever the Shiffley Construction Company had been doing in the sanctuary. Construction. An idea started forming in my mind — much more slowly than usual, thanks to the meds, but still forming.

"Just what have you guys been building, anyway?" I asked.

"A stage to fill in the area behind the altar rail," he said. "And risers for the choir to stand on. You want to come see?"

"Later," I said. "Do you have any of those construction site portapotties you could take over to the Methodist church?"

"We do," he said. "It's a slow season for construction right now, so they're not much in demand. But if you think Mrs. Dahlgren is upset now —"

"Deliver half a dozen of them," I said. "I'll ask Mother to send over some of the ladies of St. Clotilda's with some wreaths and tinsel to make them look a little more festive. Can you do that?"

"I can," he said. "If you really think —"

"HALLELUJAH! HALLELUJAH!"

We both jumped as the opening of Handel's "Hallelujah Chorus" rang out from down the hall in the sanctuary.

We listened for a few bars, and then the music abruptly stopped. We could hear angry voices instead. We both remained silent, straining to hear what was being said. Eventually Lightfoot's voice came through more clearly.

"I said get out and stay out!"

"Only Lightfoot abusing the choir," I said.

"They should get rid of him before he ruins that choir," Randall said.

"He's not a good choir director?"

"Not that I'm an expert," Randall said. "But I've been talking to some people who are. He's got good credentials from a good school. Decent knowledge of music, they say. But he's a train wreck with people. If you ask me, they were in too much of a hurry to hire when their old choir director died so suddenly. Any day now, New Life Baptist Church is going to start leaking members like nobody's business."

I thought about what Minerva had said. I couldn't repeat what she told me, but . . .

"I wouldn't worry about it," I said.

"You know something I don't know?"

"No," I said. "But do you really think the Baptists haven't noticed? Besides —"

"You need to do something about this!" Barliman Vess erupted into my office. "That man has taken over the sanctuary! He's not scheduled to start his rehearsal until three! It's only half past two."

He shook a copy of the master schedule in my face.

"We were supposed to have it for the riser construction until three," Randall said. "But we finished early, so I told Mr. Lightfoot he could get started if he wanted to."

"But that's not on the schedule!"

"Technically, no." Randall's voice sounded a little less calm than usual. I suspected Vess had already been getting on his nerves during the construction. "But since —"

"Hold on!" I swiveled back to my laptop and with a few keystrokes, changed the schedule so the choir rehearsal began at two thirty. Then I swiveled back.

"As duly appointed schedule coordinator, I hereby issue the latest revised schedule," I said. "Choir practice begins at two thirty. Would you like a clean copy?"

I pointed to the printer. Vess shook his head.

"Anything else?" I asked, in my sweetest voice.

Vess frowned down at the paper in his hand, obviously still angry, but curiously unable to argue now that Lightfoot's trespass had been legitimized. I found myself noticing all the liver spots on his bald head and how the skin on the back of his hands was crinkled like tissue. I suddenly felt very sorry for Vess. He'd been retired for at least twenty years and a widower for almost that long. Maybe fussing over the fine details of Trinity's finances and organization were the only things that kept him going.

"Hmph!" he said. He glared at me, and then at Randall for a few seconds, before stomping out.

"I guess he blames you for messing up the schedule," I said. "Though I doubt if he's too pleased with me, either. Mother will get an earful."

"Oh, Mr. Vess already had it in for me," he said. "Kept coming up and complaining about how long our construction was taking. 'How long can it take to nail down a few boards?' And sneaking up behind us to see if we're damaging any of the original 1870s woodwork. And in case you didn't have time to notice, we're not just nailing down a few boards."

"I can see that," I said.

"We designed and built a removable stage

and a set of risers that are custom fitted to the space here at Trinity," Randall said. "With all due respect to Mr. Vess, I can appreciate a fine bit of craftsmanship when I see it, and that's why I wanted a solution that didn't require driving a single nail into your beautiful hundred-and-fifty-year-old oak woodwork. After tonight's concert, it won't take more than half an hour to disassemble it so y'all can have services tomorrow morning as usual, and then after the last church service we'll put it back up again for tomorrow night's concert. If there's a single scratch or nail hole I'll personally make it good as new. And Trinity gets to keep the whole thing, so if you ever need a stage, with or without risers again, you've got one. Your minister's pleased as punch — what's Vess's problem? He's been riding us all day."

I couldn't remember the last time I'd seen Randall this provoked. My sympathy for Vess was fading.

"Robyn's sane," I said. "Vess, not so much. If the congregation took a vote on who they most wished would get fed up with Trinity and join some other church — any other church — I'm betting Vess would win, hands down."

"Just don't sic him on First Presbyterian,"

Randall said. "Sorry. Didn't mean to rant at you. I think I'll make myself scarce before he comes back."

"And as soon as I send out what I fondly hope is the final schedule, I'm going home to shower and rest," I said. "So maybe I'll be able to enjoy some time with Michael and the boys when they get back from Christmas shopping. Don't forget those portapotties."

"I won't." He stood up, nodded, and strolled out.

I scanned the schedule and made one more change. Not much I could do about today, but tomorrow? Lightfoot had a couple of hours' worth of rehearsals with his soloists scheduled for Sunday afternoon. I swapped them into the Methodist church, so Mrs. Dahlgren could enjoy his company for a while.

I sent out a group e-mail with the new schedule, sent a copy to the printer, saved the file, and packed up my things. I made sure I had the meds Dad had provided, but decided to wait until I got home to take more of them. Detachment was great for coping with recalcitrant people, but my current alert — if cranky — state seemed better for dealing with snowy driving conditions.

Just as I entered the vestibule, the choir started another song.

"There's a star in the east on Christmas morn," sang a soaring soprano soloist.

"Rise up, shepherds, and follow," answered the choir.

I stepped into the sanctuary and perched on a pew to listen, just for few minutes. The soloist and choir both sounded wonderful to me, but from Mr. Lightfoot's gestures and facial expressions, I could tell he wasn't happy.

Just as the soloist was beginning the third verse, my cell phone rang. It wasn't loud, and I had the ring tone set to a single chime, which was not as intrusive as the loud and intricate tunes so many people seemed to favor, but Lightfoot turned and glared at me as if about to shout "Off with her head."

I pressed the answer button before the phone rang a second time and ran out into the vestibule to take the call. In fact, for good measure, I ran all the way outside the church.

"Meg, dear?" Mother. "Is this a bad time?"

CHAPTER 11

I was tempted to lie and say I was busy, before she had a chance to ask whatever she was calling me to ask. But I felt a little superstitious about uttering falsehoods on the steps of a church.

"Not a bad time for me," I said. "Mr. Lightfoot may yet kill me for interrupting his choir practice."

"Mr. Lightfoot should be very grateful to you that he has a place to practice," Mother said. "Speaking of finding places . . ."

I winced. I could already see my latest carefully arranged schedule collapsing like a house of cards. I leaned against one of the bright red double front doors, brushed a aside a stray frond of spruce from the wreath that was trying to tickle me, closed my eyes, and braced myself.

"We need a place to hold a sewing bee," she said. "The cleaning company says there's nothing they can do about the seat cushions that were sprayed by the skunks. So we're going to make all new ones."

"Do we have to do it now?" I asked. "And who's 'we'?" I hoped she hadn't forgotten how meager my sewing skills were.

"The New Life Ladies' Auxiliary and St. Clotilda's Guild," Mother said. "And yes, we need to do it now because there's a chance we can get the church back in operation for Christmas Day services. If the cleaning service manages to get the smell out of the heating system and Randall's crew can finish replacing the wood that soaked up the scent and we can handle the cushions, the church will be as good as new!"

I was working on a tactful way of suggesting that once the cleaning service got the ducts clean, the Baptists could have their services back with folding chairs instead of new pews and upholstery, and maybe the sewing bee could wait until after Christmas. Suddenly the church's outdoor decoratives came on, outlining every tree, bush, lamppost, and fence post with fairy lights. No similarly sudden illumination flooded my brain — only a mild curiosity about whether someone had just turned them on or whether they were on a timer. Then Mother spoke again.

"We were thinking of using your library, dear. If that's okay with you. It's big enough, and we wouldn't really be in your way."

It sounded like such an easy solution. True, I'd resisted offering the library when I was compiling my schedule, in no small part because Michael and I were still very much enjoying having it to ourselves. We'd lent the space, along with our barn, to the county for several years during the financial crisis, when Caerphilly had lost possession of its library building and needed someplace to house the books. But now that we had it back, I wasn't keen on making it a public space again.

"And of course we'd be happy to watch the boys if you and Michael need to do a little last-minute Christmas shopping."

Mothers of twins can be induced to do many things with an offer of free babysitting.

"Fine," I said. "But just the library — not Michael's office, which is where we've hidden all the Christmas presents. Except for yours, which are somewhere else entirely and already wrapped," I added.

"Of course, dear." Mother was almost purring. "I wouldn't think of peeking. I'll be over in half an hour or so to make sure everything's ready."

"Surely you weren't planning to start tonight?" I asked. "Won't a lot of people want to be at the concert?"

"We're starting bright and early at eight tomorrow," Mother said. "For those who aren't attending early services, of course; they can come later."

"Why don't I just make sure all our stuff is out of the library when I get home?" I asked. "I'll be there soon."

"That would be perfect, dear," Mother said. "And I'll see to the decorations," she added.

" 'Decorations'? Mother, you already decorated our house weeks ago — remember?"

"Yes, dear," she said. "But that was weeks ago. Things might need a little sprucing up. And back then I was just decorating for you — not for the Ladies' Auxiliary and St. Clotilda's. See you soon."

With that she hung up.

I wasn't sure I wanted to find out what feats of decorating Mother was capable of when she was trying to impress not one but two church women's groups. At least between my bruised shoulder, my job as location tsarina, and most important, Michael and the boys, I'd have plenty of very valid excuses to avoid getting involved if Mother tried to enlist my help.

I ducked back inside. In my haste to remove my offending phone from choir practice, I'd left my purse, my coat, and the tote containing my laptop in the pew where I'd been sitting. I slipped into the sanctuary and collected my gear. Lightfoot was so busy yelling at the baritones for sloppy enunciation that he didn't notice my arrival.

As I was about to leave, I realized I hadn't collected the hard copy of the latest schedule from my printer. I plodded down the dark little hallway to my temporary office. I unlocked my door, went in, and closed it after me, because I suddenly felt a little light-headed and didn't want anyone to see me wilt into my desk chair.

Definitely time to go home and rest. Past time. And maybe a good time to take that next dose of the tranquilizer after all. I set down my tote and began to rummage through it one-handed for the water bottle I usually kept there.

Then I heard a noise from the office next door. From Riddick's office. Which had been closed when I walked down the hall, with no line of light under the doorway.

I was opening my mouth to ask who was there when it occurred to me that maybe someone who was sitting in an office with the lights off might be doing something that wasn't on the up-and-up.

I put down my tote and the water bottle and tried to stand up quietly. I was taking slow, careful steps toward the door —

And tripped over my purse. I twisted to avoid landing on my shoulder, and ended up knocking over the office chair, which landed with a noisy clatter on the linoleum floor. I scrambled up as quickly as I could, but I heard soft, rapid footsteps going down the hall.

By the time I opened the door, the hallway was empty.

And now Riddick's office door was standing open.

I walked in.

At first I thought that Riddick had made a clumsy attempt to decorate his office for Christmas. Then I realized that the decorations piled on his desk, his shelves, and his floor were actually church castoffs — broken angels, half-melted candles, an ancient fly-specked Santa. All the worn-out items Mother and the ladies of St. Clotilda had winnowed out and marked for donation or disposal when they'd decorated the church. Was he keeping the junk out of some sense of thrift or feeling of nostalgia? Or was it merely, like so many other things at Trinity, a case of Riddick just not yet getting around to dealing with the detritus?

Maybe the mounds of paper covering every horizontal surface were similar signs of neglect rather than busyness. It would take someone more familiar with them — perhaps only Riddick himself — to tell if anyone had been messing with them. But I did notice that his computer was on. Would he have gone home and left it on? Many people did, of course. If I were Riddick and knew Barliman Vess might come snooping around at any time, alert to every nanowatt of waste, I wouldn't, but maybe Riddick was used to Vess's nagging.

I stepped inside to see what was on the screen. It appeared to be the alumni directory for a prestigious school of music. Someone had done a search on the name "Lightfoot." I scrolled down to see the results. Only one Lightfoot, and he was Arnold, not Jerome. The picture didn't look right, either — the choir director was a tall, skinny, light-kinned African-American. This Lightfoot was a short, bespectacled white guy with thinning blond hair. About the only similarity was their age — at a guess, they were both in their forties.

Of course, the fact that our Lightfoot hadn't showed up didn't necessarily mean anything. I wondered if the University of Virginia, my alma mater, had an online searchable directory — one accessible to anyone who went to the alumni Web site. If they did, they certainly wouldn't have a recent picture of me. Maybe Lightfoot just hadn't signed up for the directory. It seemed largely calculated to let students and alumni look for jobs and network with people who might be interested in musical collaborations and jamming. Lightfoot had a job, and I didn't see him as the collaborating type.

Up until a few weeks ago I wouldn't have had the slightest idea how to extract any more information from Riddick's computer, but it had occurred to me that given how precocious Josh and Jamie were, all too soon they would start playing with our computers and getting into who knows what sort of trouble. One of the perks of Rob owning a computer game company was access to expert tech support whenever we needed it. Rob had been happy to send over someone from his help desk to set up parental controls on all our computers and to teach me a few basics on how to check up after the boys — knowledge I hoped I wouldn't have to use for a few more years.

As a result, I knew how to find the list of other pages this browser had recently visited. It was a moderately interesting list. Someone had searched for Lightfoot's name, alone and in combination with the music school and with the name of a Baptist church in Detroit.

Someone was suddenly very interested in Mr. Lightfoot.

Of course, this fact would be a lot more useful if I knew who was doing the snooping. It could have been Riddick, before he left. Or any of the dozens of other people who had been coming and going from the church all day, including whoever had fled when I'd knocked over my chair.

I pulled out my phone and took a picture of the history, and then another of the page showing the wrong Lightfoot. Then I turned off the computer and shut and locked Riddick's door.

I collected my purse and tote and locked up my office, too.

In the vestibule, I opened the door to peek into the sanctuary. Several dozen people were listening to the rehearsal. Including Mr. Vess, who did not appear to be enjoying himself. He was standing in the back, glaring at Lightfoot.

I closed the door and was about to leave when I heard a loud thud followed by some clanking noises to the left side of the vestibule, where another corridor led to the classrooms and the parish hall.

Two Shiffleys were each holding one end of a small stack of long boards and looking down at a small toolbox lying on the floor with some of its contents spilled out. Clearly the metal tools were the source of the clanking noises.

"What's up?" I said.

They both jumped when I spoke, and then relaxed.

"We thought you were him for a minute," one said.

"Let's get the rest of this stuff loaded before he does come out again," the other one said.

"Meg, could you put that toolbox on top of the boards?" the first asked.

"She's injured," the other said. "You can't ask her to —"

"It's okay," I said. "I can do it one-handed." I put down my stuff, dumped the tools back in the box, and set it as securely as possible on top of the boards.

"Thanks," one of them said.

"Come on," the other said, looking around nervously. "Let's go before he comes out here again."

I followed them out. They thanked me again as they threw the boards and then the

kit roughly into the back of a Shiffley
Construction Company truck. Then they
roared off before I'd finished stowing my
stuff in the car.

Had Lightfoot unnerved them so much?
Or something else?

I shoved the thought aside, got into the
car, and headed for home.

Chapter 12

It was snowing again, so I decided maybe it was a good thing I'd been distracted before I took another pill. The ride home promised to be a little slippery.

But I did enjoy the part of it that led through the town square of Caerphilly. Nearly every building was decorated, some with tasteful wreaths and natural evergreens, others with twinkling lights. The county's annual holiday parade had already taken place, but many of the floats had been installed as decorations in the town square, at the foot of the county's living Christmas tree, a specially planted Colorado blue spruce that, according to Randall, was "just a smidgen shorter than the national Christmas tree."

I was pleased to see that the town square was still covered with snow. If the snow didn't melt by Christmas Eve, Randall would set the plows to clearing out a space at the foot of the Christmas tree so the crowds could gather to watch the living Nativity pageant across the street at the Methodist church and then gather around the county tree for the community carol sing. But for now, the large expanse of snow, unbroken except for occasional footprints from birds or foxes, was magical.

A surprising number of people were trooping up and down the sidewalks and in and out of all the shops around the town square. Maybe Randall's campaign to promote holiday tourism was working. I wasn't sure why "Christmas in Caerphilly" had a Victorian theme — maybe Randall, like me, had seen *A Christmas Carol* too many times at an impressionable age — but I enjoyed it. Nearly every corner had a band of carolers in Victorian costume, entertaining passersby while collecting donations for local charities. The outdoor stalls, also for charity, were doing a brisk business in hot beverages — coffee, tea, chocolate, and cider mulled with spices — and hot snacks, including muffins, cookies, candied apples, and roasted chestnuts. There were long lines for the hay rides, in reproduction farm wagons pulled by teams of sleek draft horses, specially chosen because they weren't spooked by the constant jingling of all the bells on their harnesses. And even longer lines to have pictures taken in borrowed Victorian costumes either in front of the town Christmas tree or in a genuine one-horse sleigh with a beautiful dappled gray horse harnessed to it.

It was more peaceful when I reached the residential areas of town, although I doubt if I spotted a single house without some kind of Christmas or winter decoration. On the outskirts of town I passed by several hills and ravines bristling with sledders and snowboarders. And when I got out into the country, I passed the occasional group of people who in spite of the fact that they were rapidly traversing the frozen fields on cross-country skis still found the energy to wave their poles at me and shout "Merry Christmas!" and "Happy holidays!"

For a moment I tried to imagine trekking that way across the countryside with Michael and the boys. And then I gave it up. My arm had begun bothering me on the way home. I waited until I was safely parked in the driveway, then took the pill with a long pull from the water bottle and walked inside. Michael's car was there, which meant he and the boys were home from their shopping.

James and Josh were very glad to see me,

and only the sight of my sling prevented them from hurling themselves upon me. They kept staring at the sling and asking what it was until I finally led them into the kitchen and made each of them a dish-towel sling.

The boys were delighted, and began racing around to find someone to admire their new accessories. Mother, when she arrived, was startled.

"What have they done to themselves now?" she asked.

"Swing, Gamma!" Josh explained.

Jamie just held his sling up so Mother could see.

"They *both* fell off the swing?" Mother asked. "What were they doing outside in this weather?"

"That was 'sling,' " I pointed to my own sling. "They're fine. Monkey see, monkey do."

"Oh, I see," she said. "Very elegant. You both look quite dashing."

"Where's Daddy?" I asked. "Do you want to show him your slings?"

"Show Daddy!" both boys shouted, and ran upstairs.

"And how are you doing, dear?"

"Long day," I said. "But I'm home, and planning to rest now."

Which was intended as a subtle hint that if she was planning to enlist me in the redecorating, it wasn't going to work.

"That's nice, dear. Yes, it needs a little something." She was gazing around the hallway with a small frown on her face, so I deduced that last part was about the decor, not my napping plans.

" 'A little something'?" I followed her gaze. The whole hall was decorated within an inch of its life. Evergreen garlands alternated with gold tinsel garlands, all ornamented with red velvet ribbons. Every horizontal surface contained at least a few branches of holly sporting clusters of red berries. Several dozen poinsettias were massed along the walls — elegant silk ones, of course, rather than real ones that might be poisonous to the dogs. In the front corner was a rather elongated tree, chosen specially to reach as close to the ceiling as possible without occupying so much floor space that we couldn't open the door. It was completely decked with red and gold ornaments. We had two Nativity scenes, one small and traditional on the hall table, the other large and modernistic, on the floor beside the tree. Two handmade baskets held the Christmas cards we'd received. Special red and gold bowls scattered throughout held Rose Noire's special potpourri blends — spruce and pine scent near the tree, cinnamon and apple flanking the arch to the living room, and clove and nutmeg in the hallway leading back into the kitchen.

Arriving guests generally spent the first fifteen minutes of their visit exclaiming over the decorations, which actually wasn't as inconvenient as it might sound, since it usually took me five or ten minutes to hack my way through the decorations to get to the hall closet or the coatrack to hang their wraps. And once I finally pried the guests out of the hall, the marveling usually continued. Mother referred to her efforts in the living room and dining room as more restrained, though of course they were only so in comparison to the hall. It was all fine for social visits, but whenever anyone came on any business I'd taken to leading them to the kitchen, where they wouldn't spend their entire time sightseeing and could be more easily induced to help consume some of the surplus of holiday cake, cookies, candy, and fruit that was piling up.

Mother had even incorporated our two dogs into the decorating scheme. The original plan was to put large red velvet bows on both dogs' collars and to have them sleep on matching red velvet cushions on the hearth. I felt sorry for Horace, who'd been drafted to help with this part of the decorating. Tinkerbell, Rob's enormous Irish Wolfhound, gave him no trouble — in fact, she actually seemed to like the red bow — but Horace had ended up making a trip to the ER after trying to decorate Spike, our nine-pound furball, whose personality resembled a cross between a saber-toothed tiger and a wolverine. By the time Horace got back, Spike had established ownership rights to the wolfhound-sized cushion. The cushion intended for his use was barely large enough to fit Tinkerbell's enormous shaggy head, but she curled up on it anyway. Fortunately Mother found the resulting tableau cute, since any attempts to rearrange it would probably have resulted in more trips to the ER.

Mother had gone particularly overboard in the dining room, where she'd adopted an angel theme. Legions of angels marched up and down the dining room table, holding trumpets or songbooks or candles. More angels lolled on the sideboard and peeked out from behind the plates and pitchers in the built-in china cabinet. Angels rioted along the evergreen garlands that festooned all four walls, climbed and dangled from the chandelier. There wasn't actually a lot of room left for serving food or seating people, which hadn't been much of a problem so far — we'd just taken to eating a lot more often at our oversized kitchen table — but was definitely going to cause some tension when Michael's mother arrived to carry out her plan of using our house to prepare and serve her entry in the two dueling Christmas Day meals we were expected to attend. Mother would be serving her own meal over at the cottage, as she'd taken to calling the rambling farmhouse she and Dad had bought to stay in during their increasingly frequent and lengthy visits to Caerphilly. Was I wrong in suspecting that the decor in her dining room would be equally over the top but far less impractical in which to serve a meal?

Looking around, I tried to imagine what Mother could possibly think was missing.

"Didn't some famous interior designer say when you finished decorating you should take a look and remove at least one thing?" I asked.

"It was Coco Chanel," Mother said. "And she was talking about a woman getting dressed — not interior decorating, and certainly not decorating for Christmas, where a certain feeling of luxurious excess is quite appropriate."

She was shuffling through one of the Christmas card baskets, making sure that the top cards were all elegant ones that matched the red, gold, and green color scheme, and banishing any that did not meet her aesthetic standards to the bottom of the basket.

"I'll leave you in charge of the luxurious excess," I said. "I'm going to take a nap so I'll be fit to go to the concert tonight."

"Splendid," she said absently. She was holding up both hands making the suggestion of a picture frame and squinting through it at the stairway.

I headed upstairs, resigned to the probability that the hallway would be unrecognizable the next time I saw it.

When I was halfway up, Michael and the boys appeared.

"Mommy, go sledding!" Josh called.

Jamie just raced downstairs and began digging through the coat closet for his snow gear.

"They already napped," Michael said. "And I assume you still need to. So since there's fresh snow falling . . ."

"Wonderful idea," I said. "How about feeding them while you're out, and I'll meet up with you all at the concert?"

I helped stuff the boys into their snowsuits and boots and then climbed upstairs again, ignoring the fact that Mother was still busy with her measuring tape and notebook. I put my cell phone where I would hear it if the chief finally returned my call and fell asleep secure in the knowledge that the boys were safe, and happy, and that I could take a nice long nap before I saw them again.

My phone alarm woke me up a few hours later with just enough time to throw my clothes on and drive into town for the concert. In fact, not quite enough time, since I had to park half a dozen blocks from Trinity.

I despaired of getting a seat for the concert, and was resigned to standing in the back. Or maybe sitting on the floor of the vestibule — I wouldn't see much but at least I could hear. But when I peeked into the sanctuary, I spotted Michael and the boys, sitting in one of the front row pews, with Robyn and her husband sitting on one side of them and Mother, Dad, Grandfather, Caroline, Rose Noire, and Rob on the other. Robyn caught sight of me and waved, and I hurried to take the seat they were saving for me.

If I'd been picking the seats, I wouldn't have picked the front pew. Because of limited space, the first two rows of choir members were standing in front of the communion rail, almost stepping on our feet, so we had to crane our heads up to see them and couldn't get a glimpse of the rest of the choir. I was afraid we'd get blasted when they opened their mouths and began to sing, and the fact that Jerome Lightfoot had set up his music stand not six feet away, in the center aisle, didn't exactly make me any happier. But the boys were very excited at being so close to the choir, and it was all we could do to keep them from reaching out and grabbing the red velvet and gold lame of their special Christmas robes.

And we couldn't keep the boys from standing on the pews when a hush fell over the church and Lightfoot nodded to the organist, who had been playing soft background music. The organist struck up the first few chords of "O Come, All Ye Faithful" and the choir all lifted their hymnals purposefully.

Suddenly something shifted in the evergreens over the choir's heads, and a bright green snake's head popped out of the foliage, followed by three or four writhing feet of body.

CHAPTER 13

Scattered screams erupted from both the choir and the audience, and I was terrified that a stampede would take place. Cleopatra, by contrast, seemed remarkably calm.

Fortunately, Grandfather saved the day by scrambling up onto the seat of our pew, and then beginning to bellow out orders and exclamations.

"Cleopatra! Well done! You've found her! Quiet, everyone! She's easily startled. Get a ladder, someone! Let's get her down before she falls!"

A few people still fled out into the halls, but nearly everyone sat quietly and watched with interest as several sturdy basses and baritones lifted up other, lighter choir members onto their shoulders. Following Grandfather's bellowed instructions, they carefully untangled Cleopatra from the greenery, carried her down, and placed her across Grandfather's shoulders. The choir and congregation burst into applause as Grandfather, still wearing his scaly boa, shook the hands of Cleopatra's rescuers. He and Caroline drafted Horace to help them drive Cleopatra back to the zoo and strode out. Once Cleopatra was gone, everyone — even the people who had briefly fled the sanctuary — seemed in an unusually good humor, and Lightfoot had a little trouble getting them all to settle down so the concert could resume.

In fact, Lightfoot was the only person who seemed at all upset over the incident. He was in a completely foul humor. And kept glaring over at me. Did he suspect me of having arranged Cleopatra's appearance, to upstage his concert? Or was he just staring at the sling Dad insisted I still wear? People tended to notice it, and a lot of them came over to commiserate with me, shooting him frowning glances as they did, but I wouldn't have taken him for someone who cared what others thought.

Then again, maybe he was afraid I'd sue. That seemed more in character. I made a point of beaming graciously at him the next time I caught him glancing my way, which seemed to disconcert him more than all the whispering and finger-pointing.

The audience finally settled down, and

Lightfoot raised his baton and the concert resumed.

"O Come, All Ye Faithful!" was followed by "Hark! The Herald Angels Sing" and then "Ding Dong Merrily on High," "Go Tell It on the Mountain," "Glory, Glory, Glory to the Newborn King," "When Was Jesus Born?" "O, Holy Night," and "Children, Go Where I Send Thee."

Josh was clearly enjoying the concert immensely — he was nodding his head, tapping his feet, and slapping his knees in time to the music, even during the slow songs. I loved watching him, but I had to admit, I was glad he had crawled into Michael's lap, not mine. I was holding Jamie, who was sitting with his mouth and eyes wide open, utterly motionless, as if afraid the whole thing would vanish if he moved a muscle or made a sound.

Satisfied that the boys were having fun, I settled back against Michael's shoulder, closed my eyes, and gave myself over to enjoying the music.

It was well past the boys' bedtime when the concert ended, so rather than wait for the slow procession out the main doors, where both Robyn and Reverend Wilson were shaking the hands of the departing audience, we ducked to one of the side doors — where we found Riddick Hedges standing guard. He frowned at us.

"Good evening, Riddick," Mother said. "Lovely to see you." With that she sailed toward the door, clearly assuming he would open it by the time she reached it. Riddick blinked, and then scrambled to comply.

"Good evening, ma'am," Riddick said. He didn't quite bow, but he was clearly tempted.

We all followed in Mother's wake, wishing Riddick good evening — except for the boys who were fast asleep on Michael's and Rob's shoulders.

"I was supposed to be keeping this door secure," he muttered as I approached, bringing up the rear of our party.

"Against intrusion, I assume," I said. "Or did Robyn tell you to lock it up so no one could escape her handshake?"

"Never had such foolishness before," he muttered. "Skunks! Snakes! What next?"

"Nothing, let's hope," I said. "Or at least, with you on guard, nothing here."

"The chief sent out orders for everyone to lock up tight tonight," he said. "I remember when nobody had to lock his front door here in Caerphilly."

"I'll let you know if I spot anyone suspicious lurking outside," I said.

"Right," he said, with a grudging nod of approval as he held the door for me.

As I followed the rest of the family, I heard him testing the lock behind us.

On the first part of the way home the boys woke up long enough to serenade us with some of the songs the choir had performed. The results might have been more melodic if they were old enough to have any idea of pitch and key and if they could have been persuaded to sing the same song at the same time, but Michael and I enjoyed it anyway. I wasn't quite so sure about Rob. Still, I was relieved when both of their voices began to fade — bedtime would go so much more easily if we could just carry them to bed and tuck them in, still unconscious.

"I see your mother's been busy again," Michael murmured as he walked into the foyer with Jamie over his shoulder.

"It's like living at the North Pole," Rob muttered as he hauled Josh upstairs.

I was relieved to see that Mother hadn't rearranged everything — just added a little more of everything. More greenery. More ribbons. More tinsel. About the only annoying thing she'd done was arrange for someone to fit out the entire downstairs with little wireless speakers to pipe in an endless supply of soft instrumental Christmas music. It took me fifteen minutes to find the central source of the music — an iPod set up in the kitchen pantry — and silence it for the night.

I checked to make sure the library was ready for the sewing bee and Michael's office, with its dangerous cargo of unwrapped presents, was locked. Then, after a quick visit to the boys' rooms to plant good night kisses on their sleeping foreheads, I fell into bed. It was still dark the next morning when my cell phone rang.

CHAPTER 14

It was my phone ringing, not Michael's pager — something to be thankful for, I supposed. I fumbled to answer it.

"Meg?" It was Robyn. "I hope I didn't wake you."

I knew it was customary under such circumstances to protest that no, of course, she hadn't awakened me, I had been up for hours. But it was 6:00 A.M. and I wasn't sure I could manage the obligatory cheerful tone with any grace, so I skipped to the point.

"What's wrong?" I asked.

"Can you come in and work your magic on the schedule again?"

I blinked for a few moments, puzzled.

"Is there something wrong with the schedule everyone agreed to last night?" I asked finally.

"Of course not! It would have been perfect except there's been another incident."

Suddenly I felt a lot more awake. I sat upright and began fumbling for the light.

"What kind of incident?"

"Someone left a flock of ducks overnight in the sanctuary at St. Byblig's."

"Ducks?"

"What's wrong?" Michael muttered.

I pressed my cell phone's speaker button so he could hear what Robyn was saying.

"Father Donnelly came in to get ready for the early mass," she reported. "And he found the ducks, several hundred of them, roosting on the pews, and a few of them waddling up and down the aisles. And more down in the Sunday school classrooms. And they'd obviously been there for hours, and the place was a mess — no way they could celebrate mass in there till after a good cleanup. So he canceled the mass, and most of the parishioners who showed up for it are already on their way home to change into work clothes and start cleaning. But the cleanup could take a while, and he doesn't yet know if the building has to be reconsecrated, so he needs to know where he can celebrate mass today — several masses, actually — and you're the only one who knows the master schedule well enough to figure that out. Can you come down to St. Byblig's and help us cope?"

"Be there in half an hour," I said.

"Bless you!" With that, she hung up.

"Ducks," Michael mused. "Well, at least evicting them won't be dangerous. Geese, now, might put up quite a fight, but ducks are pretty mild-mannered."

"Does this mean you're volunteering to help with the duck removal?" I asked. I was slipping on my jeans and a fairly warm sweater, since I'd probably be spending a lot of time either outside or in a church building whose doors and windows had been flung open to bring in the fresh air.

"Someone has to watch the boys," he said.

"True," I said. "And they had a late night last night, so if by some miracle they actually sleep in, let's let them. I have no idea how long this will take, but I'll keep you posted."

"Maybe the boys and I can come over and help when they are up," he said. "But not until the ducks are gone — they'd want to bring some home, and I don't think we want any more additions to the livestock just yet."

"Agreed." I grabbed my laptop, which was still perched on top of the dresser where I'd dumped it before going to bed, and headed out.

It was snowing, but only lightly, and the roads were fine, so I made good time. And while my shoulder wasn't back to normal, it didn't hurt as long as I refrained from raising my hand too high or trying to lift anything heavy.

St. Byblig's was a quaint little gray stone building nestled into the side of a hill on the outskirts of Caerphilly. The roofs were covered with snow, the surrounding grove of evergreens all had a light dusting of snow that outlined every needle, and the whole thing looked like a picture postcard. Well, except for the long line of people well bundled in overcoats and down jackets, trudging into the church with their gloved hands empty and then out again, each carrying a snowy white duck. It was a memorable scene, and a reporter from *The Caerphilly Clarion* was taking pictures to document it.

The line continued down to a small panel truck from the Shiffley Construction Company, parked at the foot of the church steps. Here the process was reversed — people walked in carrying ducks and walked out empty-handed, to join the procession back into the church.

I parked my car as close to the door as I could, and peeked into the panel truck on my way into the church. Someone had done a quick conversion job with chicken wire and a rough door frame, transforming most of the space inside the truck into a giant duck cage.

"Morning, Meg." Inside the truck, Caroline Willner was minding the gate, holding it open just enough for each arriving human to tuck his or her duck inside, and then shutting it so the ducks already in residence couldn't escape.

"Where are they going?" I asked.

"Down to the zoo for now," she said. "Your grandfather's got his men clearing out some space."

"Odds are they won't have to stay there long," I said. "Sooner or later, some farmer is going to wake up and notice his ducks are gone."

"I'm surprised it hasn't happened already," she said. "Of course, when someone does show up, we'll need some proof of ownership. No way we're just going to turn over several hundred valuable Pekin ducks to any old person who shows up claiming to have lost some. We're nearly full here — can you stick your head out and see if the other truck's back?"

I did as ordered.

"No other truck in sight," I reported.

"Blast. Well, send in the next dozen ducks, and have the rest wait back in the church

141

till the truck's here."

I relayed her instructions to the duck-laden conga line. The first twelve queued up outside the truck door while the rest trudged back into the church, calling out "Hold up! Waiting for the next truck!" to those still emerging from the church.

By the time I reached St. Byblig's vestibule, it was filled with people standing around holding ducks in their arms and chatting cheerfully with one another — a little loudly, to be heard over all the quacking.

"There she is!" Robyn and Father Donnelly waved me over.

"Let's talk in my office," Father Donnelly said. Normally his round ruddy face would have worn a broad smile, but this morning he looked harried. "More peaceful away from all the livestock. It's the wrong season for the blessing of the animals."

"Can I see the scene of the crime first?" I asked.

"Help yourself." He shuddered, and gestured to the doors leading to the sanctuary.

I peered in. Dozens of white ducks were still waddling about the floor, resting on the pew seats and kneelers, or perched on the top of the pews. Considering the number of ducks in the truck outside, in a holding pattern in the vestibule, or already on their way to their temporary quarters at the zoo, the original duck infestation must have been impressive.

"Quite a lot of them," I said aloud.

"Hundreds," he said. "For all I know it could be thousands. I expect someone is counting them, if you're curious. I have no doubt they'll want to publish the statistic in the newspaper. At least I can report one blessing — they all seemed to have stayed on this side of the altar railing. So while there's a lot of soiling in the nave and some of the nearby meeting rooms, the chancel area, thanks be to God, seems untouched."

"And we had the Shiffley Construction workmen rig that netting to make sure it stays that way." Robyn pointed to the far end of the church, where several expanses of ten-foot-tall deer netting divided the main part of the church from the raised area with the altar.

"Good idea," I said. "Well, let's get started."

It took two hours and countless phone calls to devise a workable solution, and in the end we only managed it because the Methodist and Lutheran ministers offered to hold an ecumenical service at the Methodist church, freeing up a time slot at the

Lutheran church for one of the masses for the refugees from St. Byblig's. Also, in a novel idea, the Caerphilly Bowl-o-Rama, which didn't normally open till one on Sunday, offered the use of its space until that time and we relocated all the St. Byblig's Sunday school classes there. Father Donnelly made a quick call to his archdiocese, where a sleepy monsignor gave the chancery's approval to our revised plans.

"The Bowl-o-Rama," Father Donnelly said. "I never thought I'd see the day."

" 'Wherever two or more of you are gathered in His name,' " Robyn quoted.

"Yes," Father Donnelly said. "But thank the Lord for the Lutherans and Methodists. I'm not sure how the chancery would have reacted if I'd asked to hold the mass in a bowling alley."

I decided not to point out that it could come to that, if Caerphilly's reigning prankster continued unchecked. From the look on his face, I suspected that thought had already occurred to him.

"Perhaps I should ask now, just in case," he murmured, picking up the telephone again.

"Let's get the e-mails and telephone trees going," Robyn said.

Since it was Sunday morning and most of

the clergy were conducting services and not apt to be near their computers any time soon, I printed out two dozen copies of the schedule (version seven) and drove around to the various churches to hand deliver them. At the Methodist church, Mrs. Dahlgren, the secretary, give me a particularly poisonous look. I couldn't pretend not to know why so I just ignored it. And the portapotties didn't look that bad. Randall's crew had set them up right behind the life-sized Nativity scene on the grass in front of the church — which would, with the figures removed, be the venue for the live-action Nativity on Christmas Eve. Someone — probably at Mother's direction — had screened the portapotties as much as possible with a lot of very leafy fake palm trees. They'd even painted the white portapotties with faux doors and windows and rooftop terraces, so they looked remarkably like the little dioramas of Bethlehem I remembered building in my childhood Sunday school classes, even down to a light dusting of snow to soften everything.

Mrs. Dahlgren may have been vexed, but a great many of the congregation — particularly the children — were charmed with the dramatic addition to their Nativity scene. As I left, I could see Reverend Trask beaming as he and Reverend Larsen supervised a joint task force of Methodist and Lutheran children who were dusting the snow off all the human figures in the scene. He waved back at me cheerfully and gave me a double thumbs-up. So there, Mrs. Dahlgren.

As I drove around, I found it was gnawing at me that I still hadn't managed to tell the chief about overhearing Caleb and Ronnie. I wasn't sure whether to be irritated at the chief for not calling me, or with myself, for not persisting. I finally pulled over and called again. And once again I reached only his voice mail.

"This is Meg Langslow," I said. "Just wanted to remind you that I may have some information on who's pulling these pranks."

At the First Presbyterian Church a service was letting out. I ran into Randall Shiffley and learned that progress had been made in solving the mystery of who owned the ducks.

CHAPTER 15

"We're pretty sure the ducks belong to my cousin Quincy," Randall explained. "He's been in the hospital, recovering from heart surgery. He's a bachelor, so there'd be no one at his farm to notice someone loading up the ducks. We've all been taking turns going over to look after them, but we haven't had anyone sleeping there, so the place was wide open for the duck thief. Looks like they even used his big truck to do the hauling."

I almost asked if his nephew Caleb was one of the ones who'd been helping with the duck care, but thought better of it. I'd let the chief sort that one out.

"I gather he has a lot of ducks?" I asked instead. "So whoever was doing the feeding wouldn't necessarily miss the borrowed ones immediately?"

"Does he ever!" Randall exclaimed. "Man, but I hope he gets well before my next turn to go over there. Do you have any idea how much poop eight or nine hundred ducks can produce?"

"Yes, I saw St. Byblig's," I said.

"Maybe I should go apologize to old Barliman Vess," Randall says. "He keeps filing complaints about Quincy with the health department and the police and any other agency he can think of."

"Complaints about what?"

"The noise and the smell and the fact that occasionally the ducks get into his garden and eat his plants," Randall said. "And I understand how Vess feels — I wouldn't want to live there myself — but fair's fair. Quincy was there first, and that part of the county is zoned for agricultural use. What kind of idiot moves in next to a working duck farm and then starts complaining that his neighbors are quacking and pooping too much? City folks."

I nodded, feeling just a little flattered. Having the locals complain to you about city folks was, I knew, a distinct step up from being city folks yourself.

"I think the biggest problem is that Quincy's operating as a free-range farm," Randall said. "If he was running a conventional duck farm with the birds all cooped up in tiny little cages — which is what Vess kept suggesting — they probably could have gotten along okay. But these days, at least around here, the money's in raising free-range, organic birds for the premium market."

"And Quincy's birds are a little too free-ranging for Mr. Vess's taste?"

"Yup." Randall nodded. "Well, I should be off. Got to move the ducks back to Quincy's farm before your grandfather gets fed up and starts feeding them to his wolves."

I hoped Randall was kidding. Then again, while Grandfather was devoted in theory to the welfare of all animals, he did have a sneaking fondness for carnivores and predators.

I had saved Trinity Episcopal for last, figuring if I had any energy left I could attend the ten o'clock service. But by the time I got there, my energy was nearly gone.

Trinity was hopping. The classrooms were filled with Episcopal and Baptist Sunday school classes. Father Donnelly was galloping through a briskly paced Catholic mass in the sanctuary, no doubt confusing a few Episcopalians who hadn't gotten the word that the usual nine o'clock service had been pushed back to ten. The vestibule was filled with Episcopalians waiting patiently for their service to begin, and not seeming to mind the wait much, because they all had so much news and gossip to catch up on.

I ran into Mother, resplendent in a new red-and-gold hat.

"Meg! Would you like to sit with me and the ladies?"

"Another time," I said. "I've been up since before dawn working on the schedule, and my arm is bothering me." I realized as I said it that this wasn't a white lie. My arm was starting to ache slightly.

"We'll tell you all about it later," one of the ladies said. "When we come out for the sewing bee."

"And Michael and the boys can sit with us," Mother said.

The boys looked very fine in their little suits, including special red and green plaid ties in honor of the season. I shuddered, briefly, imagining how hard it had been for Michael to achieve their sartorial splendor, and made sure both they and Michael knew how impressed I was.

"We're staying afterward for the rehearsal," Michael said.

" 'Rehearsal'? Oh, for the Christmas pageant." Trinity always had what we called a Christmas pageant. It was actually a lot like the live Nativity that the Methodists had on their front lawn on Christmas Eve. But since we held it in the sanctuary, children in costume acted the parts of the animals, along with Mary, Joseph, the wise men, the shepherds, and the angels.

The part of baby Jesus was normally played by a startlingly lifelike doll. The year the boys were born the well-meaning volunteer in charge of the pageant decided it would be adorable to have a real baby play the part. She recruited Josh and Jamie, on the rather unsound theory that they wouldn't both be cranky and crying at showtime. In her defense, it had been at least twenty years since her own children were infants, and she was the first to admit that we should bring back the doll after the first rehearsal, when Jamie projectile vomited on Melchior and a couple of helpless sheep.

This year, Robyn had recruited Michael to read the Christmas story as the children acted it out, while the choir would lead the congregation in a few musical selections, like "While Shepherds Watched Their Flocks By Night" when all the sheep milled on stage and "We Three Kings" when the wise men made their entrance. I was looking forward to the performance, but I hadn't realized Michael had signed the boys up to participate. Though I was glad to hear that in spite of their previous attempt to turn the Christmas story into *The Exorcist* the boys were still welcome back.

"That's good," I said. "What are the boys — sheep?" Most of the smaller children ended up as sheep.

"They're going to wear their Halloween costumes," Michael said.

"But they were dinosaurs for Halloween," I pointed out. "I don't think there were a lot of dinosaurs in Bethlehem in biblical times."

"Picky, picky," Michael said. "Robyn's got a more expansive approach to the pageant. Wait till you see it."

I felt a brief twinge of guilt at weaseling out of the service, but my eyelids were drooping more and more. And if Michael and the boys were attending not only the service but also the rehearsal, I might have time for a proper nap.

With visions of soft pillows and our down comforter dancing through my head, I headed for the exit. Unfortunately I got caught up in the human traffic jam in the vestibule, as several hundred Catholics tried to leave the sanctuary at the same time that a similar number of Episcopalians tried to enter. It wasn't just the sheer numbers but the fact that everyone wanted to clump in little groups to share news and gossip with friends they didn't usually get to see on Sunday morning. And by the time I managed to escape to the parking lot, so had a lot of the departing Catholics, while late-arriving Episcopalians were cruising up and down the lanes, looking for vacant spaces that would have been a lot easier to create if the impatient new arrivals would stop blocking in the departing cars.

By the time I was finally out of the parking lot and on my way, I felt distinctly low on Christmas cheer. The words "Bah! Humbug!" kept trying to escape from my lips. Clearly I needed an attitude adjustment, so I turned on the radio and tuned in the Caerphilly College station.

Normally at this time of year KCAE radio was shorthanded because most of the student staff left for the holidays. The few who remained usually filled airtime with long, interrupted sequences of Christmas carols. My spirits rose at the prospect.

Unfortunately today the radio station appeared to have fallen into the hands of a few students who were either more enterprising or perhaps enjoying the opportunity to play around with minimal faculty or editorial supervision. I quickly deduced that

153

they'd been running around interviewing various people in town about the pranks, and then interspersing audio clips from the interviews with clips from the Marx Brothers' *Duck Soup.* I couldn't quite decide whether the juxtaposition made the interviewees sound a lot funnier or a lot less intelligent. Or both.

I finally punched the off button and tried to hum for the rest of the way home. And for some reason as soon as I spotted the first few sheep belonging to Seth Early, our neighbor across the road, I cheered up immensely and began singing aloud.

"Shepherds shake off your drowsy sleep, rise and leave your silly sheep."

Although I hoped Seth wouldn't hear me referring to his dignified Lincoln sheep as silly. And I had to admit there wasn't anything silly about them, since he'd resisted Mother's suggestion that he decorate them all for the holiday with big red bows.

At least twenty additional cars were parked up and down both sides of the road in front of our house. Several women with piecework totes or brown paper grocery bags were trotting down the path that ran along the left side of the house and led to the backyard where the library had its own entrance.

A real hostess would have gone and

greeted the ladies, made sure they had enough light, offered them coffee and tea.

Instead, I scurried up the path and let myself into the house, looking over my shoulder, and managed to shut the door just as another car pulled up.

I took a deep breath. And then another. The house wasn't quiet — soft instrumental carols were playing through the sound system Mother had set up. But it was peaceful. I inhaled the cinnamon, clove, and evergreen smells. I looked around. Mother had upped the ante on the decorations, all right. The foyer didn't look like our foyer. It looked like a set for a movie. A movie set at Christmas, back in Victorian times. Maybe a new remake of *A Christmas Carol*. Any second a director would yell action and a flock of actors would walk in, the women in crinolines and the men in frock coats and —

"Meg?"

Rose Noire was standing in the hallway from the kitchen, holding the large coffee urn we used for parties and looking at me with a worried expression.

"Is something wrong?" she asked. "You were just standing there staring at the chandelier."

"Sorry," I said. "Long day already."

"Yes," she said. "And you need to be very,

very careful over there."

"Careful?" I said. "I'm only over at Trinity. It's not exactly hazardous duty."

"Not physically, no." She set the urn down on the floor by the stairs, stood up, and clasped her hands dramatically. "But I sense unseen danger there."

"You can sense it all the way out here?" I tried not to sound too incredulous.

"I went in yesterday to take lunch to your Mother after Michael came back to stay with the boys," she said. "I sensed something at Trinity."

"Something?" I repeated. "Like evil?"

"Danger."

Her voice carried a note of firm conviction that alarmed me. I didn't quite believe Rose Noire had the psychic ability to sense danger. But I didn't ignore her premonitions, which all too often turned out to be accurate. My theory was that she was very good at observing facts and danger signs and even subconsciously adding them up but either unable or utterly unwilling to recognize that she was making deductions rather than having premonitions.

"I don't trust that man," she murmured. And then, before I could ask, she clarified: "Mr. Lightfoot. His aura is very dark and troubled. He's not what he seems. And it's infecting the whole choir. I sense nothing but pain and unhappiness around them."

"Doesn't take a psychic to figure that out," I said. "I could tell as much just from attending a rehearsal."

"Your instincts are good," she said, nodding with approval. "He has something to do with the pranks."

Not unless I was completely wrong about Ronnie and Caleb.

"Lightfoot?" I said aloud. "Seems unlikely. Why would he try to sabotage his own concert?"

"Your mother didn't believe me either," she said. "And I think the man she was talking to only pretended to. A tall, elderly man she was arguing with," she added, seeing my inquiring look. "I think he has something to do with running the church."

"That would be Mr. Vess, Trinity's resident gadfly," I said. "And I'm sure he's quite willing to believe anything negative about Lightfoot."

"I hope he takes it seriously, then," she said. "He could be in danger, too."

Perhaps he had taken her warning. Was it Vess who'd tried to look up Lightfoot's history on the computer? And was he acting on his own suspicions or because of Rose Noire's warning? I had a hard time seeing him as a believer in premonitions, but if Rose Noire hadn't bothered to share the source of her conviction that Lightfoot was not what he seemed . . .

"Well, I'm taking this to the sewing ladies," she said, stooping over to pick up the urn. "Are you going to join them?"

"Maybe later," I said. "I was up before dawn, and I need a break."

"Your arm is hurting you," she said.

"Not that much —" I began.

She frowned slightly.

"Why, yes," I said. "I hadn't noticed it till now, but I think it is hurting me. I'd better go up, take some of those painkillers, and lie down."

She smiled happily.

I glanced into the living room. Spike and Tinkerbell were curled up in front of the hearth, where a much larger than usual fire was blazing merrily — no doubt to impress the sewing circle attendees if they wandered into the living room. If Michael and I had to chop and split our own wood, I'd have protested the extravagance of the huge fire, but since I knew every log was helping put food on the family dinner table for one of Randall's poorer cousins, I just pulled out my notebook and jotted down a reminder to check the level of firewood in the barn and call for a new supply if necessary. Tinkerbell raised her head and thumped her tail on the floor in greeting. Spike opened one eye, sniffed vigorously for a few moments, and then, having detected no trace odors of anything edible, went back to sleep.

"I don't think those two have left the fireplace in days," I said. "What did Mother do, glue them to the cushions?"

"She might as well have," Rose Noire said. "They're heated cushions."

She sailed off toward the library, carrying the huge coffee urn.

Okay, now it made sense. I cast an envious glance at the cushions before trudging upstairs. Maybe it was time to break down and buy an electric blanket. I didn't like the idea of sleeping under a tangle of wires, but if the weather kept on being this cold . . .

I'd worry about it later. I fell onto the bed. In a few minutes I'd gather enough energy to crawl under the covers, I told myself.

Then I realized that I felt grungy. I hadn't had time for a shower before racing off this morning, and I'd been spending a lot of time in close proximity to duck poop.

I had plenty of time to take a shower before my nap. In fact — I felt a twinge of deliciously guilty pleasure at the thought — I had enough time to take a good, hot, soaking bath.

I ran down into the basement, because while I'd done a lot of laundry over the last several days, none of it had yet traveled upstairs from the enormous folding table I'd installed. "Getting dressed in the basement" was my own private shorthand for being woefully behind not just on niceties but on essential household chores. I needed to tackle the folding table soon.

But not right now. I collected clean clothes and a clean bath sheet. I heard voices coming down the hall from the library, and voices coming up the front step. Someone else would have to deal with them. I ran upstairs, laid out the clean clothes on my side of the bed, then dumped my dirty clothes in the hamper, snagged my fuzzy robe, and marched into the bathroom. I was trying to decide between the cinnamon-apple-spice bubble bath Michael's mother had given me last Christmas — nice enough, but not my favorite, although, it would be tactful to finish it off before she arrived, probably bearing this year's bubble bath offering — or Rose Noire's homemade rose and lavender soak, which was my favorite, and tended to vanish almost as soon as a new supply arrived. And after my bath —

I was reaching to turn the faucet when I

heard a noise behind me.

"Quack-quack-quack!"

I whirled, throwing my robe around me as I did.

A large white duck waddled out of the shower stall.

CHAPTER 16

I pulled on my robe and belted it as I peered into every cranny of the bathroom.

No one there. Just the duck. Which looked up at me expectantly.

"Quack-quack-quack!" it said again. It fluttered up to the rim of the tub and marched up and down, looking down at the tub and then up again at me.

I could see that the plug was in the tub. The old, worn-out plug, which leaked slightly — replacing it was another one of those neglected tasks. I suspected that someone had filled the tub with water, put the duck in it, and then left, not realizing that eventually our winged visitor would be left high and dry.

"No," I said. "I am not filling the bathtub for you."

I left the bathroom, closing the door carefully behind me. I put my nice clean clothes on, which seemed a bit of a waste, since I

hadn't managed to get myself clean to go with them, but I didn't fancy digging the dirty ones out of the hamper.

I pulled out my cell phone. Should I call 911? No. I put it away again. The duck didn't necessarily mean that our house had been hit by the prankster. There could be some other perfectly logical reason for the duck in our tub. Maybe it was intended as a Christmas present. Not for me or Michael, presumably, or the giver wouldn't have hidden it in our bathroom. And I had a hard time imagining anyone in my family giving the boys a duck. My nephew Eric had had a pet duck for many years, and they all knew how much trouble it had been. And they all knew we'd only just adjusted to the amount of work required by the chickens we'd acquired this fall. I'd spent the last several months making it very clear to anyone I could even imagine giving the boys a present exactly how we'd feel if they inflicted more livestock on us.

Maybe someone in the family had been helping with the duck removal at St. Byblig's and failed to notice one of the trespassers stowing away in his vehicle. And by someone in the family I mainly meant either Rob or Dad. Anyone else would have noticed a stowaway duck long before they got all the way out here or, failing to notice it, would find something a lot more sensible to do with it — either taking it back to town or stowing it in the barn for the time being. I couldn't imagine anyone but Rob or maybe Dad putting the duck in our tub.

I could tell by glancing at the cars outside that neither of my prime suspects was around to be confronted.

And I really needed that nap.

So I collected the duck, took him upstairs to Rob's bathroom, drew him an inch or so of water in the tub, and made sure the door was closed firmly.

I wasn't keen on having that soaking bath until I'd cleaned the bathroom thoroughly to remove the last vestiges of the duck's occupancy, so I settled for a hot shower before my nap.

And I actually did manage to sleep for an hour and a half before my notebook-that-tells-me-when-to-breathe began whispering in my ear that I should be paying attention to it. After that, sleep was impossible, so I went downstairs to see what was up.

I ran into Rose Noire in the hall.

"Do you have any idea why there was a duck in Rob's bathroom?" she asked.

"I put it there," I said.

She blinked.

"Okay," she said finally. "Why did you put the duck in Rob's bathroom?"

"I was afraid it would keep me awake if I left it in Michael's and my bathroom. And before you ask, I have no idea why there was a duck in our bathroom. Maybe it's left over from the church prank."

"I think we should take it outside," Rose Noire said. "I can set up a nice place for it in one of the sheds and —"

"No," I said. "It's not staying. It needs to go back to wherever it came from as soon as possible, before the boys see it and want to keep it."

"Oh, dear." Rose Noire glanced toward the kitchen.

I suddenly realized that I could hear Spike barking in the kitchen.

I had a bad feeling about this. I strode down the hallway and burst into the kitchen.

The duck was in the middle of the kitchen, inside the plastic fencing that we had used as a portable playpen for the boys before they figured out how to climb over it. The boys were inside the pen, petting the duck. Spike and Tinkerbell had deserted their heated cushions to inspect the newcomer. Tinkerbell was just sitting outside the pen, sniffing occasionally, and wagging her tail. Spike was scurrying around the outside of the pen, growling nonstop, except when he erupted into brief fits of barking. Rob was standing just outside the pen with his hands in his pockets, looking worried. Mother was setting the kitchen table. Michael was tending two pans on the stove, and Dad was slicing ham. From the haste all the adults were displaying — well, Michael and Dad, at least — I deduced that the boys had returned from rehearsal hungry and perhaps a little cranky, and they were hurrying to get food ready before the distraction of the duck wore off and they remembered their tummies.

"Rob brought him down," Rose Noire said. "And I left him there while I went out to fix a place for him . . ."

"I get it," I said. "I'm more interested in where the duck came from in the first place."

Rob and Michael both winced. That surprised me; I hadn't suspected Michael of any involvement in the duck's arrival. Mother and Dad looked as if they'd also like to hear the answer.

"Mom sent a grocery list of things she wanted for her Christmas dinner," Michael said. "I was pretty busy yesterday, so Rob offered to get everything."

"And I did," Rob said. "Except for the

duck. The market didn't have fresh ducks. And she was very specific — not a frozen duck."

"You should have gotten a frozen one," Michael said. "We could have taken the wrapper off and hid it till it was thawed. She'd never have known."

"Now he tells me," Rob said. "Anyway, I ran into one of the Shiffleys who said he could get me a fresh duck. Said he'd deliver it this morning. It seemed like a good idea at the time."

"Unfortunately, the duck is a little too fresh," Michael said.

We all looked in dismay at the boys, who were happily chasing the duck around the perimeter of the playpen while Spike kept pace with them on the outside. The duck didn't seem to mind. Dad took up a station just outside the pen and began handing the boys little bits of ham or cheese each time they passed.

"The first thing to do is to get the duck out of sight," I said. "Jamie! Josh! It's nearly time for lunch. Go wash your hands."

"Can I feed ducky?" Josh asked.

"The duck has to go outside," I said. "Ducks don't belong in the kitchen."

"Nooo!" Josh wailed.

"Want ducky," Jamie whined.

Think fast, I told myself, if you don't want to start a flock of ducks on top of all the chickens.

"We have to hide the duck," I said. "It's a present for someone else," I said.

Both boys' faces fell, and I could tell that tears, in large quantities, were moments away.

"But don't worry," I said. "You'll be able to see him all the time."

The boys looked hopeful. As I glanced around, seeking inspiration, I could see that every adult in the room was staring at me in dismay. Mother was shaking her head almost imperceptibly.

"Where is everybody? And when's lunch?"

Grandfather strode into the room.

CHAPTER 17

Although giving animals to Grandfather
made about as much sense as trying to give
Mother a decorating book she didn't already
have, he was probably the only adult in the
room who wouldn't hate me if I gave him
the duck.

"Darn," I said. "Looks as if we've spoiled
the surprise. I guess there's nothing to do
but give it to him a little early."

I picked up the duck, strode over, and
handed it to Grandfather.

"Merry Christmas," I said, giving him a
kiss on the cheek.

Grandfather stared for a few moments at
the duck in his hands as if he'd never seen
one before.

"Gampy like duck?" Josh said. He
sounded anxious.

"Why, yes!" Grandfather said. "What a
surprise!"

"Better than a tie," Rob put in.

"Wear it in good health," Michael said, lifting a water glass and then gulping down half its contents.

"And a fine, fat bird," Grandfather said. He poked the duck's ample, downy white breast and nodded appreciatively. "Well, I shall look forward to having this with —"

"With all the other animals in your petting zoo," I said.

"Not sure we need any more —" he began

"Because he's a very fine duck," I said. "I'm sure the children who come to the zoo will enjoy visiting him."

"But what's wrong with a little roast —"

"You know how much little children love ducks," I said. "The boys have already grown fond of him."

As if on cue, they both toddled over to tug at Grandfather's trousers, in a subtle hint that he should hold his present a little lower and let them enjoy it, too. He obliged.

"Ducky!" Jamie cooed happy. He was gently stroking the duck's wing feathers.

"See," I said. "They've already named him."

"That's not a name," Grandfather growled. "It's a generic description."

"Ducky Lucky!" Josh said. He was pounding the duck on the head with the same vigor one would use on a large and rambunctious dog. Ducky Lucky seemed to take it all in stride.

"I rest my case."

"Hmph!" Grandfather said.

"And see?" Michael put in. "He's obviously quite tame enough to be a great addition to the petting zoo."

Grandfather shook his head. But it wasn't a "Hell, no!" headshake. More of a "What now?" He turned his attention to Ducky Lucky and his two human acolytes.

"Feel how oily his feathers are." Grandfather demonstrated for the boys by stroking the duck's feathers gently. "You know why that is?"

Both boys shook their heads and began massaging the duck's feathers with enthusiasm.

"It makes them waterproof and keeps them warm. Come on — Let's take Lucky out to the barn and I'll teach you a few things about ducks."

He strode out, and his tiny pupils tried to follow, though we had to stop them and stuff them into their winter wraps before we let them out. Dad grabbed several newly made ham-and-cheese sandwiches and trailed after them. Everyone else in the room let out a sigh of relief.

"So I guess I should tell Michael's mother

I couldn't find a fresh duck?" Rob asked.

"Please," Michael said. "I'm not sure I'll ever want Peking duck again."

"She won't be happy," I said. "Why not call whoever you got it from and demand a replacement that's ready to cook?"

"I can't do that," Rob said. "I mean, he did deliver the duck. Besides, I don't know his name. And I paid cash. I offered to write a check, but he insisted on cash. I got the feeling maybe he wasn't really supposed to be selling the ducks. He was kind of hanging around the poultry section of the market, and came up to me when he overheard that I couldn't get a fresh duck."

"Let me get this straight," Michael said. "The night before several hundred ducks were stolen from Quincy Shiffley's farm, you made arrangements for a random Shiffley to deliver a live duck here."

"A fresh duck," Rob said.

"And sometime this morning you took delivery of what you already suspected might be a stolen duck."

Rob squirmed and nodded. I found myself thinking, not for the first time, that if Michael had gone in for law school instead of drama school, he'd have made a first-class prosecutor. And that the chief might want to check up on the Shiffley who'd delivered our duck.

"It sounds so terrible the way you put it," Rob said.

"How can you be so sure he was a Shiffley?" I asked.

"He looked like a Shiffley," Rob said. "And besides, I saw him helping build the stage at Trinity."

"So maybe he was just working for the Shiffley Construction Company."

"Do all their employees call Randall 'Uncle Randall'?"

I pulled out my cell phone and hit one of my speed dial buttons. Randall Shiffley answered his phone on the first ring.

"What's up?" he said. "Any new schedule changes?"

"Do you have any idea which of your many relatives would have sold my brother a fresh duck last night?"

A pause.

"Was there something wrong with the duck?" he asked finally.

"The duck is just fine," I said. "In perfect health, in fact; he arrived here still alive. And the twins met him, and the newly christened Ducky Lucky will soon be an exhibit at Grandfather's petting zoo rather than the main course of our Christmas dinner."

Randall sighed.

"The only Shiffley I know of who raises ducks is Quincy, and he wasn't hanging around the supermarket flogging them last night, that's for damn sure. I saw him in the hospital this morning and he hadn't been anywhere. But I think I can figure out who did this. You want a replacement duck or shall I just get Rob his money back?"

"Either would be fine," I said. "Do you already have a suspicion who did it, or do you just plan to raise Cain with all the family black sheep until one of them confesses? If it helps, Rob thinks the seller was one of the men doing construction at Trinity."

"I'm going to start with my cousin's boy Duane, who's been known to pull stuff like this before — and yes, he was on the crew over at Trinity. Consider the original duck my gift to the Caerphilly Zoo."

"I'll have Grandfather send you a receipt for your generous donation," I said. "Thanks."

"That works. Someone will drop by with the new ready-to-roast duck tonight."

"After the boys' bedtime?"

"You got it."

"Good!" I said. "And thanks."

We both hung up.

"We're getting a new duck?" Rob asked.

"Make sure there's someone here to receive it tonight," I said. "And can someone figure out what's French for 'Peking duck' and explain to Michael's mother why we all have to call it that when the boys are around."

Dad pulled out his iPhone.

"I'm going to check on the sewing bee," Mother said.

"Lunch in a few minutes," Michael said.

"Canard laqué de Pékin," Dad said, looking up from his iPhone.

"I'll come with you," I told Mother.

We left the men to finish putting lunch on the table and went through the foyer to the long hallway that led back to the library. Some ancestor of the previous owner had added it on as a ballroom, back when that was a fairly normal thing to have around the house, and we'd finally finished converting it to the library of our dreams. The boys already loved curling up in the big sofa for story time, and in due course I was looking forward to sitting with them at one of the long oak tables, supervising their homework and helping them with their science projects.

I opened the big double doors to find the entire room had been decorated to the hilt and was filled with red velveteen in various stages of being made into seat covers and curtains. Mother and whoever she recruited to help must have stayed up half the night working in here. Ropes of evergreen framed every one of the tall windows and built-in bookshelves and looped along next to the double-height ceiling. Red and gold tinsel festooned the circular stairway leading up to the second level of shelves, where the tinsel-wrapped railings seemed barely adequate to hold back a small jungle of point-settias, live spruces, and Norfolk pines. Trailing wicker baskets of red Christmas cactus hung down from the railings so far that I could see some of the sewing circle members having to duck as they bustled around the room, and the baskets were decorated with ribbons holding little silver bells that set up a constant tinkling with the breeze when anyone passed beneath them. Mother and her minions had even gussied up the books — on every shelf, two or three of the volumes had been wrapped with temporary dust jackets of red, gold, green, or purple foil paper. When you added in the soft instrumental carols playing — no doubt from wireless speakers hidden behind the books — and enough Christmas potpourri to send up an almost visible haze of evergreen, clove, cinnamon, and ginger fumes

— well, I'd bet anything that the decor stopped everyone in their tracks for at least the first half hour after they arrived.

But now everyone was hard at work. A dozen portable sewing machines were set up in a line on the right-hand table, with a dozen women sewing away busily on them. The center table was covered with cloth on which other women were fitting white pattern pieces and then cutting out various shapes — mostly the red velveteen, along with a sturdy black cotton for curtain linings and parts of the cushions that didn't need to be seen. One end of the left-hand table was piled high with bolts of red and black cloth, while at the other end Minerva Burke had set up her command center.

Mother was immediately drafted to give an opinion on some fine point of upholstering — not that she ever sewed much, apart from doing the odd bit of crewelwork, because she thought it an elegant thing to be seen doing. But she was a very expert consumer of upholstery services. I strolled over to talk to Minerva.

"How's it going?" I asked.

"I'm optimistic that we'll have everything done by Christmas Eve," she said. "It won't be a problem if we stay up rather late finishing, will it?"

"You'd have to be pretty loud out here for us to hear you," I said. "Just lock up when you leave. How's the smell removal going?"

"Slowly. If I ever catch the wretches who did that to our lovely church —" She broke off and set her jaw, as if forcibly restraining language no self-respecting Baptist matron would know, much less use in public.

"I tell you one thing," she said. "This duck thing has confounded my theory of the crime."

"I find myself wondering if your theory was also the chief's," I said. "But I know better than to ask. What is your theory?"

"That the pranks have something to do with the choir," she said.

I nodded agreement. Should I tell her about what I'd overheard? No, the chief would probably be annoyed if I tried to involve Minerva, and I wasn't at all sure a proper Baptist matron would approve of Rose Noire's premonitions. Besides, she was already keeping a close eye on Lightfoot.

"But I haven't seen any choir events scheduled in the Catholic church," she went on. "So there goes that theory."

"Maybe not," I said. "What if St. Byblig's wasn't the intended target?"

She raised one eyebrow and cocked her head.

"You're keeping the New Life building locked up pretty tight, right?"

"Tight as a tick," she said.

"And I suspect Trinity wasn't left standing wide open last night."

"No," she said. "I was one of the last to leave — I was helping make sure we'd left everything at least as clean as we found it. And your pastor was there to lock the door behind us, and when I told her she should go home and get some rest, she said she would as soon as she made sure everything was secure."

"That fits," I said. "Imagine you're the prankster, and you drive your truck full of ducks up to your intended target and you can't get in. Are you just going to give up and take them back where you stole them? Or are you going to look around for some-place else to cause trouble?"

"Ye-es," she said slowly. "But why the Catholics?"

"St. Byblig's isn't far from Trinity or New Life," I said.

"The Methodists are closer," she said.

"Yes, but the Methodist church faces the town square," I said. "Not exactly the place I'd pick to unload several hundred contra-band ducks. Way too public and visible."

"No," she said, with a note of excitement

in her voice. "But a church at the edge of town, whose parking lot is completely hidden from the road by trees . . ."

"Exactly."

"And besides," she said. "St. Byblig's has a loading dock."

"It does?"

"No idea why, but it's quite useful," she said. "That's why they're the central distribution point for the county food bank — it's so easy to load and unload. I've put a loading dock down as a feature we'd like at New Life next time we do a little expansion and remodeling. It would make handling the choir equipment a lot easier."

"So once they got into St. Byblig's, they could just drive up to the loading dock, herd the ducks out, and drive off," I said. "Maybe it was the target after all, because of the loading dock."

"Very interesting." She looked preoccupied.

"I should be heading out," I said. "If I stay much longer, someone will force me to sew, and I'd hate to ruin any of that beautiful fabric. But if you happen to talk to Henry, remind him that I have some information for him. About the case," I added.

"Will do," she said. "Thanks again for the use of the room."

I headed back to the foyer. But before I left the long hallway, I heard the library door open. Minerva stepped out into the hallway, closed the door after her, and raised her cell phone to her ear.

The chief had probably already thought of everything we'd been discussing. And maybe he hadn't called me back because he knew what I had to say — I might not be the only one who had overheard Ronnie and Caleb. But just in case he hadn't, it wouldn't hurt to have Minerva remind him to call me.

CHAPTER 18

Lunch was pleasant, if a little chaotic. Unfortunately one of the interesting facts Grandfather had told the boys about ducks was that having no teeth, they swallowed bits of grit to help grind up their food. I could tell the boys were eager to experiment with this, but fortunately our gravel driveway was currently covered with snow. Perhaps they'd forget by the time the weather warmed up.

After lunch, Michael curled up to have a nap with the boys. I checked my e-mail and voice mail and found that a few small schedule kinks had to be ironed out. Normally I'd have worked on it in Michael's office, where I could use the printer, but I was wary of getting sucked into the sewing frenzy. So I packed up my laptop and headed to town. After all, I could do some shopping while I was there. We were running low on a lot of things, particularly coffee, tea, juice, and sodas, thanks to the enthusiasm with which Rose Noire was keeping the sewing circle refreshed.

While I was at the market, I spent a little time hanging around the poultry section, frowning at everything, but no lurking Shiffleys offered to sell me illicit poultry. Evidently Randall had reined in Duane.

I dropped by the New Life Baptist Church and St. Byblig's so I could check on the progress both sets of cleaners were making. And then I went over to Trinity and settled down into my little office to sort out the schedule once more.

I'd been there for fifteen minutes or so when Barliman Vess walked in. He started when he saw me, so I deduced I wasn't the object of his visit.

"Can I help you?" I asked.

"No," he said.

I was tempted to ask, "Then why are you standing here, hovering over me?" But I decided it would be more effective to ignore him.

I was wrong. He just stood there. After what seemed like an eternity but was really only five minutes according to the clock on my laptop, I looked up again. He was staring at the junk. Or possibly at the window at the far end of the room, behind all the junk.

"It'll be nice when all that junk's gone, won't it?" I said.

"Junk?" He looked over as if startled that I was still there, and frowned thunderously. "Nonsense. Perfectly good furniture. Plenty of use left in it. Complete waste of money, replacing all of it."

He glared at me. I shrugged, because it was less likely to make him angry than saying what I thought — that he was a pig-headed old skinflint to begrudge Robyn a nice office. It wasn't as if the church was broke.

He eventually stopped scowling at me and ran his eyes across the junk filling the room one last time. Then he turned and left without saying another word.

"And a merry Christmas to you, too, Mr. Scrooge," I muttered.

I had barely turned back to my laptop screen when Riddick scurried into my office.

"What did *he* want?" he asked.

"Vess? I have no idea," I said. "Just shedding a little yuletide warmth in my direction, I suppose."

"Didn't he say anything?"

Riddick was clearly overwrought. I turned

reluctantly away from my computer again to face him.

"He just stared at all the junk," I said. "And when I said something innocuous about how nice it would be to see it gone, he nearly bit my head off."

"I'm trying to deal with it," Riddick said. "It's not my fault. Even before all these snakes and skunks there's been so much more work with the new rector here, and it's not really the right time of year for a rummage sale, and I can't just get rid of it like that." He snapped his fingers.

"Of course not," I said, in my most soothing tones. Although I couldn't help thinking that anyone with an ounce of common sense and gumption could get rid of everything here pretty quickly. Mother could do it. I could do it. And if she and I could convince Robyn to turn the two of us loose on it . . .

"He wants my job, you know," Riddick said. "Wants to eliminate it," he clarified. "Thinks what I do should be done by volunteers."

"As far as I can tell, he's the only one in the church who feels that way," I said. "I know Mother disagrees. Don't let it worry you. And if you need help dealing with the junk, I'm sure Mother will be able to help. I could, too. But let's not worry about it till after Christmas."

" 'After Christmas,' " he repeated. He didn't exactly look thrilled at my suggestion. But he did look a little less tense. "Yes. Your mother is always very . . . Yes. After Christmas."

He glanced warily at the clutter as if half afraid it would jump out and attack him. Then, with a visible effort, he straightened his spine and forced his face into an unconvincing but very determined smile.

"Thank you," he said. "And merry Christmas."

And then he scurried out.

A few moments later, when I had buried myself back in my schedule, I heard Mr. Vess's voice.

"I need to speak with you for a moment."

I braced myself and looked up, but he wasn't in my office. The words had come from out in the vestibule. Just then the organ began to play, drowning out anything else Vess had to say. According to my schedule, that would be Trinity's regular organist, sneaking in a short rehearsal between Baptist choir rehearsals. I resigned myself to the possibility that Lightfoot might barge in and complain about this minor interruption in his frenzied rehearsal schedule.

A soft instrumental version of "O Little

Town of Bethlehem" filled the air. When no one barged into my office, I relaxed and went back to my work, happily humming along with the carols.

I'd thought it would only take a few minutes, once I was finally free of interruptions, but by the time I finished juggling and e-mailing the resulting schedule, I looked up from my laptop to find that the sky outside was getting dark. And since my temporary office had only one small window at the far end of the room, behind all the boxes and old furniture, it had grown very dark indeed.

I sat up, stretched my shoulder gently, and checked my watch. Nearly time for our organist to turn the sanctuary back to the Baptists for their final preconcert prep. I didn't quite share Rose Noire's suspicions of Jerome Lightfoot, but I had no desire to talk to him. And so, time for me to go home and have some Christmas fun with Michael and the boys.

I organized all my papers, turned off my computer and my desk lamp, and was about to stand up and be on my way when I heard low voices outside my door.

"Man, are you crazy?" Ronnie Butler.

"What do you mean?" Caleb Shiffley.

I crept a little closer to the door, the better to eavesdrop.

"That thing with the ducks."

"Shut up — what if someone hears us?"

"No one here," Ronnie said. "The rev is out running the prayer meeting, and old man Hedges went home to nurse his migraine."

And if Caleb was suspicious and decided to check doors, should I try to hide behind some of the old furniture and keep eavesdropping? Or just look startled and pretend I hadn't overheard them?

Luckily I didn't have to make a decision.

"Look," Ronnie went on. "I know you're still mad at Bigfoot about the whole April thing, but enough's enough. The chief's got Horace Hollingsworth doing fingerprints and stuff. They could still catch us for the skunk thing, or the snake. We should lay off with the pranks, not do stupid stuff that might leave more evidence and doesn't have anything to do with old Bigfoot anyway."

"Wait," Caleb said. "You think I put the ducks in St. Byblig's?"

"You mean you didn't?"

There was a brief silence. Presumably Caleb had answered by shaking his head and they were staring at each other in dismay.

"This is creepy," Caleb said at last. "If you didn't, and I didn't — man, they're gonna blame this on us, too."

"If they catch us."

"When they catch us."

"And why would anyone want to cause problems for St. Byblig's?" Ronnie asked. "Everyone likes Father Donnelly."

Another pause.

"Maybe we should go to the chief," Ronnie said. "Or Reverend Wilson."

"You think they'd believe us?"

Silence.

"You know," Caleb said. "I bet it's going to be a lot easier for them to catch whoever did the ducks."

"What do you mean?"

"Think about it," Caleb said. "We were in and out of the New Life Church pretty quick, and the snake didn't even take ten minutes. But somebody had to load all those hundreds of ducks and bring them over there in a truck or something and carry them all into St. Byblig's. That took a lot more time. Which means a lot bigger chance of being seen or leaving evidence."

"Are you suggesting that if they catch whoever did the ducks, we should let them take the blame for the rest?"

A sigh.

"I guess not," Caleb said. "That would be pretty slimy. Though if you ask me, it was slimy of them to do the ducks. Everyone was kind of calming down and then the whole thing with the ducks stirred them up again."

"What makes you think they were calming down?"

A pause. A long pause.

"Well, I think they would have if the pranks had stopped," Caleb said finally.

"Yeah, right." Ronnie sounded unconvinced. "Look, no matter what Bigfoot gets up to, we just sit tight. Agreed?"

"Agreed."

Soft departing footsteps signaled that my eavesdropping was over. I decided to wait for a little bit before emerging. And as soon as the coast was clear, I should call the chief and report what I'd heard. Everything I'd heard — he still hadn't returned my call from yesterday.

And was Rose Noire right about Lightfoot having something to do with the pranks — at least the latest one? And should I relay her suspicions to the chief? I knew he shared my skepticism about premonitions, but did he also share my trust in Rose Noire's subconscious?

As I was crouching there, trying to decide how soon to take out my cell phone, it rang. Michael. I hurried to answer it before it alarmed the departing pranksters.

"Josh has been begging to come to tonight's concert," he said. "I told him I'd ask Mommy if it was okay."

"I have no idea how crowded it will be," I said. "But if nothing else, we can listen from here in my temporary office. You said Josh has been begging — does Jamie have an opinion?"

"He has no objection. He wants to see the snake again. He's asked about it several times."

"Let's hope he's disappointed. Want to meet for dinner someplace before the concert?"

"How about Luigi's?"

"My very thought. I'll head out in five minutes."

Before leaving my now completely dark little office, I called Chief Burke's cell phone. Which went to voice mail. Not knowing who might be around when he played it back, I made my message noncommittal.

"Hi," I said. "It's Meg Langslow. I really need to talk to you. I've overheard several things that I'm pretty sure are relevant to the question of who's pulling off these pranks. Would be happy to fill you in at your convenience."

With that I tucked my phone in my pocket, threw on my coat, hat and gloves, and headed for my dinner with the family.

Tonino's ducks only by promising them a visit soon to Ducky Lucky.

In honor of the season, Luigi's cousin Guiseppe, the failed opera singer, was occupying the small stage in the main room, singing Christmas carols in Italian, accompanied by Zia Filomena on the badly tuned upright piano. Jamie enjoyed the performance enormously, but Josh found it strangely disturbing to hear familiar carols with strange words, even after I explained that it was just another language.

"He's not singing the right words, Mommy!" he said loudly during one of the quieter moments of *"Astro del Ciel"* — better known to Josh as "Silent Night."

I'm not sure he bought my explanation. And I had to admit, when Guiseppe launched into the Italian version of "White Christmas," in a passable imitation of Bing Crosby's mellow baritone, even I found it a little strange.

But listening to Guiseppe was a good appetizer for the New Life choir's second concert, which was just as splendid as the Saturday night version had been, even though we did get stuck sitting in the front row again. Josh insisted on singing with the choir, which would have passed unnoticed if, at the end of "Angels We Have Heard on

High" he hadn't gotten carried away and added a few more "Glo-o-o-o-rias!" to the song, to the great amusement of both choir and audience. Jamie spent most of the concert craning his neck to look up at the overhead decorations, trying to spot a snake, but at least it kept him occupied.

Even Barliman Vess seemed in a good mood, although I doubted he was enjoying the music. More likely he was comforted by the thought that every verse brought us closer to the moment when Lightfoot and the choir would be leaving Trinity. By the end of the concert he was actually smiling.

As Michael, Rob, and I were filing out with the boys we ran into Robyn. When she spotted us, she looked relieved.

"Is there any chance one of you could do a quick check around the church before you leave?" she asked. "Make sure everything's locked up with no stragglers? I could do it of course, but for now, I have to stay here to make sure everyone really leaves — we think the pranksters got into New Life by staying after the choir rehearsal. And that's going to take a while, and —"

"And if someone checks all the doors and windows and closets while you're guarding the exit, you'll get home all the sooner." I turned to Michael. "I need to drive my car home anyway. Why don't you take the boys home and start the bedtime process? I should be there before you get them tucked in."

"Can do," Michael said. He and Rob exited.

Robyn handed me a key ring and I started my inspection on the small hallway on the right side of the vestibule that held the offices and several storage rooms. No intruders in Robyn's office, and her windows were all properly locked. Ditto for my small office, although I couldn't actually get anywhere near the window. As far as I could tell from across the room, it was latched; and if it wasn't, any burglar foolish enough to attempt entry would probably impale himself on the upturned legs of the half dozen battered chairs stored just under the window. Riddick's lair looked like a filing clerk's bad dream, untidy stacks of paper covering every horizontal surface, but it was secure and intruder-free. A couple of locked storage rooms finished off the short hallway. I unlocked the doors and peered in, seeing nothing amiss.

I returned to the vestibule, gave Robyn a thumbs-up, and crossed to the other side, where a longer hallway led to several classrooms and eventually the parish hall. I checked them all, methodically — even the bathrooms — and then headed down to the basement. Or should I work on calling it the undercroft, to please Mother and Robyn? A couple more classrooms on the downhill side, which had natural light, and on the side that nestled into the hillside was the furnace room, which also doubled as a huge storeroom.

The classrooms were a little cramped, thanks to the rows and rows of Shiffley Moving Company boxes stacked in the corners.

I had a brief anxious moment when I peered into the furnace room and thought I saw a human figure crouched against the wall at the far end. But when I turned on the light I saw that it was a coat tree covered against the dust with an old sheet that fluttered slightly in the draft from one of the air vents. There were a lot of hulking shapes in the furnace room, with and without dust covers. Like the greater part of my temporary office, it was filled with boxes, interspersed with heavy vintage furniture. Mrs. Thornefield's legacy, no doubt.

"She had some very nice things," I remembered Mother saying, when news came out that Mrs. Thornefield had left her entire estate to Trinity. "I shall look forward to the estate sale."

Presumably the nice things were in the boxes. Unless Mother's taste had changed dramatically, I couldn't imagine her coveting any of the furniture I was seeing. No antiques, nothing light or graceful or elegant. Just a lot of big, heavy, dark, battered furniture with faded, threadbare upholstery and cheap, corroded metal fittings.

And scattered in and around the boxes and furniture I could see the detritus of decades of parish life. Hideous paintings in dusty, ornate frames. Every piece of broken equipment that had ever been banished from the offices above, including an IBM Selectric typewriter, an Apple IIe computer, and what appeared to be a 1950s mimeograph machine. Hulking unidentifiable papier-mâché objects left over from bygone children's pageants. Why did we have a mini trampoline leaning in one corner?

Still, the undercroft was looking better than it had the last time I'd seen it. Shortly after Robyn's arrival, Mother and the ladies of St. Clotilda had renewed their longstanding offer to reorganize all the church storage spaces, from attic to undercroft, and unlike Father Rufus, Robyn had given her approval. The crowded shelves of food that formed the food bank were gone, reorganized into a former junk closet upstairs. The dozens — perhaps hundreds — of cardboard boxes of old files had been sorted, weeded down to the essentials, and stored in neatly labeled waterproof plastic bins in the attic. The basement really was the last bastion of disorder — well, the basement and my office — and once the Christmas season was over and the guild had time to organize the rummage sale, even those would be gone. The very thought made me cheerful.

I ended my inspection at the back door, which opened into a concrete well where a set of steep stairs led up to the churchyard. The stairwell was screened by a thick privet hedge, which made the back stairs precisely the sort of discreet entrance I would use if I were a prankster looking to smuggle ducks, snakes, skunks, or other unwanted livestock into the church. I double- and triple-checked the locks on that door.

And then, having found no stowaways and no security breaches, I took the stairs back up to the ground level and reported to Robyn.

"All secure," I said as I handed over the key ring.

"Thanks," she said. "But keep the key ring. Until the prankster is caught, we'll be locking the church a lot more. Which shouldn't inconvenience anyone with a legitimate reason to be here — we must have a million spare keys out there in various parishioners' hands — no reason you shouldn't have one set, in case you need to get into your office."

"Not that I'm complaining, but shouldn't Riddick be helping with all this checking out and locking up?" I asked.

"He's home with his migraine," she said.

"Again? He had one yesterday, didn't he?"

"He seems to be having a lot of them lately." She shook her head. "Frankly, I doubt if we'll see much of him as long as we have so many people from other congregations coming and going. Intruders, as he calls them."

"He's very protective of the church," I said.

"I'd call it possessive," Robyn said. "And frankly, it's been driving me crazy. Hard enough coming in as the new kid, dealing with people who want an older priest."

"Not to mention a male priest," I put in.

"Yes," she said. "But I seem to have gotten off on a particularly wrong foot with Riddick, and nothing I've done seems to have made any difference. Well, at least the end is in sight."

" 'End'?" I didn't like the sound of this. "What do you mean, 'end'?"

"He's retiring," she said. "Theoretically. It was supposed to be end of the year, but now he's pushed it back to the end of January. And it's his decision, not mine. Retiring and moving to someplace warmer. He asked me not to announce it until he could tell people himself — though I think with only a month to go it's about time we said something to the congregation. I mean, people will want to throw him a good-bye party, won't they?"

We both thought about that for a few moments.

"We'll all feel bad if we don't," I said. "It's the right thing to do."

Robyn shook her head sadly.

"So much for my New Year's resolution to find a way for us to get along better," she said. "I've been talking to Reverend Trask over at the Methodist Church. He has some wonderful wisdom on how to get along with difficult people."

With Mrs. Dahlgren to deal with, no doubt he did. Reverend Trask must be a saint.

"I confess," Robyn went on. "I resented Riddick at first — he had it within his power to make my arrival at Trinity so much easier, and instead he seemed to be putting up obstacles at every turn. But then I took a step away and looked at the situation. He's served the parish for twenty years — all of them under Father Rufus. I'm sure my arrival can't have been easy for him."

No, I suspected it hadn't — particularly since Dr. Rufus J. Womble had been a mild-mannered, easygoing sort, perfectly content to leave all the practical matters to Riddick's marginally more capable hands. The three of them — Riddick, Father Rufus, and Trinity — had quietly moldered away until Father Rufus, while walking around the rectory, as usual, with his nose in a book, had fallen down a flight of stairs and broken both legs, prompting the bishop to decide that he was overdue for retirement. And along came Robyn, with her huge supply of enthusiasm and energy. Even those of us who adored her sometimes felt a little tired. How must it have been for Riddick?

"There's so much I could have learned from him," Robyn said.

"Yes," I said. "Sometimes he's the only one who can get that window in the kitchen to open when it gets stuck. And every year, the decorating committee nearly has a nervous breakdown until he figures out where the boxes of decorations have gotten to."

"I was thinking more of the wisdom he must have learned from working with Father Rufus for so long," Robyn said. "And his deep knowledge of the congregation. But yes, those things are useful. Although Randall Shiffley's promised to find me a carpenter who can fix the window, and once we have that yard sale and clear out thirty years' accumulation of pure junk, finding things around here won't be nearly so difficult."

I could understand why Riddick was leaving, even though I was very much in favor of Robyn's plans.

And it occurred to me that although very few people knew it yet, two of the most annoying people in my life right now — Riddick and Mr. Lightfoot — were probably leaving town soon. Could life get any better? Well, possibly if Barliman Vess decided to convert to one of the other denominations in town. Unlikely, and I didn't really want to wish him on any of them.

And if Michael's mother would go back to her longstanding tradition of taking a cruise to some warm climate for Christmas and showing up with armloads of presents for Epiphany, thus avoiding the dueling holiday dinner crisis we were having this year. But that was a problem for another day.

"Speaking of clearing out," I said aloud. "Time we both did that."

"Not quite." She closed her eyes briefly, and I could see how tired she was. "I'm not leaving until the night watch gets here."

"Night watch?"

"A small group of parishioners have agreed to stay here in the church overnight," she said. "To guard against any more pranks."

"Smart idea," I said.

"All the churches are doing it," she said. "Just until Chief Burke catches who's pulling these pranks. And did you know the temple has a guard who stays there every night? Times being what they are I'm sure that's wise, but isn't it sad for a house of worship to have to do any of this?"

"Very sad," I said. "How soon are our volunteer guards coming?"

"They were supposed to be here at ten."

We both glanced at our watches. The volunteers were fifteen minutes late. And no doubt at this time of year Robyn had a busy day tomorrow.

"Don't worry," she said, as if reading my mind. "They should be here any minute."

"I could wait for them," I began.

"But you have Michael and those sweet little boys waiting for you," she said. "And when I go home it's to a cold house — my husband had to dash down to North Carolina to see about his great-aunt again."

"Oh, no," I said. "But he'll be back for Christmas, I hope."

"Of course," she said. "And I rather think Matt will be bringing Great-Aunt Brynhild back this time — and not just for Christmas. But tonight I'm footloose and fancy free, so I might just stay here with the watch for a while. For the company."

I wished her a good night and headed home, feeling reassured that Trinity was locked up tight and would soon be watched over by a vigilant group of parishioners.

CHAPTER 20

I got home in time to hear the last few pages of *How the Grinch Stole Christmas* and participate in the usual bedtime ritual — made somewhat more prolonged by the fact that the boys, who had only the vaguest idea of time, had to be told several times that no, Santa was not coming tonight. Soon, but not tonight. And perhaps they weren't sleepy enough, given all the napping they'd done during the day to allow them to stay up for the concert. But once we were sure the boys were asleep, we assigned Rose Noire to keep an eye on them, and Michael and I retreated to the library to wrap presents.

It was going a lot slower than usual, thanks to my still wonky shoulder — in fact, half the time it was Michael doing the wrapping with me providing sage advice and an occasional finger to hold a ribbon in place.

As we wrapped, I told Michael about what

I'd overheard after the concert.

"So we know who the pranksters are," he said.

"One set of pranksters," I said. "They didn't do the duck prank."

"Maybe," he said. "Or maybe they just didn't *both* do it."

"Michael, they both denied it. Strenuously. And they had no idea anyone was listening."

"Except each other. What if one of them did it, thinking the other would approve, only to find out the other was furious. Would he admit to pulling the prank? Or would he pretend to be baffled?"

I closed my eyes and tried to remember their voices.

"They sounded so sincere," I said.

"So would I have at their age," he said. "At least we have a better idea why they did it. Some kind of retribution against Lightfoot — I assume that's who they meant by 'Bigfoot.'"

" 'Mad at Bigfoot about the April thing,' " I repeated, as I collected a stack of presents Michael had already wrapped and moved them out of his way. A small stack, that I could carry one-handed. "I'm sure that's what they said. What happened in April?"

"Easter? The New Life choir gave that big

sunrise concert down at the lake. Did Light-foot dislocate anyone else's shoulder for the occasion?"

"Easter was in March," I said.

"Would they remember that? Most people think of Easter as being in April."

"Maybe," I said. "But if Lightfoot did something to upset them back then, why not call it the Easter thing? And why wait nine months?"

Michael shrugged and shook his head.

"Well, I'll tell the chief," I said. "Assuming he ever calls me back. He's in the New Life congregation — maybe he'll have some idea just what happened in April."

"Or maybe he'll convince the boys to spill all," Michael said. "Anyway — you know, we could do this tomorrow."

He'd caught me yawning prodigiously.

"Tomorrow is cutting it awfully close, isn't it?" I asked. "Especially since we've got your *Christmas Carol* performance tomorrow night. And I want to get everything possible wrapped beforehand, so we can save Christmas Eve for assembling things."

"Do we have any more gift tags?" Michael said, holding up a present. "I need to tag this one before I forget who it's for."

"Hand it to me — I'll make some more tags." I grabbed the scissors and a scrap of

209

foil paper and began carefully cutting little rectangles that I could fold into tags.

"And don't forget," I went on. "We'll be helping both mothers with their dinners."

"Right," he said. "So we persevere. It would help if our respective mothers-in-law could work together and throw one big Christmas dinner instead of two."

"It was a major feat of diplomacy to get them to schedule their meals at different times," I said.

"Understood," he said. "And believe me, your diplomatic skills are much appreciated. So is it lunch with your parents and then supper back here with whatever Mom comes up with? Or vice versa?"

"Please!" I said. "They would both be mortally insulted at hearing their banquets described as lunch or supper. Early dinner and late dinner, noon sharp and six p.m."

"And Pepto-Bismol at midnight," he said. "Please tell me they're going for something easy to digest."

"Mother's doing turkey," I said.

"Fabulous! I like a traditional holiday meal."

"Which she is cooking in some odd way she read about on one of those food blogs," I said. "Stuffed with crab, oysters, and lobster."

"Sounds delicious!" And then his face fell. "For those who can eat it. Is she having a seafood-free option, or has she forgotten your allergies again?"

"Mother doesn't approve of my being allergic to anything as elegant and expensive as crab, oysters, and lobster," I said.

"Well, there should be plenty of side dishes."

"And with any luck she won't gussy up all of them with seafood."

"Or if she does, you'll have all the more room for Mom's feast," he said.

"Yes." I tried to sound enthusiastic, but Michael knew me too well.

"So, what's Mom serving?" he asked.

"She's going pan-Asian," I said. "Cantonese-style lobster is the main course."

"Oh, dear."

"Accompanied by Peking duck, squid pancakes, spicy pig's blood soup, thousand-year-old eggs, and charcoal-grilled eel."

"She's clearly trying to impress everyone," Michael said. "She always goes to Asian dishes with . . . unusual ingredients when she wants to impress."

"She said she knew people would be tired of ordinary holiday fare by the time they came to her dinner," I said.

We wrapped in silence for a few minutes.

"You know," I said finally. "I just don't get it."

"Get what?"

"The whole idea of getting tired of the usual holiday fare," I said. "I like holiday fare. Turkey. Gravy. Mashed potatoes. Pumpkin pie. I like them."

"I assume everyone does. Or almost everyone."

"And I never understand all the fuss about how to use up leftover turkey. What's wrong with just eating it the way it comes, at least while the gravy lasts? I'm always a little sad when the turkey runs out."

"I agree," he said.

"But unfortunately neither of our mothers does," I said. "And please don't repeat this to them —"

"Of course not."

"Because I feel horribly ungrateful complaining about this. They're going to a world of trouble, and fixing us fabulous, gourmet fare."

"That you can't eat."

"Some of which I can't eat, but that's beside the point. Even if they fixed something I could eat — something I liked, like steak — I'd still kind of miss the traditional fare. Turkey, cooked in a normal way, not

212

stuffed with crustaceans. And with good old artery-clogging southern gravy. Mashed potatoes. Cranberry sauce. Pumpkin pie. Tomato aspic. Don't make a face — Mother's tomato aspic is more like Bloody Mary-flavored Jell-O."

"Still — aspic?" Michael still sounded dubious. "Did you like it that much?"

"I didn't hate it," I said. "And it was traditional. What I'm trying to say is that I miss all the things I used to have at Thanksgiving and Christmas when I was growing up. Back when Mother drafted Mrs. Fenniman to do her cooking. Mrs. Fenniman was an excellent plain cook. Forget losing weight on her cooking, and if you valued your life, you didn't make a suggestion about how to do something differently, but if you liked good, plain southern cooking, Mrs. Fenniman was the queen."

"I remember," Michael said. "Who's helping your mother this holiday?"

"Some poor cousin from Matthews County whose husband is spending Christmas on the USS Harry S Truman," I said. "She's wonderful cook, and willing to put up with Mother's strangest suggestions, and I'm sure it will all be delicious. But it's — it's not the tradition I grew up with. And I feel terrible complaining to you, because I know having strange and unusual food is your Christmas tradition."

"Some tradition," he said. "Every year something different, from some other part of the world. The first time I had a holiday dinner with your family, I thought I'd died and gone to heaven."

"Really?" I put down the scissors and stared. "You never told me. Or if you did, I assumed you were just being polite."

"Your family had the kind of holiday dinners I always longed for," he said. "The kind every other kid on base — or later, in the neighborhood — got to eat. Real old-fashioned meals, like the Pilgrims ate. I wish we could go back to that."

"Yeah," I said.

We fell silent again. I wasn't sure what Michael was thinking, but I was pondering the fact that I already felt better about our mothers' strange and over-the-top holiday menus, knowing Michael didn't like them any more than I did.

"I have a plan," he said finally. "To satisfy the longing we both have for an old-fashioned Christmas dinner."

"We run away and eat with Mrs. Fenniman?"

"Better," he said. "We cook our own."

"And have three Christmas dinners?" I

shuddered slightly. "I'm not sure that's much of an improvement."

"We could do ours on Christmas Eve," he said. "Remember that little basement apartment we lived in before we found the house?"

I nodded.

"It's vacant at the moment. And the owner of the house is a friend. He's trying to decide whether to rent it out again or remodel it as part of his house. I'm sure I could arrange for us to borrow the apartment."

"And do what?"

"Cook our own Christmas dinner," he said. "Just you and me and the boys. Not a big dinner — the kitchen's pretty tiny. But I can drop by the turkey farm and get a small bird."

"It takes a while to cook even a small turkey," I pointed out.

"And you'll probably be swamped with more church-swapping chores," he said. "So I'll pick up the ingredients, and the boys can help me get it started, and then you can join us in the basement apartment for our own little Christmas dinner. The four of us. And then when the tryptophan in the turkey starts working on the boys, we bring them home, put them to bed, and assemble the train tracks and whatever else in a fabulous mood."

"It's a crazy idea," I said. "Let's do it."

We took time off from our wrapping to run to the kitchen for a few cookbooks and make a list of utensils and ingredients we'd need. And by the time we'd finished that, it was well past bedtime, but we lay awake for quite a while, inventing ever more fantastic tales to tell our families about our absence on Christmas Eve, and giggling until I was afraid we'd wake the boys. It was nearly one by the time we fell asleep.

And half past three when Michael's pager went off again.

CHAPTER 21

"Where is that, I wonder?" Michael asked, after Debbie Anne had rattled off the address. "Someone really should explain to Chief Featherstone that a lot of people in town barely know their own street addresses, and at least half of his firefighters don't own a GPS."

"Temple Beth-El," I said. "I have now memorized the addresses of every church and synagogue in town, and I've practically memorized the phone numbers of all the priests, ministers, and rabbis."

"The prankster again?" He looked grim.

I went up to make sure Rob was stirring. I found Rose Noire knocking on his door, which popped open just as I reached her side.

"All right, all right," he muttered. "Why didn't someone tell me so many of these fires would be in the middle of the night?"

He popped back into his room and from

the thumping and scuffling noises, he appeared to be hauling out and donning his gear.

"I'll fix coffee again," Rose Noire said.

"And after that, could you watch the boys again while I trail after the firefighters?" I asked. "I have at least a dozen events scheduled in one or another of the temple's meeting rooms today, and if I'm going to have to rework the schedule again, I'd like to know sooner rather than later."

"Oh, dear," she said. "So it's the prankster again? Of course."

She flitted downstairs and into the kitchen. I went to throw on my clothes. Warm clothes, in case we were in for another long stretch of standing about in the cold.

Temple Beth-El was also on the Clay County Road, a little farther out of town than the New Life Baptist Church. It was fairly new, and very modern, with a lot of floor-to-ceiling glass windows looking out over the surrounding woods. In any other season, the view from those windows was magical, since members of the congregation had subtly improved the natural beauty of the woods by planting dogwoods and redbuds at its edge for spring blossoms and Japanese maples for fall color.

But as I pulled into the temple parking lot

and picked my way through the mounds of snow to find a good stopping place, I glanced up at the glass windows and shuddered. Even if they'd gone in for the kind of thick, energy-efficient glass that would make the inside toasty warm in this weather, just having a view of the snow and ice outside would chill me on a night like this. And knowing that every time I walked in front of one of those windows some lurking prankster might be watching me —

"Stop spooking yourself," I muttered as I parked the car.

And my stomach tightened when I realized that this time the fire engines weren't standing idly by. Michael and Rob and their colleagues were unrolling hoses and hauling equipment out of various compartments and then dashing off into the woods to the right of the temple.

Most of the deputies who had arrived on the scene were following them, although I could see a pair of deputies slowly working their way around the left side of the building, checking behind every twig. And my friend Aida Butler was talking to an excitable man in a fur-trimmed down jacket. I strolled over to eavesdrop.

"— and Chief Burke told us all to be on the lookout for the prankster," the man was saying. "So when I saw the flames out in the woods, I called."

"Did you go out to investigate?" Aida asked.

"I didn't dare leave the temple," he said.

Flames in the woods. I watched until the last fireman had disappeared into the woods, then followed the path of the hoses, keeping a good ten feet away from the nearest one. A half-moon shone down from the cloudless sky and reflected on the snow, making it easy to see where I was going.

Pretty soon I spotted the firefighters in a clearing. No flames, but a lot of steam rising from what had probably been a campfire before the hoses had gotten to it. Three hoses were still pouring water into the clearing — Rob was wielding the nozzle on one of them — and a couple of other firefighters were hacking at logs and turning over piles of leaves, presumably to uncover any lingering sparks.

Chief Burke and Chief Featherstone, the fire chief, were standing at the edge of the clearing, watching the excitement.

"You think maybe you could call them off now?" Chief Burke said. "I hate to dampen their enthusiasm, seeing as how for most of them it's their first real fire —"

"But the fire's long gone, and all they're

doing now is washing away any evidence that you might like to find," Chief Featherstone said. "I hear you."

He lifted a bullhorn to his mouth and barked out an order. "Stand down! Turn off your hoses and stand by to assist the deputies if needed."

It took a few seconds, but the hoses cut off, and all the firefighters gathered around the clearing, except for a few who were running through the woods shouting "All clear here!" at intervals, and were probably too far away to hear their chief.

Two of the deputies sprang into action, searching the sodden leaves and ashes in the clearing.

"Found something," one called. "Beer bottles. And the contents are still a little fizzy."

He held up a bottle of Gwent Pale, a local microbrew.

"Never heard of that brand," Chief Featherstone said.

"It's not really sold anywhere but Caerphilly," Michael told him. "Two retired agriculture professors from the college started a microbrewery as a hobby. The quality varies wildly, but since they're not trying to make a profit, they keep the cost dirt cheap — making it the beer of choice for a lot of the college students who are old enough to drink."

"And a lot who aren't," the chief added. "But most of the college students have gone home. This looks like teenagers."

I had to agree. I tried to think of a reason why someone old enough to drink legally would take to the woods with a six-pack of Gwent Pale on a night like this, and failed miserably. I saw several other firefighters or deputies nodding as if having the same thought.

"Let's finish up here before all that water freezes over again," the chief said. "And —"

A harsh buzzing broke out, as if a tribe of giant, angry, mutant bees had suddenly descended on the clearing. All the firefighters began digging in their pockets. Chief Featherstone pulled his pager out first and pressed a button.

"Box fourteen oh four for the structure fire. Seventy-two Church Street. Engine companies fourteen and two, truck twelve, rescue squad two, ambulance fourteen respond. Oh three twenty-three."

"Church Street," the Chief Featherstone said. "Let's go."

"Which one is it?" one fireman asked.

"Trinity Episcopal Church," I called over

my shoulder. I was already making tracks for the parking lot.

CHAPTER 22

Since I wasn't hauling heavy equipment, I beat all the firefighters and most of the deputies back to the parking lot. But since I was only a civilian, I made sure not to get in the way of any of the emergency vehicles as they roared and squealed out of the parking lot. So I was, of course, the last to arrive at Trinity.

When I pulled into the parking lot, not that far behind the last of the fire engines, I saw five people standing around, stamping their feet and blowing out plumes of vapor as they breathed. None of them was wearing coats, so I suspected they were the night watch, and had evacuated the church in a hurry. And yes, I could see smoke coming out of the church. Out of the basement stairwell, in fact. Not a whole lot, but still. A real fire.

I pulled up to the group of onlookers — I recognized several of them as frequent church volunteers — and rolled down my window.

"Anyone need to warm up?"

They all took me up on it. Four of them, three men and one woman, climbed into the back. It was a tight squeeze, even after we stowed the boys' car seats in the trunk. The fifth, a plump elderly woman, joined me in the front seat.

"What happened?" I asked, as I rolled my window up again.

"We were playing Parcheesi in the social hall," one of the men said. "To help keep awake."

"And we took a break every hour and patrolled," the plump woman said. "Inside, of course — what a beastly night!"

"And just a little while ago, we smelled smoke coming from the undercroft," the man went on. "Hank and I went down to check things out, and there was a fire in the furnace room!"

"We emptied the fire extinguishers on it without doing much good," said another man — Hank, I supposed. "So we called 911."

"And evacuated," the plump woman said. "And would to goodness we'd taken the time to grab our coats."

"Good thing we didn't," the first man said.

"Wouldn't have hurt," the woman said. "Church hasn't burned down yet."

"You didn't see that fire," Hank countered. "Meg, can you pull a little closer to the church so we can see what's going on?"

I started the car again, and carefully crept through the parking lot until I found a spot with a better view of what was going on. Some of the firefighters — including Michael; I recognized him by his height — were dashing in through the front door, dragging hoses behind them while others had gone down into the basement stairwell. But they appeared to have halted there. I could see several of them standing at ground level, holding the hose or their axes, peering down. Then I heard a smashing noise, and the firefighters set up a cheer, and they all disappeared into the basement.

We watched in silence for a few moments.

"Looks a bit more serious than ducks and skunks," one man finally said.

More smoke billowed out of the basement door, and a little out of the front door of the church. Was that a bad thing? A sign that the fire was spreading? More likely it meant the firefighters were pouring water on the blaze.

I noticed two of Chief Burke's deputies working their way around the left side of the church, giving the clouds of smoke a wide berth. The chief himself was standing in the parking lot, well out of the firefighters' way, but visibly impatient for them to finish their job so he could start his.

After a while he spotted my car and strolled over. I rolled down my window.

"Evening, Chief," I said.

"Morning, I think," he said. "One of these days you're going to have to let Michael and Rob go to a fire all by themselves. Are these the folks who called in the alarm?"

My passengers poured out their story, interrupting each other in their haste. The chief heard them out, then took their names and numbers.

"I hate to ask it, but would you good people mind staying here until the fire's out and I can get into the church?" he asked. "I'd like to take your detailed individual statements as soon as possible."

"No problem," Hank said.

"We're the night owls," the plump woman said with a small laugh. "We were planning to stay up all night to watch over the church."

"Looks as if we failed," another man said.

"I wouldn't say that," Chief Burke said. "Looks as if you called 911 in time to save the church."

He pointed to the front doors, where fire-fighters had begun trickling out. I felt a sudden wave of relief when I saw Michael's tall form among them.

"Is it the same prankster, Chief?" one of the men asked.

"Too early to tell," he said. "Were the five of you the only people in the church?"

"Yes," said the plump woman.

"As far as we know," muttered one of the men.

"The doors and windows all locked?" the chief asked.

"And checked every hour," the plump woman said, nodding vigorously.

"And you didn't let anyone else in at any time?"

The members of the watch all shook their heads, some of them frowning uneasily.

"Good." The chief nodded absently. He appeared to be lost in thought. I hoped the watch members were reassured by the fact that he was staring into space, not at any of them. I know I would have been relieved.

Chief Featherstone came over.

"We're still finishing up in the basement," he said. "But the fire's out, and you're welcome to come in and start your investigation. And I expect these folks would like to get in out of the cold. Okay with me as long as they stay out of the basement."

"And with me as well," Chief Burke said. He turned and strode toward the church. My passengers all murmured thanks to me and scrambled out of the car to follow. I decided to tag along.

Since the night watch had all been in the social hall when the fire broke out, the chief sent them there, with orders not to talk to each other until he'd interviewed them — and a deputy to watch over them and make sure they followed orders. I went along and busied myself making a pot of coffee so I'd look useful enough that they wouldn't kick me out. In fact, I decided, I'd fill the big pot we used for receptions. The firefighters might want some before they went home, and there were bound to be more deputies showing up soon, not to mention curious parishioners.

When the coffee was ready, I grabbed a cup with my good hand and went out to hand it to one of the firefighters or deputies, so I'd have a good excuse for taking a look around. I spotted the two chiefs in the vestibule, talking intently about something. I headed their way.

Then I saw my dad appear in the vestibule, medical bag in hand. He said a few words to the two chiefs, then trotted briskly in my direction.

"Morning, Meg," he said when he spotted me. "Terrible business."

He disappeared down the basement steps.

I went to the head of the stairs and peered down. A deputy was standing at the foot of the stairs. He turned, and I recognized him as Vern Shiffley, one of Randall's many cousins.

"No one's allowed down here," he said.

"Not sure I even want to go down there," I said. "Coffee?"

"Thanks." He trudged up the stairs, looking glum, and took the cup from me.

"What's wrong?" I asked. "Is it bad down there? Was anyone hurt?"

"We have a body," he said. "Looks like the prankster went too far this time."

CHAPTER 23

"A body?" I flinched at the thought. "Who?"

He looked for a moment as if he were about to tell me to mind my own business, then his face fell.

"It'll get out soon enough. That old gentleman who used to run the First Farmers Bank of Caerphilly before it got bought up by that out-of-state bank."

"Barliman Vess?"

"That's him." Over Vern's shoulder I could see the chief had spotted us talking and was heading our way. I braced myself to be kicked out.

"I gather Mr. Vess works here or something?" Vern asked.

"He's a vestryman."

I could tell from Vern's face that he didn't know the word.

"The vestry is very similar to what you Presbyterians would call the session," I said. "Group of people elected from the congre-

231

gation to help govern the church."

"So he's what we'd call an elder?" Vern asked.

"Yes," I said. "Hello, Chief," I added.

"Any idea what Mr. Vess was doing in the furnace room at three in the morning?" Chief Burke asked.

"None whatsoever," I said. "We had a night watch staying here in the church — those people who were warming up in my car. They were keeping a lookout in case the prankster came back. But they were all in the social hall, as they told you, playing Parcheesi between patrols. You can ask them if Mr. Vess was with them — though I think they'd have mentioned it if one of their number never made it out of the church."

The chief nodded.

"The only thing I can think of —" I began. And then I stopped myself, because what I had been about to say suddenly seemed foolish.

"Go on," the chief said after a moment.

"Mr. Vess was kind of a gadfly," I explained. "Particularly on church financial issues."

"Useful to have a retired banker for that," the chief said.

"Except he drove everyone crazy," I said. "He was always going on about overspending, and trying to catch people being wasteful — or worse, dishonest. Mother said last year he was putting marked bills in the collection plate to see if the people adding up the offering were honest."

"What could he have been trying to find out in the basement?"

"No idea," I said. "Robyn — Reverend Smith — might know. Or my mother. She's on the vestry with Mr. Vess."

The chief turned to Vern.

"It would help if we knew whether Mr. Vess was killed in the furnace room or whether his body was moved there later," he said.

"I'll ask Dr. Langslow." Vern headed down the stairs.

"So you think he hid in the church after the concert and then came out to do — whatever he came to do," the chief said.

"No, he couldn't possibly have been hiding in the church after the concert," I said. "I locked up for Robyn while she was seeing people out, and I'd have found him."

"He could have been hiding in a closet," the chief said. "Or the men's room."

"The bathrooms are one-person and unisex," I said. "And I checked them all. And all the closets. I remember one time Mr. Vess hid in the broom closet for hours so he could find out who was constantly leaving the lights on after choir practice. So I checked everywhere."

"You were checking for Mr. Vess?" The chief looked confused and a little suspicious.

"No, I was looking for potential pranksters, but I remembered how easily he'd hidden in the closets, so I figured if he could hide in closets, so could they."

"I suppose you checked all the doors," the chief said. "Including that little door at the far end of the basement."

"The door that would be just perfect for sneaking in with a small cage of skunks?" I said. "Absolutely."

"Actually, this time it was rabbits," he said. "And they're fine," he added hastily, seeing the look on my face. "A little frightened, but they were at the far end of the furnace room. The fire didn't get that far."

I nodded, and found I had to blink back tears. For the rescued rabbits, or Barliman Vess? I wasn't sure.

"Only two of them," the chief went on. "Not much of a prank compared to the others."

"Maybe Mr. Vess interrupted the perpetrators while they were unloading the rabbits and they fled with most of them," I said.

"You could put out an APB. See if you can find anyone in possession of a suspicious number of rabbits. Just kidding," I added, seeing that the chief didn't seem to like my suggestion.

"Indeed," he said. "Actually, since the rabbits turned out to be stolen from the fifth grade classroom at Caerphilly Elementary, which only had two to begin with, I don't think we'll be uncovering any hoards of contraband leporids."

I decided to wait until he looked less stressed before making my other, more serious suggestion — that perhaps whoever had killed Vess had left the rabbits to make it seem as if Vess's murder was connected to the other pranks. Although the odds were, the chief had already thought of it.

"By the way," I said aloud. "I know no one was hiding in the church when I left, but I'm not sure it's all that significant. I don't think the locks have been rekeyed in twenty years, and both Robyn and Father Rufus have been pretty quick to give a key to anyone with a legitimate purpose. Including some of the people from other churches who were here at Trinity over the last few days. Like Lightfoot and Randall's construction people."

The chief sighed and nodded.

"It's the same at New Life," he said. "The reverend is always more interested in bringing people in than keeping them out. We won't be solving this one based on who has access to my crime scenes. But thanks."

"Chief, there's something else," I said. "Did you get my call last night?" I decided that was more tactful than "Why the heck haven't you returned my last three phone calls?"

He nodded. I looked around to make sure no one else was nearby.

I noticed he did, too.

"You have some relevant information?" he asked, in a low voice.

"Do you know Caleb Shiffley and Ronnie Butler?" I asked.

"Yes." He nodded slightly. "Both fine young men. I believe they're seniors this year. Both on the basketball team, in fact. Ronnie is a member of the New Life congregation, and I believe Caleb, like most of the Shiffleys, attends First Presbyterian. What about them?"

"They were the ones who put the skunks in the choir loft. I overheard them talking about it. And the snake here."

The chief looked at me for few moments, expressionless.

"Yes," he said finally.

236

"You already know?"

"I didn't quite know," he said. "But I suspected. In fact, I was suspicious of Caleb almost from the start."

"You were?" I exclaimed. "Why?"

"Caleb helps his father out at the Shiffley Exterminating Service. His father usually assigns him to go deep into the woods to release the animals that are being returned to the wild. The most plausible explanation I could come up with for the sudden appearance of so many skunks was that some of the rescued skunks had not been released as planned over the last few months. And Caleb and Ronnie are inseparable. Have been since grade school. I figured if one was in on it, it was almost certain the other was."

"So you were just gathering evidence?" I asked. "Before confronting them or arresting them or whatever?"

He sighed.

"Gathering evidence, yes, but frankly, I was hoping when they realized how much trouble they'd caused, they'd both come forward and offer to make amends. But after the duck incident, I had no choice. I was already planning to bring them and their parents into the station this morning. If only I hadn't waited."

"So you didn't return any of my calls

because you already knew about them," I said. "Makes sense."

"I'm sorry." He seemed to be wincing slightly. "There was also the fact that I've gotten at least a hundred calls over the last day and a half, all from people who were sure they knew who had committed the pranks."

"Now I feel guilty, adding to the avalanche," I said. "I probably should have just relayed the information I had to Debbie Anne. Or one of your deputies."

"Actually," the chief said. "I suspected, with all the time you'd been spending around the New Life choir, that your suspicions might be a lot more accurate than most, but I wanted to see if I could induce the boys to come clean first."

"Before I gave you concrete information that forced you to take more drastic action."

"I was . . . well, yes. Precisely. I wanted to handle it privately, with apologies to Reverend Wilson and Father Donnelly, complete financial restitution, and a stiff unofficial course of community service to the two churches."

I nodded. I hoped Josh and Jamie never did anything as stupid as the pranks, but if they did, I hoped the chief was still around to help us deal with it.

"I was wrong," the chief went on. "I let myself be swayed by my good opinion of the young men. My desire to avoid ruining their futures. If I'd only brought them in after the duck prank, perhaps they'd have stopped, and whatever tragic sequence of events happened here last night would never have taken place."

"But they didn't do the duck prank," I said. "And I doubt if they did this. They did the skunks and the snakes — I overheard them talking about it on Saturday. But they had nothing to do with the ducks. That's what I was calling last night to tell you."

Chapter 24

"Didn't do the duck prank?" The chief looked surprised, and a little skeptical. "Are you sure? And how do you know?"

I relayed what I'd heard in the hallway at Trinity on Saturday, what I'd seen on Riddick's computer, and then what I'd overheard Sunday afternoon.

"So you see why I don't think Caleb and Ronnie did anything after the snake incident." I didn't realize until I was finishing up my account how much the information had been weighing on me.

"You believed them, then?"

"Yes," I said. "They had no idea anyone was listening, and they sounded utterly truthful. They were both reproaching the other for committing the duck prank — doing something so stupid, something that was likely to get them caught, after they'd agreed to lie low."

He pondered for a few moments. I glanced

down the hallway and saw that a couple of the deputies were looking at us, obviously impatient, but not about to interrupt the chief when he was so intent on a conversation.

"Anything else?" he asked.

Should I tell him about Rose Noire's premonition of danger in the church and her suspicions of Lightfoot? He'd probably only find it annoying. And what good were premonitions about something that had now already happened? I shook my head.

"Keep this to yourself for now," he said finally.

I nodded.

"It's possible that whoever did this is hoping the blame will fall on the boys," he went on.

"And you want the real culprit to think that he's succeeded so you can catch him off his guard. Or her."

"Or them," he added. "Precisely. So tell no one."

"Not even Michael?"

He frowned for a moment.

"I think we may rely on Michael's discretion as well," he said finally. "But no one else."

"Especially not my dad," I said. "Who would probably manage to tell the whole county within a few hours — swearing them all to secrecy, of course."

That got a slight smile out of him.

"Speaking of your father, I need to talk to him. Stick around, if possible. I may need your help to sort out what went on here."

With that he started down the stairway toward the basement. I headed back for the parish hall, to wait with the others there. Just as I was about to enter it, Horace dashed through the front door. The deputies in the vestibule pointed him toward the stairway.

He waved to me before disappearing into the basement.

In the parish hall, four of the watch members were once again playing Parcheesi at one of the long tables we used for meals, while the older woman was seated a little farther down the table, reading an Agatha Christie paperback.

They all looked up when I came in.

"The investigation continues." I slumped in a chair at the same table, but at the far end from the Parcheesi game, and closed my eyes as if too exhausted to speak. I wasn't sure they knew about Vess's death, and if they didn't, I was sure the chief would want to break the news himself and watch their reactions.

A few minutes later the chief came in, accompanied by Robyn. Several deputies came in after him and stood along the wall.

"Are all of you okay?" Robyn exclaimed. The chief stood by watching while she went around to give each of the watchers a few words and a quick hug. She ended up with me.

"So sorry," she said. "I have a feeling we're going to be rearranging again."

I nodded.

"Ladies and gentlemen," the chief said. "I want to have a brief word with each of you. But first, I have to tell you that tonight's incident is more than just a prank. There's been a murder."

The watch and Robyn all reacted with gasps and exclamations of "Oh, no!" or "Who?"

I just watched, trying to detect any false notes in their reactions — probably just what the chief and the deputies were doing. Maybe the chief spotted something suspicious but I didn't.

"We've identified the deceased as Mr. Barliman Vess," the chief added.

I don't think I was imagining the looks of relief that crossed all of their faces — quickly replaced with looks that clearly said, "Of course, it's still a terrible thing."

"May I remind all of you not to discuss what you heard and saw tonight until after I've interviewed you?" the chief said.

The watchers and Robyn all murmured their agreement.

"You, too, Ms. Langslow," the chief added. "Michael asked me to tell you that he's heading home and will see to the boys till you get back."

I nodded. So much for going home and catching up on my sleep.

The chief left with one of the watchers — the Christie reader — while the Parcheesi players seemed to have lost interest in their game.

"What on earth was he doing here?" one of them asked. "Sorry, forget I said that," he added, glancing up at the deputy.

"We could talk about what's going to happen with our Christmas services," the remaining woman watcher said. "That's not against the chief's orders, is it?"

The deputy shook his head.

"That will depend on how long the church is unavailable to us," Robyn said. "If it continues to be a crime scene after today, we must trust Meg to find us a solution."

"But having a death so close to Christmas," another watcher said. "Surely that will cast a pall over all our celebrations."

"Not if we remember the true meaning of those celebrations," Robyn said. "The reason Christ was born among us."

" 'Born that we no more may die,' " one of the men sang softly. I recognized the tune and some of the words from the little-sung third verse of "Hark! The Herald Angels."

" 'Born to raise us from the earth,' " the singer went on. Two of the others joined in on the next line, " 'Born to give us second birth.' "

Another deputy stuck his head in, looking a bit surprised, but apparently warbling Christmas carols wasn't against the chief's orders, so both deputies joined in the last two familiar lines: " 'Hark! The herald angels sing, Glory to the newborn king!' "

"Very good," Robyn said. I wasn't sure whether she meant the singing or the sentiments, but everyone seemed more cheerful. "Charles Wesley did have a way with a hymn, didn't he?"

"On a practical note," the remaining woman said. "If we get the church back in time, will we need to reconsecrate it after this?"

The others all glanced over at the deputy, as if checking to see if this line of conversation was allowed.

"I think not," Robyn said. "I'll have to

check with the bishop, of course, but I think the appropriate action is a prayer service for the Restoring of Things Profaned."

"I don't recall seeing that in the Book of Common Prayer," one of the men said.

"Book of Occasional Services," Robyn said. "I've actually used it once at my previous parish — one of the parishioners had a psychotic episode and willfully injured himself."

The watchers all nodded. One of them walked over to a bookshelf, picked out a volume, and walked back to the table with it.

"Here it is," he said. "Book of Occasional Services." Two of the others crowded around to look over his shoulder.

"Does Mr. Vess have family?" I asked Robyn.

"A son on the West Coast." She pulled out her Day-Timer and scribbled a few items in it, and then glanced at her watch. "I'll check with the chief to see if I should do the notification or wait until after he makes the call. I do hope he doesn't declare the whole church a crime scene, although I suppose we should be prepared for that."

"I think the best thing I can do to prepare is rework the schedule again," I said. "After which I hope no one will think me rude if I try to nap."

"Would you like my laptop?" Robyn reached into her oversized purse and pulled it out. "I've got your latest schedule on it, and you should be able to access the network from here. Or if you really need to sleep, do!"

She gestured toward the far end of the room where there was a nest of cast-off armchairs and couches.

"Thanks," I said. "That would be great. And while I'm thinking of it, do you think perhaps it might make sense to rekey the church? Since by now we have no idea where most of those million spare keys have gone."

"I hate the idea," Robyn said. "But it's probably necessary. Long overdue, in fact." She pulled out her Day-Timer.

I curled up on one of the couches and pulled up the latest schedule. A quick call to Father Donnelly confirmed that St. Byblig's was back in play, and I was now so thoroughly familiar with all the available spaces in the local churches that it took me only a few minutes to move all the events scheduled today in Trinity to the equivalent spaces in St. Byblig's. Of course it helped that since today was Monday, and only the twenty-third, it was a relatively quiet lull between the weekend and the holiday itself.

And then, after e-mailing my ever-growing list of people who needed to be informed of every single change in the schedule, and recruiting one of them — the office manager at the Unitarian church — to print out and drop off some signs that would tell anyone who showed up at Trinity where to go, I curled up on the most comfortable-looking couch. Napping was probably not going to happen, but at least I could rest my eyes. Yes, lovely to rest my eyes, and . . .

"Meg?" I woke with a start to find a uniformed deputy looming over me.

Chapter 25

Evidently I had napped. For two hours, unless my watch was wrong. The room was empty except for me and the deputy. It was Sammy Wendell, one of Rose Noire's many beaus.

"Meg?"

"Sorry," I said. "I was fast asleep. I gather the chief wants to see me."

"No, the chief just took off," Sammy said. "We're locking down the building. I'm afraid you need to leave."

"Locking down the building? For how long?"

Sammy shrugged apologetically.

I followed him out. Our steps echoed in the empty building. It was so quiet that I started when I heard the sound of hammering coming from downstairs.

"One of the Shiffleys is boarding up the basement door," Sammy said. "The one the firefighters had to break to get in."

Out in the parking lot I could see groups of people. Some were standing and staring at the silent, empty church, as if unwilling to accept that the drama was over. Others were turning to leave and climbing into their cars. I saw Riddick standing on the sidewalk, wringing his hands and leaning forward slightly as if poised to run back into the church if the chief changed his mind and took away the crime scene tape.

Robyn, Mother, and several ladies I recognized as members of St. Clotilda's Guild were standing in a cluster. Robyn was holding open what appeared to be a prayer book.

"If you've been reduced to holding services in the parking lot, maybe it's time I woke up and got back to my job," I said.

"The new schedule's fine," Robyn said. "We're just making plans for the Restoring of Things Profaned. Though I think we've done all we can do until we learn when we're getting the church back."

"Poor Horace is still in there working," Mother said.

"And covering every inch of the inside with that horrible fingerprint powder," one of the ladies exclaimed.

"Which we all think should be cleaned up before we have the ceremony," Robyn said.

"Of course, that's not liturgically necessary."

"But it just won't really feel restored if we don't," one of the ladies said.

"And it's going to be difficult, first getting out the news about the cleanup, and then the ceremony," Robyn said.

"Why not schedule your cleaning and ceremony for some specific time?" I said. "Like seven a.m. tomorrow morning for the cleaning, followed by nine for the ceremony. If we have to postpone, we can, but at least people can get it on their schedules. And I'll talk to the chief and see what his timetable is. Would it work to have the upstairs back if he still wants to keep the basement — sorry, undercroft — off-limits for a while?"

"It would be fine if we just had the upstairs," Robyn said. "That's a brilliant idea."

"Yes, dear." Mother looked pleased, and all the ladies were murmuring agreement. It didn't seem like a particularly brilliant plan to me, but by now I suppose they were all accustomed to having me schedule things for them.

"And we've decided to hold Barliman's funeral on Friday the twenty-seventh," Robyn said to me. "Apparently his son is the only family he has left, and we're to make all the arrangements as we think his father would have wanted them. He'll be flying in Thursday afternoon."

I scribbled a note in my notebook to add that to the master calendar when I got back to my laptop. I was hoping the master calendar wouldn't be necessary by Boxing Day, but that wouldn't happen until all the churches were back in working order and the pranksters caught.

"If anyone needs me, call my cell phone," Robyn said. "I'm going to drop by the hospital and then visit my shut ins. Meg, if you need a room to work in here in town, Father Donnelly has one for you."

"I think I'll try working from home for a while," I said.

Robyn hurried off.

"Poor Mr. Vess," Mother said.

Quite a change from "that wretched miser" or "that horrible man."

"To have no more family than that," she went on.

I had to admit, I sometimes thought I had a little too much family, at least on Mother's side. But I wouldn't have traded with Vess.

"We shall have to do him proud at the funeral," one of the other ladies said.

"And we should plan a really nice buffet for afterwards."

"Let's go out to Meg's house," Mother said. "We can join the sewing bee and plan the buffet at the same time."

This proved a popular idea, and they all hurried over to their cars.

"I'm surprised we're waiting till Friday," one of the ladies said, pausing with car keys in hand.

"Tomorrow's Christmas Eve," Mother said. "We can't very well have it then or on Christmas Day. I suppose we could have it on Boxing Day, but I gather his poor son can't get here any sooner."

I decided not to mention the possibility that if the chief hadn't solved the murder by Friday, he might not release the body. They could always have a memorial service without it.

"The chief will be disappointed at the delay, won't he?" the lady asked. "Don't the killers usually show up at the funerals of their victims to gloat?"

"I'm not sure they do outside of the television shows and mystery books," I said. "But even if they do, I expect the whole town will show up to gawk at Mr. Vess's funeral, so the killer would be lost in the crowd."

"Yes," Mother shook her head sadly. "Everyone who feels guilty about having uncharitable thoughts toward him will show up at the funeral. We might need to borrow the Baptist church to hold everyone."

"He did have a gift for inspiring uncharitable thoughts, didn't he?" I said.

"The vestry meetings will certainly be much less stressful," the lady said. "I can't believe the amount of time and energy we spent on trivial expenditures."

"All that fuss over how fast the toilet paper disappeared." Mother shook her head.

"And that ninety-cent phone call he wouldn't stop harping about."

"And his ongoing crusade to get rid of poor Riddick."

We all glanced over at Riddick, who appeared to be working off his anxiety by picking up bits of litter in the parking lot.

"Remember what a fuss poor Mr. Vess used to make if he found so much as a gum wrapper on the grounds?" the lady said. "So much fuss over such trifles."

A thoughtful look crossed Mother's face.

"Of course, every once in a while, poor Mr. Vess did uncover something genuine," she said. "Petty, but genuine."

"But can you imagine him uncovering anything worth killing over?" I asked.

"No," she said. "But still. He had been acting very smug and cheerful lately. I've never seen him that way unless he was about to expose someone's sins. You don't suppose he had uncovered something that led to his death. If —"

"No," I said. "I'm sure it was just an accident. He was probably down in the undercroft counting dust bunnies or something when the prankster came in."

"I'm sure you're right, dear," Mother said. "I'm sure it's nothing to worry about."

"But if you think it's a possibility," I added. "Tell the chief."

"Of course, dear. I'm sure it's nothing."

I could tell she was lying.

Just then Rob ambled up.

"Hey, Meg, can you give me a ride?" he asked. "I came in with Michael."

"You can come with us, dear." Mother pulled out her car keys and headed for her own car.

"I'm not going home," Rob said. "I need to get over to Judge Jane Shiffley's farm ASAP. I have a client out there."

"A client?" Although Rob had graduated from the competitive and not inexpensive University of Virginia School of Law and subsequently passed the bar exam with a bare minimum of study, he hadn't ever actually practiced law. "No offense intended, Rob, but —"

"Yeah, I know," he said. "My legal prowess isn't exactly legendary. But the chief has arrested a couple of teenagers for pulling the pranks —"

"Ronnie Butler and Caleb Shiffley?" I asked.

"Wow, word really gets around fast," he said. "Yeah, and Caleb is Randall's second cousin once removed, and Randall's having trouble getting hold of any of the local defense attorneys, so he's hired me to go down and hold the kid's hand till the big guns get there."

"Rob, I don't want to cast aspersions —" I began.

"I know I'm not qualified to represent the kid in something that could turn into a murder rap," he said. "But I can make sure he keeps his trap shut until a real defense attorney arrives. I know my limitations. And so does Randall. He's still making calls."

"If the Butlers are having the same problem finding a lawyer, keep an eye out for Ronnie, too," I said.

"I will if I can get there," he said. "I wish someone would tell me why half the time Judge Shiffley insists on holding court in her barn when there are several perfectly good courtrooms over there in the town hall."

"Because she can," I said. "And she likes barns better than courtrooms."

"Whatever," he said. "Can you take me?"

"Let me check with Michael," I said, pulling out my phone.

"He and the boys went to pick up his mother at the airport," Rob said. "They're going to keep her out of your hair until this evening."

"Did he actually say that?"

"No," Rob said. "But that's what he meant."

I called Michael anyway.

"We're just waiting for Mom's luggage," he said. "And once we get her settled at the house, she wants to take the boys down to the pond, so we can start teaching them to ice-skate. Want to join us?"

"I do, but my shoulder doesn't," I said. "I'll see you back at home later."

I hung up and turned to Rob, who was glancing at his watch and dancing from foot to foot.

"I assume if you're out there representing Caleb and Ronnie that the chief is out there, too."

"Far as I know," he said.

"Good," I said. "I need to talk to him, so I'll take you out there. Assuming the roads are clear that far."

"Awesome," he said. "Let's go."

CHAPTER 26

Maybe Rob thought I was kidding about the roads. I wasn't. Judge Jane Shiffley's farm was about as far as you could get from the center of town and still be in Caerphilly County. To go there, you drove along the Clay County Road to within a mile of the county line, then turned off onto a smaller, gravel-paved road for several grueling miles, and then onto an even smaller dirt road for the final stretch. I was fully expecting the plowed roadway to end long before we reached the county line.

But I was surprised. The main road continued clear until we got to the point where we turned off on the gravel road to Judge Jane's farm. After that, I could see that we'd have needed a sleigh to continue on the main road, but fortunately the gravel road was as neatly and thoroughly plowed as the main road had been up to the turnoff.

"Well, why not?" Rob said when I pointed

this out. "After all, why would anybody want to go to Clay County at the best of times?"

"Someone could want to go through Clay County," I suggested. "To Tappahannock, maybe?"

"Then they'd be out of luck when they hit the county line," Rob said. "I don't think Clay County has working snowplows anymore. They figure anyone who can't be bothered to buy a truck with four-wheel drive can just wait till it thaws."

He had a point. But here in Caerphilly, even the final stretch of dirt road was pretty clear — obviously the Shiffley clan, who had the plowing contract, took good care of their aunt Jane. Or maybe they'd gotten into the habit of plowing her road this way a few years ago when the county had temporarily lost possession of its town hall and Jane's barn was the only courthouse available — just as she was the only judge not either in jail or under indictment.

I could recall summer days when court was in session in her barn and the entire dirt road would be lined with cars. You could see lawyers and their clients pacing up and down in the pastures, since that was the only way to have a private conversation, given the absence of conference rooms.

People waiting for their cases to be called would often picnic by the side of the road, and a couple of deputies would patrol the area, making sure defendants and the witnesses against them weren't thrown too close together. Some of the local churches and civic organizations set up stands to sell lemonade and sodas, while the children took turns riding the several gentle old horses Judge Jane kept around for her own grandchildren.

Even though the town had reclaimed its courthouse, the judge still often preferred to hear cases in her barn, and most of the time, nobody much minded.

Things were slow today, no doubt in part because of the weather. Only a few cars and trucks were parked in her farmyard, mostly patrol cars and the chief's blue sedan.

I saw two figures, both heavily bundled, pacing up and down in the snow nearby. One I recognized as a local attorney who specialized in representing drunk drivers. He appeared to be lecturing the other figure, and I noticed a deputy standing just outside the barn door, watching them. This time of year, the lack of conference rooms made for some pretty brisk attorney-client meetings.

Rob nodded to the deputy and hurried

inside. I stopped to say hello — it was Vern Shiffley.

"She in a good mood?" I asked, nodding toward the barn.

"With one of her own family arrested for something like this?" Vern shook his head. "Man, will I be glad to get out of here."

I braced myself and stepped inside.

The interior of the barn was warm, and humid from the breath of all the two- and four-legged creatures within. I inhaled the rich farm odor, a composite of hay, feed grain, and manure.

This end of the barn was a wide corridor flanked by stalls and boxes. Several of Judge Jane's Morgan horses or prize Guernsey cows peered over the stall doors as if interested in the proceedings going on at the far end. I started slightly when I heard a duck quack almost underfoot, but it turned out to be a large buff-colored duck — presumably one of the Saxony ducks I'd heard Judge Jane raised, rather than yet another refugee from St. Byblig's.

Judge Jane was sitting in state on the judge's bench, which was formed by putting an antique captain's chair on the bed of an old farm wagon. The chair was pulled up close to the raised driver's seat, so the judge would have a place to stow any documents she needed close at hand — and more importantly, so she'd have a good solid surface on which to pound her gavel, which she tended to do a lot when presiding.

A dozen or so of the judge's black-and-brown hound dogs lay sleeping in piles of hay, either in the bed of the wagon or on the barn floor, as close as they could get to the judge's feet. The dogs weren't fond of loud voices, overlarge gestures, or anything they suspected was a threat toward their mistress. Their menacing stares and occasional low growls usually kept most defendants and attorneys from getting anywhere near a contempt of court citation. Judge Jane called the dogs her assistant bailiffs.

Rob was already sprawled on one of the hay bales that served as seating, talking quietly to Caleb Shiffley and Ronnie Butler, and absently petting a couple of the hounds. Nearby, I recognized Ronnie's and Caleb's parents, huddled on several other hay bales, looking anxious. I tried to imagine what I'd feel if I were in their place — if Josh or Jamie had committed what he thought was a harmless prank only to have everything go so completely wrong.

Judge Jane was reading a document with

a fierce scowl on her face, Chief Burke and several of his deputies were waiting nearby.

Chief Burke looked up and saw me. He pursed his lips and shook his head with a sad expression on his face.

Did that mean that he was sorry, but he didn't believe the conversation I'd repeated to him, the one that seemed to clear Caleb and Ronnie of everything but the first two pranks? Or that he did believe it and was telling me to shut up because this was all part of a plan — perhaps a plan to scare the boys straight, or smoke out the person who'd really committed the last few pranks, or maybe both?

I strolled over and sat on the other end of the chief's hay bale.

"Do you have any idea how much longer you'll be keeping Trinity closed off as a crime scene?" I asked. "Not that we're trying to hurry you or Horace or anybody, because we completely understand that you need to process all the evidence to catch whoever killed Mr. Vess, and we can work around whatever timeframe you give us —"

"But you have a whole bunch of Christmas events coming up and it would be nice to know if you can hold any of them in your church," he said. "I understand."

"It's the sanctuary we need the most," I

said. "We could live without the undercroft if need be."

"The what?"

"Sorry," I said. "The basement. Mother and the rector and a lot of the gung ho parishioners seem to prefer the medieval term 'undercroft.' "

"Ah." He nodded. "Getting back to opening up the church — I discussed that very issue with Horace not half an hour ago. He's working to finish up in the main floor within a couple of hours. We'll probably keep the basement — er, undercroft — a little longer, till tomorrow, at least."

"That helps. Thanks."

He seemed to be preoccupied, so I retreated to a bale farther back and tapped out a quick text message to Robyn. I had just finished sending it when Judge Jane rapped her gavel nine or ten times on the wagon seat. All the dogs woke up — a few of the younger ones scrambled to their feet — and they stared out at the rest of the courtroom as if daring us to get up to something.

"All stand," the bailiff bellowed, and we all bolted to our feet — even the remaining dogs — and stayed there while he continued with his rapid fire chant. "Oyez, oyez, oyez! This honorable court is now open and sit-

265

ting for the dispatch of its business. God save the state of Virginia and this honorable court. Judge Jane Shiffley presiding. You may be seated."

The dogs kept a keen eye on the rest of us until we'd all seated ourselves on the hay bales. Then they began the traditional canine ritual of turning around three times and settling down again in the hay. The judge waited until the prolonged rustling had stopped before continuing.

"Let's pick up where we left off," she said. "Are the defendants now represented by counsel?"

"They are, your honor," Rob said. "Robert James Langslow, attorney-at-law, appearing for Caleb Shiffley and Ronald Butler."

Rob was wearing what we called his Lancelot expression — the male equivalent of Mother's Joan of Arc look. Judge Jane regarded him dyspeptically.

"You represented many clients on potential death-penalty cases?" she said at last.

One of the defendants uttered a small squeak. I couldn't tell which one.

The county prosecutor stepped forward. She was dressed in jeans and a red-and-white Rudolf the Red-nosed Reindeer sweater rather than her usual elegant pinstriped suit, but somehow it didn't make her less imposing.

"The district attorney's office is not asking for the death penalty, your honor. In fact, at present, we're not filing any changes related to the death of Mr. Barliman Vess."

"But you could be eventually," the judge said. "What if in the course of his investigation the chief finds out these two little hooligans had it in for poor Mr. Vess? And you two decide the whole thing was not the unfortunate accidental consequence of a stupid prank but a deliberate, premeditated murder?"

More squeaking from at least one of the defendants.

"Your honor," Rob said. "I'm only representing the defendants for the purposes of arraignment and, dare I hope, bail. They will be represented by experienced defense attorneys as soon as possible. Seems as if every other lawyer in the county is off spending the holiday in a warmer climate."

"And every other judge," Judge Jane growled. "Or I wouldn't be hearing this." She glared at Rob for a while. He stood, wearing the sort of innocent, trustworthy look he used to put on as a teenager when he was trying, against all odds, to talk Dad into letting him drive the car. His two clients looked anxiously from him to the judge and back again.

"Let's get this over with, then," Judge Jane said, with a few whacks from the gavel to underline her point.

In a matter of minutes, Ronnie and Caleb were arraigned on charges of trespassing, vandalism, statutory burglary, assault and battery, grand and petty larceny, arson, cruelty to animals, and illegal possession of a wild animal. And denied bail.

"But your honor!" Rob protested.

"I'm going to have to recuse myself from this case, so in the morning you — or your replacement — can ask my replacement to reconsider bail. It'll probably be Judge Brodie, and he'll probably give it to them, but I'm not going to have it said that those young rapscallions had it easy because one of them was my kin. So — bail denied."

"Has your honor considered the effect on the community?" Rob went on. I had to admit, I was pleasantly surprised that he had the nerve to stand up to her.

Judge Jane looked surprised, too, though not necessarily pleasantly.

"To have these two boys torn from the arms of their loving and very large families this close to Christmas!" Rob went on. "A holiday that's all about family, not to mention peace on earth and good will to all people. A holiday —"

"Chief," Judge Jane snapped. "You got any of those electronic bracelets you can put on these two? The kind that will raise holy hell if either of them sticks his nose outside his parents' door?"

"We do, your honor," Chief Burke said. "The ones we have are actually anklets. We can program them to notify us the second they leave their houses."

"Make it so," the judge said. "Caleb Shiffley!"

"Ma'am?" Caleb jumped up, as if someone had run an electric charge through his hay bale, and stood bolt upright before the judge.

"Ronald Butler?"

"Your honor?" Ronnie yelped, following Caleb's example.

"I'm releasing you two into your parents' custody," the judge said.

I heard sighs of relief from the hay bales where the parents were sitting.

"You're under house arrest," the judge went on. "I don't want either one of you to set foot outside your parents' houses without Chief Burke's permission. And I want you both to do some long, hard thinking tonight. Do I make myself clear?"

The two murmured assent.

"Chief, fit them out with the anklets and then release them to their parents' custody. Anything else?" Judge Jane looked around as if daring anyone to speak up.

"There's that DUI," the bailiff began.

"Tell that son of a gun he's getting a continuance until after Christmas, and he should be glad of it," she said. "Way I feel now . . . Anything else?"

No one else spoke up.

"Court adjourned," she said, with a single powerful thud of the gavel.

"Oyez, oyez, oyez," the bailiff began chanting.

"Meg Langslow!" Judge Jane snapped.

CHAPTER 27

When Judge Jane barked out my name, I didn't react quite as badly as Caleb and Ronnie, but I couldn't help looking startled.

"Your honor?"

The judge was climbing down off the bench, with the help of a nearby deputy. The dogs all rose, and the ones who had been reclining in the wagon bed poured over the side to join the others in a happily milling pack around her feet.

"I need a drink. And I don't believe in drinking alone. Your brother can ride back to town with his clients. Come have an eggnog."

With that she strode toward the exit.

Not the most gracious invitation I'd ever received, but I fell in at the tail end of the pack. Once we got outside the barn she waited for me and we walked side by side up to the farmhouse.

The front door opened into the great

room, as she called it; a huge combination kitchen, dining room, and family room with a roaring fire in the oversized hearth. I sat down on a chair near the fire — a battered-looking armchair that probably only looked tweed because of the dog hair, but proved to be utterly comfortable.

The judge hadn't gone overboard on decorating. A wreath on the door, and a big spruce Christmas tree in the corner covered with multicolored ornaments, most of them old-fashioned and a little chipped or tarnished. Mother would have described them as vintage and enthused over their patina. I just found it homey and comfortable.

But where she beat all Mother's efforts was in the smell department. The whole house teemed with authentic Christmassy scents — the sharp evergreen odors of the tree and the wreath and the mouthwatering scents of gingerbread and cinnamon-spiced cider.

"What the hell is going on here, anyway?" Judge Jane asked. "Let me hang your coat up, and then I'll get the eggnog. Did those two boys actually kill that poor old man?"

"I don't think so." I leaned back and put my feet up on a well-worn footstool. "But why ask me?"

"Because I can't ask any of them." She

was standing at the stove, and gestured over her shoulder in the general direction of the barn. The smell of warming eggnog joined the other holiday scents. "It would be completely irregular. Ex parte communication. Hell, I couldn't ask you if I hadn't just recused myself. But I'm off the case now, and you're a civilian. Does Henry Burke really think they did it?"

"He knows they did the first two pranks," I said. "The skunks and the snake. He has a witness who overheard them discussing it."

"A reliable witness?"

"I don't know," I said. "Do you consider me reliable?"

She sighed. Then she handed me a glass of eggnog and sat down on another dog-tweed armchair with her own glass in hand.

"Tell me what you heard. Please," she added, as if remembering that she wasn't wearing her judge's robes at the moment.

I gave her the gist of what I'd overheard last night, in between sips of her delicious and highly potent eggnog.

"Interesting," she said when I'd finished. "Of course, it doesn't rule out the possibility that one of them was lying to his friend."

"Agreed," I said. "But I don't think either of them is that good a liar. That phrase Ronnie used — 'I know you're still mad about the April thing' — do you have any idea what happened in April to upset them?"

She frowned and shook her head.

"No idea," she said. "Must have been something pretty bad if they're still upset about it eight months later."

"Or maybe it's something that they're trying to prevent happening this coming April," I suggested.

She continued to frown and shake her head. Then her face cleared.

"Of course," she said, with a chuckle.

"You know what the April thing is?" I asked.

"It's not a what," she said. "It's a who. April Hardaway. Her father owns the John Deere dealership in town. Caleb has been sweet on her for a year or two. Cute little redhead. No idea what she has to do with the pranks, though."

"I think I might know," I said. "Does she sing in the New Life Baptist choir?"

"She does," the judge said. "I confess, I was surprised and a little disappointed that the choir director didn't pick her for a solo."

"He didn't pick Kayla Butler either," I said. "Ronnie's cousin."

"You think those two rascals pulled the whole skunk stunt because Lightfoot didn't pick Ronnie's cousin or Caleb's little sweet-heart?"

I nodded.

"Then why the ducks?"

"You're asking why a duck?" I said, in my best Chico Marx accent. "Why not a chicken?"

Judge Jane frowned. Evidently she wasn't a Marx Brothers fan.

"There is no 'why the ducks,' " I said, in my normal voice. "Not with Ronnie and Caleb. Because they didn't do the ducks. Someone else did. And if we knew why, maybe we'd know who."

"Cui bono," she said. "Which is Latin for 'follow the money.' "

"Technically, Latin for 'who benefits?' " I said. "And I'm not sure anyone benefits financially from the pranks."

"Same thing." The judge sipped her egg-nog slowly. "Mark my words, somewhere down the line, someone will."

A thought came to me and I turned it over in my mind, sipping my eggnog, until I decided that it was something I could safely bring up with the judge.

"It's not just the fact that Caleb is your nephew, is it?" I asked. "There's been bad blood before between Barliman Vess and some of the Shiffleys, right?"

275

"There has," she said. "Quincy Shiffley is damned lucky he was in the Caerphilly Hospital hooked up to a bunch of machines last night. Otherwise he'd be Henry Burke's prime suspect. He's a known hothead, and he and Vess had exchanged high words more than once."

"And you're worried someone in your family might have been mad enough to do this to Vess?"

"Yes." She shook her head in dismay. "Quincy and Vess have been sniping at each other for years. And a lot of the family blame Vess for Quincy's coronary. Never mind the fact that Quincy has spent the past forty years eating, drinking, and smoking too much and ignoring all his doctors' advice. Just because Quincy keeled over after their latest argument doesn't mean it was Vess's fault. And in case you were wondering, yes, Chief Burke knows about the bad blood. I made sure of that, when I told him I was going to recuse myself."

I wondered how the chief had felt about finding out an as-yet-unidentified Shiffley might be one of his prime suspects. The Shiffleys were a large and very close-knit family. Most of the ones I'd met were honest and law-abiding, and I couldn't imagine them trying to protect a murderer, even if he was family.

But I didn't know all the Shiffleys. Every family had its black sheep. And while I wasn't exactly city folk — an insult that fell somewhere between carpetbaggers and horse thieves in the minds of the locals — I wasn't originally from around here, either. Maybe I wasn't in the best position to judge what one Shiffley would do for another.

"Chief's got to get to the bottom of this one," the judge said softly. "If he can't figure out who killed Mr. Vess, those boys are going to have suspicion hanging over them the rest of their natural lives."

I nodded and sipped the last of my eggnog. Then after a diplomatic pause I got to my feet.

"I'd love to stay —" I began.

"But you have a million things to do and I've already taken too much of your time," she said.

"On the contrary, you've given me a very relaxing break," I said. "And since you're constrained by your office from asking too many people what's going on, if I find out anything interesting, maybe I'll drop by for a little more eggnog."

"It's a deal," she said. "And bring the boys next time. The dogs love playing with kids."

Halfway back to town my cell phone rang:

Michael. I pulled over and answered it.

"And where are you and the boys and Granny Waterston?" I asked. "Still skating?"

"No, Mom stole all our wrapping paper and locked herself in her room to wrap things," he said. "The boys are home, being looked after by all the sewing ladies. I asked your mother if I could leave them there while I went out looking for a Christmas present for you."

"I thoroughly approve."

"Yes, except I lied," he said. "I'm not looking for a present for you — I'm out at the free-range organic turkey farm."

"It wasn't a lie, then," I said. "If you're picking up that small turkey for tomorrow night, you're definitely getting what could end up being my very favorite present."

"It's not going to be that small a turkey," he said. "Apparently they don't come all that small these days. This bird would be plenty to feed a family of twelve."

"Even better," I said. "Then it can feed our family a couple of times. As long as it's fresh."

"Very fresh," Michael said. "I just barely avoided being introduced to it. And they're still off . . . um . . . preparing it. Which means unless I want to come all the way back into town and back out again later, I'll be stuck out here a while. Could you do something for me?"

"Sure."

"My friend Charlie — the one who owns the basement apartment — is waiting for me in his office," he said. "As soon as he hands over his spare keys, he's free to split, so if there's any chance you could swing by the college —"

"I'll be going right by it soon," I said. "Where's his office?"

"Peake Hall, room two twelve," Michael said. "Thanks."

I started the car again, and as I drove the rest of the way back to town, I figured out the quickest route to Peake Hall. Wasn't it an administration building rather than an academic one? Odd — Michael's friends tended to come from the faculty rather than the administrators. Then again, since the current chair of the drama department was grooming Michael to be his successor, maybe I should be overjoyed if my husband was making friends in the bureaucracy.

Although as I climbed the stairs to the second floor, I wondered if I should call back and ask Charlie's last name.

CHAPTER 28

One mystery was solved when I reached room 212, which was a rather imposing office with a sign on the door that read CHARLES GARDNER. REGISTRAR. Aha. Michael's friend Charlie was a moderately important bureaucrat.

The secretary who would normally have been guarding his door against all comers had apparently already started her holidays. I knocked, peered inside, and instantly recognized the occupant as one of the actors in a production Michael had directed last spring.

"Polonius!" I cried.

The distinguished-looking fifty-something man with touches of gray at his temples and in his neatly trimmed goatee looked up with the unmistakable pleasure of the amateur actor whose role has been remembered.

"Only Charlie, now that the play's run is over." He stood and held out his hand, glancing briefly at my sling. "How are you, Ms. Langslow? Not a broken arm, I hope."

"Meg," I said, taking the outstretched hand. "And the sling's only to help my semidislocated shoulder heal faster. Michael sent me to release you from your vigil."

"Ah! Thank you," he said. "They're predicting more bad weather. My plan is to put a few hundred miles between me and the closest snowflake by nightfall."

He fished into his pocket and handed over a key ring with an elegant bow that would have been fully in character for the courtier he'd played in *Hamlet*.

"Mi casa, su casa," he said. "At least the subterranean part of it. And I told Michael to feel free to use the refrigerator upstairs or the dishes if you need to. Hope the private getaway is a success. Is there anything else I can do for you?"

"No, I think — Wait. Yes," I said. "Could I ask you a couple of questions? Quick ones," I added. "I know you have a storm to miss."

He looked surprised, but gestured to the chair in front of his desk and sat down again himself.

"Ask away," he said.

"You're the registrar," I said. "Is your office where someone would check to make sure a job applicant really had a degree from

Caerphilly?"

"Not anymore, thank goodness," he said. "All the paperwork involved in sending transcripts used to be the bane of our existence, but these days we outsource it. There's a central national clearinghouse for degree verification. We send them the data on all the degrees we award — and then every year when our hundreds of graduates send out thousands of resumes in their initial job searches, the clearinghouse answers all the queries from interested employers — for a modest fee."

"So if I suspect someone has lied about his degree, I should start by finding out if his employer bothered to check with this clearinghouse."

"Correct," he said. "Most large employers do. Smaller ones . . ." He shook his head. "The most common mistake is to take everything a job applicant provides at face value. We had an applicant show up here once with a stellar résumé, complete with what looked like copies of completely authentic reports from the clearinghouse on both his undergraduate and graduate degrees. Fortunately, we ran a check anyway. And did not offer employment. Here" — he picked up a pen, jotted something on a notepad, then handed it to me — "if you really think someone is committing degree fraud, you could start by checking him out here."

"Or advising his employer to." I took the paper, which contained a Web site's URL. "Thanks."

I stood, and Charlie followed suit.

"I hope your suspicions are unfounded," he said, offering his hand.

"Caerphilly would be a better place if they are," I said as we shook hands.

"Ah! Then I hope you get the sneaky degree forger dead to rights," he said with a laugh. "I'll ask Michael all about it when I'm back. Have a merry Christmas and a happy New Year!"

He bent down and picked up something from behind his desk. A small cage containing a rather large white duck.

"A present for my nieces," he said, seeing my startled look. "I'm told they make wonderful pets."

I tried to figure out a tactful way to ask him if he was sure it wasn't a stolen duck, but inspiration failed me, so I just wished him a merry Christmas and watched him hurrying down to his car with his cage in hand.

I hiked back to my own car in a thoughtful mood. Should I say something to someone at the New Life Baptist Church? I gathered from what Minerva had said that Lightfoot's departure was already a settled thing. Would it make any difference whether or not he'd lied on his application?

No, but he didn't know he was already on an exit path. So if he had lied and then found someone checking up on him, it could be very material to the chief's murder investigation.

Of course, how could I tactfully ask anyone at the New Life Baptist Church if they'd failed to do an adequate job checking out their new choir director?

I decided to talk to Minerva Burke.

Who, as I recalled, was at my house now, supervising the sewing circle and helping keep an eye on Josh and Jamie.

I got into my car and headed home. I made the mistake of taking a route that led me past some of the dorms where many of the high school and college students attending the debate and basketball tournaments were now packing up to go home. Buses, vans, and cars clogged the roads, and the departing students darted everywhere — laughing, shouting good-byes and holiday greetings, taking pictures of each other, holding impromptu snow battles. Obviously they hadn't all won their games or competitions, but I didn't see any discouraged faces. Only happy kids, excited at the prospect of going home for the holidays.

Their enthusiasm lifted my mood, even while I was dodging them. And that was even before it occurred to me that the end of their events meant that any number of rooms at the college might now be available if any more pranks put any more churches out of commission. I should keep that in mind while working on my schedule.

Back at the house I was relieved to find that except for the sewing circle, no one was around. Before going down to the library, I seized the opportunity to fill a few bags with things Michael and I would need for our Christmas Eve dinner, and managed to get the bags into my trunk without being seen.

And then I made myself a cup of tea — the old-fashioned way, by boiling the water in a kettle and steeping loose tea in the pot instead of nuking a mug of water with a tea bag in it — and sat down in the living room with one of the baskets of Christmas cards.

For a minute or so, I had to fight the urge to be doing something useful with them. Entering any new addresses or e-mails in my address book. Or checking the cards against my list of Christmas cards we'd sent so I could fire off belated greetings to anyone we'd forgotten.

"Breathe," I told myself. It took a minute or two, but I managed to relax and see the cards not as looming chores but as what they were supposed to be — expressions of love and friendship from people we might not be able to see this holiday season.

I found myself just looking at the pictures. The Blankes — a retired colleague of Michael's and his wife — posing at sunset on a beach in Bali. Eileen and Steven, whose wedding had been partially responsible for Michael's and my meeting in the first place, on the porch of their North Carolina farm with their five kids, all in matching Christmas sweaters. Dr. Smoot, Caerphilly's former medical examiner, standing in front of Bran Castle in Transylvania, smiling so broadly that you could easily see his fake fangs. A lovely action shot of the Mountain Morris Mallet Men, a troupe of friends who were croquet-loving Morris dancers. A picture of my friend Karen and her son Timmy — could he really be seven now? — in front of Neuschwanstein Castle. Pictures of other friends with children who seemed to shoot up faster than was possible from year to year.

I decided to stick to looking at the pictures and read the printed Christmas letters and handwritten notes later. Plenty of time to figure out if Eileen and Steven and their tribe were planning to arrive the same week as the Morris men, who'd established a tradition of camping on Mother and Dad's farm for a week or two every summer and challenging all comers to freewheeling games of Xtreme croquet. And to learn if this was the year single-mother Karen got transferred back to the States and announced her intention of once again leaving Timmy with us for an unspecified number of months until she got settled. To read the note from cousin Wesley, which would probably once again ask us to come and testify at his bail hearing. Or the Christmas letter from cousin Dolores, who made Job seem fortunate and Eeyore cheerful. For now, I decided, it was a time just to enjoy looking at the familiar faces and thinking of all those who were dear to us.

" 'A good time,' " I found myself murmuring — by now I knew *A Christmas Carol* as well as Michael. Even the boys could quote bits of it. " 'A kind, forgiving, charitable, pleasant time; the only time I know of, in the long calendar of the year, when men and women seem by one consent to open their shut-up hearts freely, and to think of people below them as if they really were fellow travelers to the grave, and not another race of creatures bound on other journeys.' "

I finished up my tea, reluctantly replaced the card basket in the front hall, and headed down the long hallway to talk to Minerva and check on the boys.

When I peeked into the library, the boys were nowhere to be seen. And Minerva seemed delighted to see me. She hurried over to the door, and I braced myself to remind her of my nearly nonexistent sewing skills.

"There you are!"

"Where are the boys?"

"They're fine," she said. "They were getting a bit restless, so your father and grandfather took them out to the zoo."

I decided not to ask exactly what she meant by "restless." Minerva would have used stronger words if either blood or broken valuable objects were involved. She shooed me back into the hall, followed me out, and closed the door behind her.

"Good Lord, but your mother's been on quite a tear," she said.

"She has? About what?"

"Barliman Vess. If you'd asked me yesterday what your mother thought of him, I'd have said she couldn't stand the man."

"And you'd have been right," I said. "What makes you think she's changed her mind now that he's dead?"

"She hasn't really. But now she's convinced he was onto something."

" 'Onto something'?" I echoed. "Like what?"

"She doesn't know," Minerva said. "As she keeps saying to anyone who will listen, he was cut off in his prime because he knew something dangerous or was asking the wrong questions or some such thing."

"And she could be right," I said. "Not about the cutting off in his prime — the man was eighty if he was a day. But he could very well have been killed because of something he knew."

"Seems that way to me, too," Minerva said. "I'm not arguing with her on that. I just question how wise it is to go around saying so to every blessed person in creation. *And* promising she's going to pick up Mr. Vess's mantle and carry on his crusade, whatever the dickens it was."

"Oh, good grief." I lowered my voice and took a step closer. "You do realize what she's trying to do, don't you?"

"Of course." Minerva followed suit, and looked around to see if anyone were eavesdropping. "Trying to flush out the killer by making herself a target. And a damn fool thing to do, if you ask me."

"I agree." I suddenly felt enormously tired. "I'll try to talk some sense into her. Where is she, anyway?"

Minerva pursed her lips as if almost too exasperated to speak.

"After carrying on like that here for near an hour, she suddenly announced to the whole world that poor Mr. Vess's cat must be starving, and she was going to go to the rescue. I called Henry the minute she left, but it's not as if the department doesn't have a few other things to do. And he can't very well put out an APB on a law-abiding citizen. For what? Intent to commit feline nutrition?"

"I'll go after her," I said.

CHAPTER 29

From the look on Minerva's face, I could see she approved.

"I doubt if your mother went straight to Mr. Vess's house," she said. "Because obviously there's no guarantee that the killer's here at the sewing bee."

"I'd be pretty surprised if the killer was here," I said. "Of course, maybe she knows something we don't."

"More than likely she's carrying on the same way all over town. Back at your church, if they've opened it up again. Over at the Caerphilly Market. And the post office. And the garden store. And —"

"Understood," I said. "Which gives me time to get over to Mr. Vess's house and intercept her. Where does he live, anyway?"

Minerva handed me a sheet of paper on which, in her neat handwriting, she'd written not only Mr. Vess's address but also detailed instructions, including the landmarks that would tell me I'd overshot my target.

"Before I go," I said. "May I ask you something?"

"Of course, dearie," she said. "Ask away."

"How carefully did the church vet Mr. Lightfoot's credentials before hiring him?" I asked.

She blinked and frowned slightly before answering.

"Not carefully enough, by a long shot," she said finally. "Although if you ask me the problem's with the man, not the credentials. We should have paid a lot less attention to the fancy school he went to and a lot more to what a miserable human being he is. Why — do you know something we don't?"

"No," I said. "But someone was suspicious enough of Lightfoot to start checking him out." I explained what I'd seen on Riddick's computer, and what I'd heard from Michael's friend the college registrar.

"Now that's interesting," she said. "And I purely don't know if the search committee did the kind of check you're talking about. In fact, knowing who was on the committee, I'd be surprised if they did. They spent a lot of time interviewing him, and a lot more time praying for guidance."

"Both very good things to do," I said.

"But we fell down on the practical part," she said. "Although I do know they called all his references, and they all gave him a glowing report."

"Which is why he picked them," I said.

"And of course we only have his word for it that they're really people from his old church," she said. "I will certainly have a thing or two to say when we start forming the committee to find Mr. Lightfoot's replacement. Right now we're arguing over how soon to tell him. Some people think we should wait till August, when his contract's up, but I think we need to start a lot sooner than that. And yes, we should check out his credentials — properly, this time. Won't do us any good now, of course, but if we were bamboozled, I'd like to know the whole of it."

"Better yet, if he got the job with false credentials, you might be able to get rid of him a lot sooner than August," I said. "Most contracts have escape clauses in case one party's committing fraud."

She blinked for a few moments, and then a smile slowly crept across her face.

"So how do we go about vetting his files?" she asked.

I was about to fish in my pocket for the slip of paper Charles Gardner had given me.

Then a thought hit me.

"You know," I said. "I bet the chief could find out today. Seeing as how this could be related to a homicide."

Her face fell.

"It's an interesting theory," she said. "But I'm not sure I see Lightfoot as a killer. He's a blowhard."

"He didn't dislocate your arm," I said, glancing down at my sling.

She flinched slightly, and nodded.

"Look, I agree," I said. "I can't see Light-foot carefully plotting something and flaw-lessly executing it. But losing his temper?"

She nodded.

"And lashing out at Vess?" I went on. "Striking him down in the heat of anger and then, when he realized what he'd done, starting that fire in the furnace room as a clumsy attempt to make the whole thing look like a prank?"

"You're right," she said. "It's a possibility. I'll call Henry." She pulled out her phone but remained pensive, looking at it.

"But?" I asked.

"Obviously you think Barliman Vess is the one who was looking up Lightfoot on the computer."

"You don't think so?" I asked. "Why not? Was he not very computer savvy?"

"Oh, he was savvy enough," she said. "Surprisingly so for such an old . . . old-fashioned person."

I suspect she'd been about to say "old codger," or possibly "old coot."

"According to Henry, he was always sending things he'd printed out from the Internet to justify all his suggestions and complaints," she said. "But I can't imagine why he would care that much about Lightfoot."

"I suppose it could have been Riddick, since it was his computer, but I think he'd gone home by then," I said.

"Or it could have been one of those Shiffleys," she said. "The two who were hanging around after the construction finished. Cleaning up, they said. Seemed to take them a right long time for a simple cleanup job."

"Perhaps they had to move slowly to keep the noise level down when the choir was singing," I suggested. "Mr. Lightfoot doesn't like noise during his rehearsals."

"I caught one of them coming out of that hallway where your office was," she said. "Duane Shiffley, I think it was. Maybe it wasn't my place to say anything, but he looked a little furtive, so I asked him what he was looking for, and he said the bathroom. I pointed it out to him and kept an eye on him till he went in."

"You think Duane was up to something?"

"Maybe," she said. "What if he did come back Sunday night to snoop around some more, and Mr. Vess accosted him the way I did?"

"We should tell the chief," I said. "Not our job to sort all this out."

"Thank the Lord!" With that she began dialing.

I hurried out to my car and set out.

Barliman Vess lived along the Richmond Road — so called not because it led all that directly to the state capital, but because before the interstate came through north of town, it was the first road you took on your long, roundabout journey there. Thanks to the interstate, Richmond Road had remained a pleasant country road, winding around hills through mile after mile of rolling green farmland.

Vess's house was small and unpretentious but well maintained. It had obviously once been a farmhouse, and had just as obviously been sold off separate from the farm itself — not unlike the much larger farmhouse Michael and I now lived in. A neatly whitewashed picket fence separated a modest yard from the pasture that surrounded it on three sides. A detached garage sat to the right of the house, and to the left about a third of the yard was set off from the rest by its own stretch of picket fencing — no doubt the garden, in summertime. The bushes around the house looked tidy and well pruned under their caps of snow. The driveway and front walk had been neatly shoveled before last night's light dusting of snow had fallen on them.

I walked carefully up to the door in case there was any ice hidden under the dusting, because I had a good idea how much it would hurt if I fell on my shoulder and undid whatever healing it had done. No lights in the house. I knocked on the door, hoping Mother was inside. No answer.

Maybe Mother hadn't gotten here yet. Or had come and gone.

No, there were no footsteps on the walk or the front stoop other than my own. And none marking the expanse of virgin snow around the house.

I pulled out my cell phone and called. Mother's voice mail answered.

"I'm at Barliman Vess's house," I said. "I need to talk to you before you get here. Call me."

Should I go back to town or wait here for Mother?

Or should I see if I could get into the

house myself?

I looked under the doormat to see if he had left a key. No luck. But then when I dropped the coconut-fiber mat back down it hit the brick stoop with a dull but metallic ping. I flipped it up again and looked at the underside. A key was neatly affixed to the bottom of the mat with a small strip of duct tape. A slight improvement over just tucking the thing under the mat, I supposed.

What I was contemplating was, of course, trespassing. But I could always say that I'd misinterpreted some message from Mother and believed she had asked me to feed Mr. Vess's cat. Minerva would back me up.

I pulled the key off the mat and unlocked the front door.

I'd half expected the cat to greet me at the door, but the front hall was empty and unnervingly still. The loud ticking of a huge antique grandfather clock to my left only emphasized how quiet everything else was. Was there really a cat, or was Mother just making one up as an excuse to come out here?

I closed the door behind me and locked it. I reached for the light switch, then stopped. Why advertise my presence? I began fumbling in my purse for the flashlight I always carried.

Of course, with my car parked in the driveway, I was already advertising. I gave up the flashlight search and flipped on the lights.

My first thought was that Mr. Vess clearly had taste and money, but his life must be a little lonely. Well-worn but expensive-looking oriental rugs covered small patches of the polished hardwood floors. The furniture all looked either antique — mostly Colonial — or of good quality, if very understated. But while I couldn't put my finger on the reason, I had the strong sense that not a lot of people ever came here.

To the right of the door was the living room, which looked chilly, underused, and a little brittle, as if everything might crumble if I turned even one of my boys loose in it for a few minutes. To the left, a small dining room that looked a little less as if everything was glued in place. Over the sideboard hung a modern oil painting of an attractive woman in her fifties. The late Mrs. Vess, no doubt. She was smiling slightly and her eyes looked warm and kind. If the artist had accurately captured her personality . . .

"Poor man," I said aloud. She was clearly someone who had been missed.

The kitchen was also small, with no

breakfast area, so Mr. Vess probably had to eat in the dining room. It was neat and functional, but not very personal. Maybe it was sexist of me, but I couldn't help thinking that a woman would have had more decorations in her kitchen. More individual touches.

Upstairs were two bedrooms and a small bath. One bedroom was clearly Mr. Vess's. The bed was covered with an old-fashioned white chenille spread. The bedside table to the left held a lamp, a vintage fifties electric alarm clock, a small water carafe with a top that doubled as a glass, three library books, and a pair of reading glasses. The right bedside table held only a lamp identical to the left one.

The other bedroom was fitted up as a study. A comfortable-looking reading chair stood by the front window, and the table beside it and the floor around it contained more books. At the other side of the room was a small mahogany secretary with a sleek modern laptop perched incongruously on its writing surface. A wooden file cabinet sat nearby.

I couldn't resist scanning the books first. They were a mix of well-worn literature, apparently from Vess's own library, and brand-new spy thrillers in plastic library covers.

Then I made a beeline for the desk.

Not surprisingly, most of the papers had to do either with Mr. Vess's investments — which were not unimpressive — or his work with the Trinity vestry. Fat files of paperwork from the search for the new rector. Notebooks full of financial reports going back fifteen years. More fat files of memos Vess had sent to the vestry about various issues, like the cost savings to be gained from installing lower wattage lightbulbs in the hallways and the shockingly extravagant use of toilet paper in the ladies' toilets.

I wondered if Vess had built his comfortable home through lightbulb and toilet-paper economies. I hadn't noticed any dimness in his lights, and I checked his bathroom and found that he had used fairly cushy double-ply toilet paper.

His desk file drawer contained what I assumed were his active projects — a series of files, each in its own neatly labeled hanging folder. LIGHTING USAGE SURVEY — that must be his project of hiding in the closet to see who was leaving lights on. COSTS/ DAMAGES FROM CHRISTMAS INCURSIONS — good grief; he had already started a file with his complaints about our church-swapping activities. RECTOR PERSONNEL EVALUATION NOTES — I glanced through that to see that it was a laundry list of petty or imaginary transgressions by Robyn. He also had files on all the vestry members — including Mother. I had to leaf through that one. The gist of it was that he found Mother extravagant and much too insistent on having her own way, so he wasn't completely incompetent at judging character.

I hoped his executor consigned these files to the shredder. I had trouble reconciling their pettiness with this house, with its mix of elegant functionality and quiet, understated beauty.

Maybe the house was Mrs. Vess's creation. I remembered Mother talking about how Vess had fought the rest of the vestry tooth and nail over the very minor expenditures involved in sprucing up Robyn's study — mainly a few gallons of paint, to be applied by volunteer labor.

"The man doesn't seem to understand," Mother had said. "Even if the styles haven't changed, things just wear out."

Maybe he'd kept the decor here untouched after his wife's death. I hadn't seen anything that couldn't have been here for ten years, or even twenty. I could see him living here, blind to the house's beauty but well aware of its comfort. Keeping everything unchanged not out of sentimentality but because that was the cheapest and easiest option.

Odd that one hanging folder was completely empty — the one marked THORNEFIELD INVESTIGATION.

I searched the rest of the file cabinet and the desktop. No THORNEFIELD INVESTIGATION misfiled under OFFICE SUPPLY INVENTORY or HOUSEKEEPING SAVINGS PROPOSAL or any of the other projects.

I was deeply immersed in the files when I heard a loud bang outside and started.

CHAPTER 30

I slipped over to the window on the side of the house where the sound had come from and peered out, careful to stay back far enough to minimize the chances that I'd be seen.

The back windows of Mr. Vess's offices had a sweeping view of rolling pastures leading down to a large pond and a series of long, low, whitewashed sheds. One of the barns had a faded sign on the side reading PLEASANT VALLEY DUCK FARM.

A tall, lean figure in jeans and a faded corduroy coat came out of one of the sheds and I heard the loud noise again — it was the shed door being slammed closed.

I was willing to bet that I was looking at Quincy Shiffley's farm, with one of his cousins dropping by to tend the ducks. A cousin who was slamming doors in a bit of a temper because he really didn't want to be out in the cold feeding a bunch of ducks.

I was a little alarmed when the cousin began striding across the snow-covered pasture in my direction. But I soon realized he wasn't aiming for the house. Two large white ducks were perched on the fence between Vess's yard and the duck farm. In summer, no doubt they'd have fluttered down into the garden and begun foraging, but now they merely stared down at the snow as if disappointed. I watched from behind the curtain as the visiting Shiffley captured them — they looked cold and not really all that eager to escape — and strode back up the hill to the barns with one under each arm.

I peered out the front windows to make sure there was nothing there, and then went back to hunting.

Vess hadn't been prone to clutter, so it didn't take long at all to search the small house and confirm that the missing file wasn't anywhere else. Not in the office. Not in the dresser or the bedside table. Not in any of the closets. Not in the attic, which was actually empty. Not in the garage, which contained only a bare minimum of lawn and garden tools.

Of course, that didn't necessarily mean the file was missing — only that it wasn't here. Perhaps Vess had left it in his car. Or had lent it to another member of the vestry, seeking their support.

I drifted back up to his office and wondered it I should turn on his computer. Not that I would expect to find much there — I'd already noticed that apart from the occasional letter or memo, most of the contents of his complaining files were handwritten.

And I was no computer forensics analyst, so why muddy the waters if the chief eventually did send someone to check the laptop. I left the laptop alone. It was time to go.

Though not before I fed the cat. If there even was a cat.

I went back to the kitchen. There, on the floor of the utility room, was a beige plastic mat with two bowls on it, both empty. You couldn't even tell which was the food bowl and which was the water — both had been licked clean and dry.

There was dry cat food in a cabinet overhead. I rinsed out both bowls, shook a decent amount of food into one, and filled the other with water.

Just then the doorbell rang. I hurried to peer out a window and spotted Mother's car. I opened the door to let her in.

"Hello, dear," she said, giving me a peck on the cheek as she came in. "Did you also come to look after poor Barliman's cat?"

"I came to look after you," I said. "Given the fact that we don't have any idea who killed Mr. Vess, don't you think it was a little foolhardy to make such a fuss about continuing his quest, once you found out what it was, and then letting the whole world know you were coming out here by yourself to feed his cat?"

"I knew you'd come after me as soon as you heard," she said. "And didn't it give you a lovely excuse to come out here and poke around? Did you find anything interesting?"

"Maybe," I said. "I'll show you."

I led her up to the office and pulled out the drawer containing Mr. Vess's files.

"Good heavens," she said. "I wish I could say I was surprised, but I'm not. Someone should destroy these files — the way J. Edgar Hoover's blackmail files were destroyed after his death."

"I was thinking more about Sherlock Holmes burning Charles Augustus Milverton's files," I said. "And I'd be in complete agreement except for the small fact that there might be some clue in these files to help the chief find Vess's killer."

"Then why are you taking this file?" she asked, tapping one manicured nail on the hanging folder labeled THORNEFIELD IN-VESTIGATION.

"I'm not," I said. "It was already missing when I came. Do you have any idea what it could be about?"

"He usually kept his little investigations close to the vest," she said. "I have no idea. But if he thought there was anything the least bit suspicious about Mrs. Thornefield, he's very much mistaken. She was a gracious and generous lady with impeccable taste."

"If you say so," I said, thinking of that heavy furniture in the church basement. "Maybe Vess was inspired by her generosity and was investigating how she went about arranging her legacy to the church. Maybe he was thinking of following suit."

"Maybe." She glanced around with an appreciative air. "It would be nice, of course, but I'm not holding my breath. Maybe he has — had — some bee in his bonnet about the legacy causing us a tax problem. Or an insurance problem, from storing all that stuff in the undercroft. Though that would be his own fault — he was the one who vetoed short-term storage, even though the Shiffley Moving Company would have given us a bargain rate."

"Keep your eyes open, then," I said. "And

let's get out of here before someone catches us trespassing."

"Did you feed the cat, dear?"

"Yes," I said. I walked down the hall to the kitchen and poked my head in. I could see, in the utility room beyond, the hindquarters and tail of a small gray cat, and by the sound of it she was bolting down her food. I backed away as quietly as I could.

"Mission accomplished," I told Mom. "By the way, what will happen to the cat?"

"Robyn has half a dozen volunteers to take her if the son doesn't want her," Mother said. "She'll be fine."

She looked around and shook her head.

"Such a lonely man," Mother said.

"At least he had a cat for company," I said.

"He was always complaining that she was an incompetent mouser," Mother said.

"But did he get rid of her because of that?"

Mother held her hands up as if conceding my point.

"I can think of one thing that his missing file could be about," she said. "It was just after Mrs. Thornefield died that our former rector broke his legs, poor dear. And with him laid up, and not the most practical soul at the best of times, he put Riddick in charge of disposing of Mrs. Thornefield's belongings. And since Riddick had no idea whatsoever what any of it was worth, he was just going to call in a junk dealer to give him a bid on the lot. Imagine how much we would have lost if he had and the junk dealer he'd called had been a sharp or dishonest operator!"

"And Mr. Vess found out about it and sounded the alarm?" I asked.

"He most certainly did not," she said. "He was as clueless as Riddick. But I'd been to see Mrs. Thornefield often enough, and I knew she had some very nice things, so I put a stop to the junk dealer plan."

She was back to her Joan of Arc pose.

"So we're having a rummage sale instead?"

"A very elegant auction and estate sale," Mother said. "Poor Riddick took it hard. He was so mortified at the mistake he'd been about to make that he handed in his resignation. Dr. Womble talked him out of it, of course — made him promise that he'd at least see the new rector in. Maybe the missing file is about that whole unfortunate episode. But of course even Barliman could see that it wasn't Riddick's fault. He blamed Dr. Womble for not supervising him properly."

"Do you think that's what led to the rector's retirement?"

"Oh, no," she said. "The bishop had been ignoring Barliman's complaints about dear Dr. Womble for years. It was the broken legs that made him realize the poor man just wasn't up to it any more. And now that Robyn's here, perhaps Barliman archived the missing file and just didn't yet remove the hanging folder."

"It wasn't in any of the file drawers," I said. "Maybe he just moved the contents to the file he's keeping on Riddick."

"He's keeping a file on Riddick, too?" Mother exclaimed.

"He keeps files on everyone," I said. "He's even got one on you."

Mother insisted on going back up to the office to see her file. She seemed to find its contents alternately amusing and exasperating. I was feeling a little down because my one potentially exciting and significant find seemed to be dwindling to just another of Vess's petty, misguided crusades. Riddick's file did contain a lot of notes about how he'd almost mishandled the Thornefield estate, although from reading the file you'd have gotten the idea that it was Mr. Vess, not Mother, who'd saved the day. So Mother might have explained away the one interesting thing I'd found.

When Mother had finished laughing over

her own file and the general petty nature of Vess's files, we left the house, and I locked up and taped the key back under the mat. And then I scuffed the snow around enough to disguise the fact that the mat had been moved.

"Doesn't make much of an effort for the holiday, does he?" Mother said.

She was right. No wreaths, no candles, no tree — not even any Christmas cards lying about. Maybe that was what had made the place seem so curiously forlorn.

"How does he get away with it, I wonder," I said. "Doesn't Caerphilly have some kind of ordinance requiring every household to make at least a minimum holiday decorating effort?"

"I wish it did," Mother said. I had been joking. She was probably serious.

"Speaking of making an effort for the holiday," I said. "I'm heading back to town. I have things to do."

"I'm going to get the groceries for my Christmas dinner," Mother said. "Your brother was going to help me carry everything — I don't suppose you could —"

"I'll help you hunt him down, no problem," I said, hoping to head off a request that I take her shopping. "Just don't ask him for any fresh ducks."

"What are you doing now, dear?" she asked.

If that was an attempt to enlist me in the shopping, I was prepared.

"I'm going to drop by and talk to the chief," I said. "And figure out some way to get him to look for that missing file without getting both of us thrown in jail for trespassing and interfering with an investigation."

"The file we noticed was missing while we were looking for Mr. Vess's poor starving cat?" Mother said.

"Yeah, that will work," I said. "And then I'm going to go home, take another pain pill, and rest my arm until it's time to get the boys ready for Michael's show."

"Feel better, dear," she said. "And I'll see you at the theater."

Chapter 31

I did feel better on the way back to town. Partly because my arm, although only giving me occasional twinges of pain, was proving to be such a useful tool for weaseling out of things I didn't want to do. And partly because the college radio station was back to its usual policy of nonstop Christmas music, and was playing a wonderful program of medieval carols. I was singing along with "The Holly and the Ivy" when I pulled into the police station parking lot. I was lingering in the car to hear the ending when my phone rang. I was in such a good mood that I answered it without thinking.

"Hello?"

"I don't have any animals!"

I pulled the phone away from my ear, turned down the radio, and looked at the caller ID. It was the Methodist church. Almost certainly Mrs. Dahlgren.

"I beg your pardon," I said into the phone.

"I didn't quite get that."

"I don't have any animals! I'm supposed to be getting some animals! Where are they?"

Were the Methodists — or at least Mrs. Dahlgren — feeling slighted because the prankster hadn't hit them, too?

"Most of the churches that have received animals have been rather glad to get rid of them," I said. "I'm not sure I understand why you're complaining."

"For the live Nativity!" she shrieked. "We need cows, sheep, pigs, goats, donkeys, and some ducks or chickens. The rehearsal's in two hours."

"I'm afraid I'm still confused," I said. "Where do you usually get the animals?"

"Usually we get them from farmers who belong to the congregation," she said. "But they're upset because of the pranks, and none of them want to risk their animals. I assumed you'd be getting me some animals."

"Me?"

"Aren't you in charge of taking care of all the problems caused by these ridiculous pranks?" she demanded. "Didn't you get my message?"

"No, I didn't get any kind of message from you," I said. "And I'm only in charge of scheduling, to make sure everyone's holiday events can go on in spite of the pranks."

"Well, we're an event! And we won't go on if you can't schedule us some barnyard animals."

With that she hung up.

I took a deep breath and muttered several very uncharitable things about Mrs. Dahlgren.

And then I reminded myself that the live Nativity pageant wasn't just a Methodist event. They hosted it, because they were the only church that faced the town square, but like the New Life Baptist concert, the Nativity was more a community event. And in a farming community, a live Nativity pageant with no animals wasn't much of a show.

And clearly Mrs. Dahlgren was in no state of mind to make any practical arrangements. So if I wanted the town's holiday celebrations to continue successfully . . .

It occurred to me that sheep were one of the mainstays of biblical agriculture. And Michael and I did live across the road from a sheep farm. I called home and found Rose Noire.

"Do you think you could talk Seth Early into bringing a few sheep to town for the live Nativity pageant rehearsal," I asked her.

316

"Of course!" she said. "How many?"

"I don't know." I tried to remember last year's pageant. "Half a dozen, maybe? The more the merrier, actually. The Methodist farmers are nervous about bringing their animals in, so the sheep might be the main friendly beasts there. And make sure Seth's okay with it."

"You know how he loves to show off his sheep," Rose Noire said.

Yes, and I also knew that he was one of the legion of men who were smitten by Rose Noire — that was the main reason I delegated the sheep roundup to her.

"And bring a few of our chickens in," I said. "Whichever ones you think are likely to behave during the pageant."

"Of course!"

Okay, so there would be sheep and chickens for the rehearsal. Maybe I should rest on my laurels. Though it would be nice to find someone to bring a few cows, goats, and maybe even a donkey. And surely with all the ducks that seemed to be popping up all over town, I could find one or two to grace the stables.

It occurred to me that Grandfather had all of those in his petting zoo. I called him.

"The boys are fine," he said, before I even asked. "James is making sure they don't go

317

near any of the carnivores."

"That's good," I said. "I was calling to ask if the Methodists could borrow some animals for the live Nativity scene."

"Hmmm," he said. "I've only got the two camels right now, but I suppose it's better than none."

Camels! Mrs. Dahlgren certainly wouldn't be expecting the camels. I began to feel almost smug, imagining the look on her face.

"That would be excellent," I said. "And is there any chance you could bring a few docile barnyard animals from the petting zoo? A donkey, a cow or two, and perhaps a few goats."

"Yes, yes," he said. "But why stop there? Let's make this thing impressive!"

I liked his enthusiasm, but I wasn't sure what he had in mind.

"I could bring the wolves," he said. "They make quite an impression, especially the Arctic Wolf."

"I'm not sure wolves are quite what people are expecting at the Nativity," I said. "It's not really biblical."

"The wolf also shall dwell with the lamb, and the leopard shall lie down with the kid," Grandfather quoted.

"Yes, but not at the Nativity," I said. "I

know you find wild animals a lot more interesting, but people will be expecting domestic animals. It's tradition."

"I've even got a fairly tame leopard," he said.

" 'Fairly tame'?" I repeated.

"You're missing a wonderful opportunity to put a whole new multicultural spin on this thing." I could almost see him pouting.

"Cows. Goats. Donkeys."

"Oh, all right. When and where do you need them?"

I gave him the time and place of the pageant rehearsal, thanked him, and hung up. Then I took a couple of deep, calming breaths.

"You okay?"

I looked up to see Randall Shiffley peering into my window. I nodded, grabbed my purse, and opened the door.

"I'm fine," I said. "Just settling my temper before going inside, because I figure on general principles you should never be thinking murderous thoughts when walking into a police station."

"I'm going in to see the chief myself," Randall said, and we fell into step together. "So who's your intended victim, and when do you need an alibi?"

"Mrs. Dahlgren, and I don't know yet."

He winced.

"Okay, so I guess you already heard about how she needs some animals for the live Nativity."

"I have now."

"I'm sorry." He pulled out a small notebook — his equivalent of my notebook-that-tells-me-when-to-breathe — and frowned at it, as if the missed signal was the notebook's fault instead of user error. "I was supposed to tell you about the animals, and I was going to just as soon as —"

"Life happens." I stopped about ten feet from the entrance. "You want to make it up to me? Answer me something."

"Sure thing."

"What's Duane Shiffley's story?"

Randall stiffened, then closed his eyes and shook his head.

"What's he done now?" he asked.

"You tell me."

"Nothing, lately," Randall said. "That I know of. Apart from appropriating a few ducks from Quincy's flock and selling them, but you already knew that. He seemed to think Quincy owed him something for pitching in to help at the farm. We straightened him out on that score, and he's paying Quincy back."

"You were awfully quick to suspect him

when I called to ask who might have sold Rob a duck," I said.

"Was I?"

I just waited.

"Black sheep," he said finally. "Every family has a few. Duane had a drug problem. Did some prison time, and some time in a residential treatment facility. He's clean now. Far as I know. If you know different, tell me, so we can deal with it."

"He's been seen lurking around Trinity," I said.

"He works for Shiffley Construction," Randall said. "Hard for someone with his record to get hired anywhere else. He was one of the workmen who got the place ready for the choir concert."

"I figured," I said. "Couple of people thought he was behaving a little furtively."

"If these were people who know about his problems —"

"Not all of them," I said. "Because one of them would be me, and I didn't know. I didn't even know his name at the time."

"Yeah," Randall said. "Duane's other problem — well, one of his minor problems — has always been that he looks guilty, even when he's behaving himself. I'll look into it."

"Does he go to twelve-step meetings?" I asked.

"All the time," Randall said. "It was a condition of his parole and still is a condition of his employment."

"That could partly explain it," I said. "Trinity hosts a lot of them."

"Yes." Randall sounded angry all of a sudden. "So if you're suggesting maybe Duane wandered out of a twelve-step meeting, ran into Mr. Vess and killed him —"

"Not what I was suggesting." I held up my hands in a gesture of surrender. "I was just thinking that if someone spotted Duane when he was on his way to a twelve-step meeting, he might have looked a little . . . uncomfortable."

"Try anxious and guilt-ridden and yes, more than a little furtive," Randall said. "I like that theory better. He hates going, but he knows he has to. Look — I don't think Duane was up to anything. But I can't swear to it. All I can say is that if he was, we're not going to protect him. And in case you're curious, yes, the chief knows what he's been up to with the stolen ducks. And I aim to find out if he's been up to anything else."

He looked upset.

"As you say, every family has its black sheep," I said. "Remind me to tell you about some of ours some time."

He smiled slightly.

"When things are quieter, I just might take you up on that."

He nodded and strode off.

CHAPTER 32

I wasn't sure if I felt reassured or more anxious about Duane Shiffley. I felt sure Randall would find out everything his cousin had been up to. And a good thing, too, since nothing Randall had said explained why Duane would have wandered down the hallway that housed only a few offices and locked storage closets.

Though maybe I could come up with an explanation of my own. Yes, Trinity hosted a lot of twelve-step meetings, but every church in town hosted a few, along with a variety of outreach and support groups. They'd all been pieces on my schedule — smaller pieces, pieces I'd tried to move as little as possible, because I sensed the attendees might be a lot less comfortable about relocating than catechism students or participants in the quilting circle. Maybe Duane was trying to find someone he could ask where to find a meeting he'd been planning to attend. Or looking for a posted schedule.

I realized I hadn't even asked Randall about the incredible coincidence of Duane's selling Rob — and presumably a few other people — stolen ducks on the same night someone had stolen all those hundreds of ducks from Quincy's farm.

And I wondered what Randall had been coming to see the chief about. Not, I hoped, something important, since he was now driving away. Going to deal with Duane, perhaps?

I strolled inside the police station. On the counter inside was a little two-foot Christmas tree that looked pretty normal until you got close enough to realize that instead of ordinary ornaments it was festooned with gold-colored toy police badges and tiny silver guns. The silver garland wound around it was made of dozens of miniature silver handcuffs linked together, and the angel on top was actually a blond police officer Barbie doll with glitter-flecked gossamer wings attached to the back of her blue uniform.

"Hey, girl!" It was my friend Aida Butler, one of the chief's deputies, who was sitting behind the front desk. "What did you think of Kayla at the concert?"

I enthused for a while over the concert. I wanted to ask about her nephew Ronnie, but I couldn't figure out a good way to bring it up. I settled for praising her daughter.

"I don't understand why Kayla didn't do the solo," I said. "The girl who did it was okay, but Kayla's better."

"Yeah," Aida said. "Of course, the soloist's father is the church treasurer — maybe Lightfoot's angling for a raise. Or it could just be that Kayla's mouthy. And before you say it, yeah, she takes after her mother that way. She made the mistake of talking back to Lightfoot and now fat chance of her getting a solo while he's in charge. And she's not the only one. The man is ruining our choir."

"Maybe they won't renew his contract." I was dying to tell her what Minerva had said, but I didn't dare.

"Let's hope so. Lord forgive me, when I heard about the murder, I couldn't help wondering for a moment if Lightfoot was the victim. Not hoping, mind you, but wondering. And I wasn't a bit relieved when I found out it was that harmless old man instead."

"He wasn't that harmless," I said.

"A lot of people wished him ill, then?"

Aida perked up as if she found this interesting news.

"The chief already knows that he was not well liked at Trinity," I said. "I couldn't stand him myself. But I didn't wish him ill — just elsewhere."

"Same with me and Lightfoot," she said.

"Speaking of the chief, is he very busy?" I asked.

"I don't actually know," she said. "He's over at your church — checking out whether Horace is finished and we can release it."

"Great!" I said. "That's actually what I wanted to ask him about." Well, one of the things. "I'll head over there now."

"Don't push him about it," she said. "He knows you need the church back but he's cranky as all get-out. See you later?"

"Thanks for the warning," I said.

There were two police cruisers and several other cars in the Trinity parking lot. Vern Shiffley was on duty at the door.

"I dropped by to see if you had any word on when we get the church back," I called out when Vern opened the door.

Before Vern could answer, the chief appeared in the vestibule.

"Meg," he said. "Can I talk to you for a minute?"

Vern held the door open, and I stepped

inside. The chief led the way down the hall and into my temporary office.

"Hope you don't mind," he said. "Horace and I have been using your office while we've been working here."

"My temporary office," I said. "And you're welcome to it."

The chief was sitting at my temporary desk, and he had added a folding chair for his interview subjects.

"I won't keep you long," he said. "I just have a few questions."

"And I have something to tell you," I said.

"Yes?" He picked up his notebook and pen.

"I have no idea if this has anything to do with his murder, and you probably know this already, but it could be significant that Barliman Vess kept files on stuff."

From the look on the chief's face, I could tell he found this revelation underwhelming.

"I'm not sure I see the relevance," he said. "I myself keep a modest filing system — financial records, family information, professional development materials. I should think everyone does."

"Barliman kept files on problems," I said. "And the people he thought were causing them."

A pause.

"Are you suggesting these were blackmail files?"

I hadn't been but it was an interesting thought.

"More like harassment files, I hope," I said aloud. "He was a would-be whistleblower cursed with a shortage of major smoking guns. If he didn't like how something worked around the church, he'd start keeping a dossier on the situation. And sending memos to the vestry."

"Yes," the chief said. "I believe your mother refers to them as 'Barligrams.' And it wasn't just the church. He maintained an active correspondence with the mayor, the health department, animal control — pretty much every agency in town. I have a folder full of them myself. Everyone in the town and county government got their share of Barligrams."

"So you don't think the files are significant?"

"I didn't say that." He leaned back, rubbed his forehead as if noticing the start of a headache, and looked at me for a few moments. "I understand you went out to Mr. Vess's house. Did you notice anything interesting in his files?"

"I didn't go out there to read his files!" I

protested. "I fed his cat." It wasn't technically a lie.

"And completely resisted the temptation to snoop around?"

I gave up.

"No," I said. "But it's not as if I read all the files. The only thing unusual I noticed was that one of his files was missing." I explained about the empty hanging folder marked THORNEFIELD INVESTIGATION.

"I might know what happened to that folder," the chief said. "Apparently a few days ago Mr. Vess reported the basement of Trinity Episcopal as a hazard to our new fire chief — who, as you probably know, doubles as the new county fire marshal."

"Because of all the stuff from Mrs. Thornefield's estate?"

The chief nodded.

"The jerk. It was Vess's idea to put it all there."

"That would seem consistent with Mr. Vess's modus operandi," the chief said. "I'll check with Chief Featherstone to see if the missing file happens to be in his office."

"So what's happening with the church basement?" I said. "Please tell me Chief Featherstone isn't going to close the church down." If he did, Robyn would expect me to come up with yet another iteration of the

330

schedule, and I wasn't sure there were enough rooms left in the county.

Chief Burke sighed.

"Chief Featherstone was dragging his heels on doing the inspection," he said. "Because he knew this was the worst possible time for Trinity to have to deal with a major basement cleanup. But after the fire, he couldn't very well look the other way."

"Blast," I said. "How soon is he doing his inspection?"

"He and Reverend Smith are down there as we speak," the chief said. "I gather he's giving Trinity a week to resolve the problem before he has to close you down."

"A week!"

"I know it's not very long —"

"On the contrary, it's more than enough time." I suspected Mother and Robyn would try to enlist me to deal with the problem, and I already had some ideas. My fingers were itching to pull out my notebook and start a page for the project.

"But wait," I said. "How can Chief Featherstone expect us to deal with the basement when the whole building's still a crime scene?"

"It won't be in a few minutes," the chief said.

"That's good," I said.

"Nice to see someone happy." He was frowning and staring into space.

"If I wasn't afraid you'd think I was prying, I'd ask how your investigation was going," I said.

"Very oddly," he said. "I have to confess, it's not often I get to interview someone just before he becomes a murder victim."

"You were investigating Mr. Vess?"

"I said interviewing, but yes," he said. "I know you assumed I was ignoring the information you gave me —"

"That Ronnie and Caleb didn't pull the duck prank —"

"But I did listen. And I wasn't focusing only on the boys. Mr. Vess also seemed a credible suspect for the duck theft."

I nodded. He seemed to be talking to himself as much as to me.

"It's a little hard to figure out the motive for such a peculiar prank," he said. "But he certainly had means and opportunity. And it's difficult to imagine anyone else getting away with it without Mr. Vess noticing."

"Yes," I said. "From his back windows, he'd have had a grandstand view."

"And last night was a cloudless night with a half-moon," the chief said.

"And it must have taken quite a while to load all those ducks," I said. "And caused considerable commotion."

"Yes." The chief nodded. "Mr. Vess's unfortunate demise does nothing to prove or disprove the possibility that he committed the duck prank. But there's also the possibility that he witnessed the theft of the ducks and was killed because he was trying to confront — or even blackmail — the persons responsible."

"Persons," I said. "Are we back to suspecting Caleb and Ronnie?"

"Not necessarily," he said. "But they're not out of the woods. Their fingerprints were on the half-empty beer bottles near the campfire at Temple Beth-El. And we found two more bottles near Trinity. No fingerprints, but same brand."

"And they're the only underage drinkers in town who favor Gwent Pale?" I asked.

The chief nodded as if conceding the point.

"They are, however, the only underage drinkers already known to be responsible for some of this week's unfortunate events," the chief said.

"So you think Mr. Vess was blackmailing them?" I asked.

"Or perhaps he caught them in the act of staging another prank," the chief said.

"Or someone is trying to frame them," I

said. "But why?"

"I have no idea," the chief said. "Not yet, anyway." He was staring at his notebook.

"Is that it?" I asked, after a minute or so.

"Is what it?"

"You said you wanted to talk to me," I reminded him. "Was that what you wanted to talk to me about?"

"No." He sat up straighter in his chair, turned a few pages in his notebook, then looked back up at me. "Is Trinity thinking of hiring Jerome Lightfoot away from the New Life Baptist Church?" he asked.

CHAPTER 33

I blinked for a moment in surprise.

"Not even on the list of questions I thought you'd be asking," I said. "Not that I know of. And if anyone at Trinity had been thinking of it, I should think watching Lightfoot in action over the last several days would have made them think better of the notion. No, don't start thinking the New Life Baptist Church can get rid of him by pawning him off on us. It's not that easy."

The chief smiled slightly. Then his face turned somber.

"Then do you have any idea why Barliman Vess would have called the church where Lightfoot worked before he came here to check him out?"

"Did he?" I asked. "And why not ask them?"

"I did," he said. "I know what he told them. I also know what several members of your vestry think. I was asking you."

"That he was probably trying to cause trouble for Lightfoot," I said. "It's the only reason I can think of. Our Trinity choir director's a volunteer, and as far as I know everyone is completely happy with her. Hiring someone would be overkill — the most we do is have the choir rehearse and sing one hymn each week. But Vess really clashed with Lightfoot once the choir rehearsals moved over here. I can well imagine him trying to dig up some dirt. That's the way his mind works."

The chief nodded. He pointed to an object that was standing on the desk beside him, a two-foot-tall Arts and Crafts–style candlestick made of silver and oak.

"Recognize that?" he asked.

"It looks like one of the candlesticks that stand at either end of the altar. Here at Trinity," I added, since over the last few days we'd been talking about more than one church.

"Where is it stored?"

"Stored? I don't think it is. I think they leave the candlesticks on the altar. They're heavier than they look — why would anyone haul them around if they didn't have to?"

"Someone wouldn't take it away to be polished or something?"

"The Altar Guild fusses over the church

every Saturday afternoon — I expect they give the candlesticks a dab of silver polish most weeks, so they never really need major cleaning. Although come to think of it, I suppose someone had to move the candlesticks before the concerts Saturday and Sunday nights. The New Life choir took over the whole area behind the altar rail."

"And if you were someone helping move things, where would you put the candlesticks?"

"In the sacristy," I said. "Which is that small room off to the right behind the altar. They store the chalices and all the other altar equipment there."

"No one would have a reason to haul it into the basement?"

"Why would they?" I asked. "And even if they did, the Shiffley Construction Company team took the stage and the risers down last night. I assume someone from Trinity would have been there to put everything back to get ready for any services today."

The chief nodded. From his reaction — or lack thereof — I deduced that I wasn't telling him anything he hadn't heard before. He leaned back and studied something in his notebook.

"You can ask Robyn if it was there at the

altar last night," I said. "She was staying till everyone left but the night watch. I expect she'd have noticed if anything was amiss in the sanctuary."

I suddenly realized there was something attached to the candlestick.

"Is that an evidence tag?" I asked.

He nodded. I stared at the candlestick for a few moments.

"It's the murder weapon, isn't it?" I asked.

"We don't know yet." He tightened his mouth. "Probably."

"I hope not," I said. "Mother will have a conniption fit."

"We'll know soon enough," he said. "I'm expecting — Ah, Dr. Langslow. Welcome."

Dad bustled in.

"So, you think you've found the murder weapon?" Dad sounded very excited at the thought.

The chief pointed to the candlestick. Dad's face fell.

"Oh, dear." He glanced at me. "Your mother will be very distressed."

"Meg already suggested as much." The chief was holding out a pair of gloves. "Here. Take a look and see if you think it matches the wound."

"Is that fingerprint powder on it?" I asked.

"Yes," the chief said. He was holding the

candlestick while Dad tugged on the gloves. "Horace has already processed it for finger-prints and other trace evidence."

Dad took the candlestick and examined it from top to bottom, both through and over his glasses. Then he raised it up in the air and brought it down in a slow arc.

"Yes," he said. "It's the right size and shape. If you like I can borrow the match-ing candlestick and Horace and I can run a few tests. But if this isn't the murder weapon, you'd be looking for something very like it."

Vern and Horace appeared in the doorway.

"We're in luck, Chief," Horace said. "We've got a match on the fingerprints."

Horace paused. Was he merely being dramatic, or was he giving the chief a chance to kick me and Dad out?

"Well," the chief prompted.

"Jerome Lightfoot."

CHAPTER 34

The chief didn't seem thrilled to hear this.

"I can see the headlines already," he said. " 'Baptist Choir Director Bludgeons Elderly Man in Church Basement.' "

" 'Elderly Blackmailer,' " I suggested.

"Not much better," the chief said. "We need to pick him up. Vern, Horace — hang on; I'll get his exact address from Debbie Ann."

"And she can put out a BOLO, in case he's not home," Vern said.

The chief nodded. He was already punching buttons on his cell phone.

"Debbie Ann," he said. "I need an address on Jerome Lightfoot . . . One fourteen West Street. Right. He's a suspect in the murder. . . . Right."

I pulled my latest schedule copy out of my purse and scanned it.

"He's supposed to be over at the Lutheran church right now," I said. "He had me schedule another rehearsal with some of his soloists. Of course, there's no guarantee he'll be there, especially if he suspects you're on to him."

"You heard the lady," the chief said. "Horace, you go to West Street. Vern, hit the church."

Vern and Horace nodded and disappeared.

"Who's going to direct the choir at services tomorrow and on Christmas Day if you arrest Lightfoot?" I asked.

"That's for the choir to decide," the chief said. "Though I do know Minerva has been saying for weeks that she could do a better job than Lightfoot even if she was blindfolded with one hand tied behind her back. Well, the place is all yours." The chief stood up and rubbed his back as if it ached. "I'm going to break the news to Minerva and Reverend Wilson."

I pulled out my cell phone. I should probably call a few people and tell them that Trinity was available. Or have a small celebration that I didn't have to do yet another draft of the schedule to move all of Trinity's many Christmas Eve events to someplace else. Or notify Randall and Aida that at least their nephews were off the hook for the murder.

No time to do any of it. I glanced at my watch and realized it was high time I headed home. Michael was performing his one-man show of *A Christmas Carol* in a few hours, and between now and then I had to get myself and the boys fed and dressed.

Probably best just to let today's schedule run its course. And luckily I'd left tomorrow's schedule alone, hoping that the chief would finish with Trinity today, so I didn't have to rearrange that at all.

I turned out the light, left my office, and trudged down to the parish hall where the coffee machine was kept. I decided a little caffeine would help my trip home.

As I waited for the water to trickle down into my cup, I dug into my purse and dropped some change into the jar kept for that purpose. As dark and quiet as the church was, I could well imagine the ghost of Barliman Vess appearing to chide me if I didn't.

I sipped my coffee as I headed back to the vestibule.

And just as I was about to go out the front door, I noticed that the lights were back on in my little office.

I walked down to it as quietly as I could, more than half expecting to find it filled with sheep or wombats.

Instead I found Robyn and Chief Featherstone.

"Oh, dear." Robyn was shaking her head while looking around at all the furniture and boxes that filled all but the tiny space around my desk.

"What's wrong?" I asked.

"Hi, Meg. I'm afraid the fire chief isn't happy with your office."

"It's a fire hazard," Chief Featherstone said.

"It's not Meg's fault," Robyn hurried to say. "She's only been using it a few days."

"I had a report last week that there were parts of the church that constituted a fire hazard," Chief Featherstone said to me. "I told the reverend here that I'd try to put off inspecting it until after the holidays. But now, with what's happened . . ." He shook his head.

"I assume the basement is also in your sights," I said.

He nodded.

"I completely understand," Robyn said. "I know we should have done something about it weeks and weeks ago."

"By 'we' don't you mean Riddick?" I asked. "Wasn't he the one who was supposed to arrange the estate sale?"

"Yes, but he was clearly in over his head,"

Robyn said. "I've been trying for weeks to figure out a way to reassign the project without hurting his feelings."

"Do you have someone willing to take it on?" I asked. Clearing out the basement was one thing, but arranging an auction and an estate sale? I had a premonition that the church-swapping schedule was suddenly going to need more work — at least it would if she was planning to enlist me.

"Your mother seems quite willing to take it on," she said. "She's already started planning — she thinks we'll raise more money if we have an auction for the more valuable stuff. It all sounds fabulous to me. I've just been trying to bring Riddick around. But we can't wait any longer, so even though he's out sick —"

"Again?" I asked.

"Or still," she said. "I never can tell. At any rate, since Chief Featherstone has only given us till New Year's Day to get this done, we can't afford to wait any longer."

I had the feeling that far from being unwelcome, the chief's ultimatum had given her the solution to one of her knottiest problems.

"I'll leave you to it," Chief Featherstone said. "Merry Christmas to both of you, and apologies again for delivering such unseasonably bad news."

With that he left.

"So if Mother's going to take on the project, have you told her about the deadline?" I asked.

"A few minutes ago," she said. "She seemed to have a plan for where to put the stuff."

"And did she say what her plan was?" I was willing to bet I already knew.

"She thought it would be nice to have the estate sale in a barn," Robyn said. "Or possibly two barns — I gather the one on your parents' farm is on the small side for all the stuff we've got, so we'd need either a second barn somewhere else, or possibly some tents for the yard — though that would mean waiting till it's warmer, and I gather she's as eager to hold the sale as I am to see all this stuff leave. She's going to look around and see if she can find a barn large enough to hold it all."

Just then my cell phone rang. I glanced at the caller ID. Mother. I answered the phone and put her on speaker so Robyn could hear.

"Yes, Mother," I said, before she could say anything. "You can use our barn for the estate sale."

"Thank you, dear," she said. "Now all I

have to do is figure out some way to get everything out there."

"I have some ideas about that," I said. "December twenty-sixth is Boxing Day, right? Let's ask everyone who's got a truck or a large trunk to come and move a few boxes. And you and the ladies of St. Clotilda can supervise."

"Everyone in the congregation?" Robyn said. "What a great idea!"

"And anyone in any other congregation who wants to help out," I said. "With any luck we've built some bridges over the last few days."

"Lovely, dear," Mother said. "And I can probably recruit a few cousins to help."

The last time Mother had recruited a few cousins for a project, we'd ended up fixing sandwiches and finding beds for fifty people. But the project did get done, and in record time.

"I think we have a plan," I said. "Talk to you later."

"Good night, dear," she said, and hung up.

"I hope that's not too inconvenient for you," Robyn said. "Having all that stuff in your barn."

"It won't be for long," I said. "Mother's been champing at the bit, waiting to get her chance to bid on some of Mrs. Thornefield's stuff."

"Then I will eagerly await Boxing Day and the opening of all those boxes," Robyn said. "Goodness! This has certainly been the most unusual Christmas season. Do you suppose I should warn the bishop I'm a murder suspect?"

"Are you?" I asked.

"I quarreled with the victim," she said.

"You'll have to stand in line behind half the congregation on that one," I said. "Most of us have been quarreling with him a lot longer than you have."

"And I knew he was plotting to get me kicked out of Trinity," she said. "He told me as much. My first parish as rector, after all those years as an assistant, and a mere six weeks after I arrive, one of the vestry is already plotting my downfall. That's motive, isn't it?"

"Yes, but nothing like the motive Mother has," I said. "He called her proposed design for redecorating the parish hall 'fussy and old-fashioned.' "

"Mercy!" Robyn said with a smile. "I wouldn't blame her for killing him after that. I'd have helped! So you think I should wait a while before telling the bishop?"

"Probably. Then again, Mr. Vess was

always complaining to the bishop about things, and for all I know he could have complained about our bishop to the presiding bishop. Maybe you should tell the bishop to make sure he has an alibi."

Robyn giggled and shook her head. And then her face grew sad.

"Seriously — what a terrible thing, to leave behind such a legacy. I don't think I've met a single person who is genuinely saddened by his death. I'm already fretting over what to say in his eulogy. I can honestly say that he worked hard for the vestry, and took seriously his responsibility of stewardship, but beyond that, I confess, I am stumped."

"Have you seen his house?" I asked.

"I've dropped him off there a time or two, but no, I've never been inside."

"I suspect it's unchanged since his wife's death," I said. "Perhaps some of the oldtimers can tell you more about her — from her portrait, I suspect she was a kind person. And he bought expensive cat food for his cat, in spite of being disappointed in her mousing abilities."

"Thank you," she said. "I can use all that."

"Go out and look yourself," I said. "You'll get a better sense of the man. The key's taped to the underside of the mat."

"I will," she said. "Thank you. I'm tempted to go over there right now."

"Why not?" I said.

"Because first I've got to find Riddick and tell him I'm taking the rummage sale out of his hands."

"Mother can't possibly schedule anything till January," I said. "Why not wait till after Christmas to tell him?"

I could tell from her face that she was tempted.

"No," she said finally. "I think I'd rather not have it hanging over me. And your mother needs to be able to start planning and organizing without any secrecy. Besides —"

We both started slightly on hearing a door slam in the distance.

"Front door, I think," Robyn said. "I suppose the crime scene tape is down. People will start coming for events."

"We don't have any scheduled here for tonight," I said.

Just then Riddick came into view. He glanced into the doorway and nodded to us.

"I see you heard the news," Robyn called out.

Riddick stopped and turned.

"I heard we finally got our church back to ourselves," Riddick said. From the way he was glowering at us, I wondered if he was blaming me and Robyn for all the unfortunate events that had disturbed his normal routine. And then he put his hand up and massaged his temples, wincing, and I realized that maybe he was just still feeling his migraine.

"All the congregations have their churches back, and everyone's Christmas Eve and Christmas Day services can go on as planned," Robyn said. "Isn't that wonderful?"

Riddick nodded glumly and turned to leave.

Robyn took a deep breath, gave me a brisk nod, and stepped out into the hallway.

"If you have a moment, there's something I'd like to talk to you about," I heard her say.

She and Riddick disappeared into her study. I silently wished her luck and turned to leave.

CHAPTER 35

I felt surprisingly cheerful on the way home. Or maybe it wasn't so surprising. The chief had solved the murder, and Lightfoot was probably already in custody. Caleb and Ronnie had undoubtedly learned their lessons, which meant the pranks would almost certainly come to an end. I would probably see Randall at Michael's performance tonight, and could apologize to him for casting any aspersions on his cousin Duane's character.

My spirits fell a little when I arrived home and found Horace dashing out of our front door, chewing on a sandwich.

"I thought you'd be down at the station with Jerome Lightfoot," I said.

"So did I," Horace said. "He's flown the coop. Probably sometime last night from what his neighbor said. We're all doing double shifts until he's caught. I just dropped by to grab a bite on my way out to search Caerphilly Creek."

He dashed back to his cruiser.

Rose Noire was standing in the doorway, waving to him as he hurriedly took off.

"Poor thing," she said, as I came in. "He's going to miss Michael's show."

He was also going to be scouring the county for a dangerous killer in twenty-something weather at a time of year when most people would rather be indoors with their families preparing for the upcoming holiday. But I was glad to see she had her priorities straight.

"How is everybody?" I asked.

"Michael is in his office doing his vocal exercises," she said. "The Baptist ladies have finished and taken all the new curtains and seat cushions over to the church. They'll be back tomorrow to clean up and take away the sewing machines. Rob and the boys are in the playroom, watching cartoons. Michael's mother is in the kitchen."

"I should go and say hello," I said. "To Michael's mother, that is."

Rose Noire winced, but I wasn't bothered. These days I actually liked my mother-in-law. Before Michael and I were married, her habit of referring to me as "her" and my family as "the outlaws" had rubbed me the wrong way. She seemed to grow a lot fonder of me once Michael and I had gotten married — though I found myself wondering if she was just resigning herself to the inevitable. But eventually, after a conversation with Rose Noire, I made a resolution to consider everything Mrs. Waterston said to me in a positive light — even if it sounded like criticism.

So if she commented, "You've gained a few pounds, haven't you?" I would say, "Why yes! Thank you!" as if pudging out was something I had been working frantically to achieve. If she mentioned that the boys were a grubby mess, I would beam and say "Yes, isn't it nice that they're so active!" If she mentioned how loud they were I would enthuse, "Yes, is there anything more delightful than hearing the happy voices of children at play?" If she commented on any shortcomings in the housekeeping, I would pretend to think she was complimenting me on achieving a comfortable, unstuffy, lived-in house.

I'd gotten to the point where playing the lemonade game, as I called it, was actually quite enjoyable, and these days, for whatever reason, she gave me far fewer opportunities to do so. I wasn't sure if she was making fewer snide or critical remarks or if I was just less apt to misinterpret random remarks as intended slights, but either way, we got along better.

I strolled into the kitchen. Michael's mother was standing on the stepping stool, rummaging through one of the cabinets. Was she looking for something in particular or just planning to rearrange them again?

"Hi, Mom," I said.

"Hello, dear." She stepped down off the stool and we exchanged kisses on the cheek. Then she held me at arm's length, studied my face for a few moments, and nodded as if I'd passed some test.

"You're looking well," she said.

The old me would have wondered why she had to sound surprised. The new me just noted with pleasure that she sounded sincere.

"Thanks," I said aloud.

"Where's your colander?"

"We have several that live in that cabinet." I pointed to the proper one. "But Rose Noire's been doing rather a lot of soap and potpourri making lately. She may have borrowed them."

And one had gone out to my car in the bag of things we needed to cook our contraband Christmas dinner, but I wasn't about to tell her that.

"I don't need it right now," she said. "Just

making sure you have everything I need for my dinner. I'll put it on my list. When I'm finished, you and Rose Noire can take a look. There may be things you have that I'm not finding, and anything else we can buy."

"Good plan." This was the side of Michael's mother I liked. She always checked to see that she had everything she needed before leaving the house. She never started a project without making sure she had all the tools and supplies she required. Most people thought I was a good organizer, but I had to admit, Dahlia Waterston had me beat.

Of course, she'd only had Michael to raise. Perhaps if she'd had to cope with twins —

"What did you do to your arm?" she asked.

"A rude person barged into me and dislocated my shoulder on Saturday," I said. "It's still a little bruised."

"Ah," she said. "You might want to get a new sling for the performance. This one has red stains on it."

She turned her attention back to her list and then darted over to the spice cabinet.

She was right. The sling had red stains. Red wine or marinara sauce? In either case, not suitable for wearing on Michael's big night.

I went out to the library and hunted around until I found a scrap of the black lining fabric that was the right size for a replacement sling. Might as well look a little elegant for tonight's performance, and I was sure the sewing circle wouldn't mind. Then I took a deep breath and went upstairs to face the task of getting the boys ready for *A Christmas Carol.*

At least I didn't have to stuff them into little suits and ties again.

We'd left the boys home last year, and probably should have this year, but hearing Michael practice had stirred them up, and the prospect of being left behind provoked tempests of misery.

So we'd agreed to bring them. After the last two late nights, we'd come up with a new plan. Tonight they would wear pajamas under their snowsuits. And we'd cautioned them that if they got tired of listening to Daddy, they should tell me quietly so I could take them home to bed. Rose Noire and I were driving separately, so if the boys faded at different times we could each ferry one home.

To my delight, the idea of dressing up in pajamas and then going outside in them had just enough flavor of forbidden fruit to delight the boys, so they cooperated unusually well. Then I left them and Rob to continue watching *It's a SpongeBob Christmas* and went upstairs to get cleaned up and dressed myself.

I was wearing a long black dress, and the black sling was almost invisible against the fabric. Was that a bad thing? Should I perhaps go back and borrow a scrap of red velvet, so people could see the sling and perhaps avoid jostling me? No, I decided on elegance. If I got jostled a bit — well, we all have to suffer for beauty.

We all had a quick supper — ham-and-cheese sandwiches and Rose Noire's potato-leek soup. Well, all of us but Michael, who preferred not to eat too close to a performance. But Rob, Grandfather, Caroline, and the boys more than made up for any self-restraint on Michael's part.

"So you do this *Christmas Carol* thing every year?" Caroline asked.

"Every year for five years now," Michael said.

He'd started doing it because he wanted to help to raise money for the local food bank whose supplies usually ran particularly low at the holiday season, and had come up with the idea of doing a dramatic reading of

Dickens's *A Christmas Carol.* Not the whole book of course, but luckily Dickens himself had created a condensed version that he could perform on his frequent tours of America.

The first year, a brave fifty or sixty of us filled the first few rows in one of the college's smaller auditoriums. Last year it had been standing-room only in the drama department's main theater. I hoped they didn't have to turn too many people away tonight. Next year we might need to schedule two performances, unless the new drama department building, now under construction on the north side of the campus, was finished slightly ahead of time. The J. Montgomery Blake Center for the Dramatic Arts — Grandfather had donated a good chunk of its cost and browbeat a number of friends and foundations for the rest — would have several performance spaces, including an enormous state-of-the-art theater that could hold twice as many people as the hall we were in tonight. But since it wasn't scheduled to open for another year . . .

We could worry about having two performances — complete with two sets of prep-erformance jitters — next Christmas.

"And this is the first year the boys are old enough to go!" Michael added, beaming at his sons.

Actually, I wasn't all that optimistic about their chances of staying the course, but they were so eager that I thought we'd at least give them a chance. And if I had to leave early with one or both of them — well, it wasn't as if I hadn't seen the performance before. Thanks to all that rehearsing, I could have recited it along with him.

"And it's time we all took off," I said. "Daddy needs to get there early," I added to the boys.

I drove, since in his preperformance state Michael tended to forget about boring, practical things like turn signals and stoplights. The boys chattered happily about SpongeBob and Frosty the Snowman, which I hoped was enough of a distraction to keep his nerves from starting to fray.

We dropped him off at the stage door of what people were already calling the Old Drama Building. It was built in the overly ornate Gothic-revival style that made the Caerphilly campus so popular for film crews looking for locations for music videos and low-budget vampire films. Fortunately the snow and the addition of wreaths on the doors and candles in the windows created more of a festive Victorian Christmas atmosphere.

"Bweak a leg, Daddy," Jamie said. I'd been coaching him on the fact that it was bad luck to wish an actor good luck.

"Two yegs," Josh said, competitive as usual.

I parked in one of the faculty spaces and then led the boys around to the front door. We probably could have slipped in with Michael, but I wanted the boys to see all the people lining up and paying money to see Daddy. To keep down expenses we didn't print tickets for the show — just took contributions at the door, and attendees could donate any amount they felt comfortable with. Last year we'd taken in a lot more fifty and hundred dollar bills than fives or ones.

Of course we were early, so there weren't too many people lining up. Still, we formally handed over our contributions to the ushers, who were clad in Dickensian costumes. I recognized the one in front of us as one of Michael's graduate drama students.

"Thank you, my good man," the usher said as Josh handed over his dollar. "At this festive season of the year, it is more than usually desirable —"

"That we should make some provision for the poor and destitute," Jamie rattled off.

"Bravo!" Our usher and several others

nearby applauded.

"Bah, humbug!" said Josh, not only competitive but contrarian tonight.

The drama students all found this delightful and applauded some more.

"I take it this means that Professor Waterston has learned his lines," our usher said.

"If he forgets any it's not from want of rehearsal," I said, handing over my contribution.

"Thank you, madam," he said, with a bow. "Enjoy the performance. And I look forward to seeing you the day after tomorrow."

"On Christmas Day?"

"Your mother has very kindly invited those of us who cannot go home for the holiday to share in your Christmas dinner. Christmas orphans, she calls us."

"Lovely," I said. And since I wasn't hosting the dinner and had every intention of dodging all attempts to suck me into cooking, I meant it.

The lobby was decorated with whole forests of greenery festooned with red ribbons and flickering faux candles, and with all the ushers and ticket takers dressed in Victorian costumes, the effect was quite splendid. In a far corner, a costumed string quartet was playing a lively version of "Good King Wenceslas."

"Meg, dear!" Mother was standing just inside the door, also dressed in period costume, though her red velvet gown was much more elaborate than those worn by the women ushers. "Come have tea. And some hot cider for the boys."

"Gamma in play, too?" Jamie asked

Josh just trotted past her to the stand where volunteers — mostly women from St. Clotilda's Guild and the New Life Ladies' Auxiliary, resplendent in hoopskirted Victorian dresses in jewel tones — were selling hot tea, coffee, and cider to benefit the cleanup and renovation of the churches of Caerphilly, according to the signs posted nearby. I had a feeling this would be only the first of many benefits.

"Nice to see you," said a familiar voice.

CHAPTER 36

I had to do a double take before recognizing Robyn, also in a Victorian gown, although I recognized hers as one borrowed from the drama department's wardrobe collection.

Riddick Hedges was also there in costume, which was unfortunate, because unlike Michael and the other men from the drama department, he had no idea how to carry it off well. He was squirming as if the whole outfit was profoundly uncomfortable, and if I'd been casting David Copperfield he'd have been a shoo-in for Uriah Heep. It was perhaps a measure of his discomfort that he was not only willing but eager to fetch pitchers of water to refill the urns, haul away bags of trash, or perform any other chore that allowed him to disappear from view. In between errands he appeared to be attempting to fade into the wallpaper along one side of the lobby. No doubt he was unaware that he was standing directly beneath one of the dozen ornate Victorian mistletoe balls that dotted the room. I suspected he'd be mortified if anyone pointed this out.

I shelled out for tea for me and cider for the boys. Josh bolted his and had to be told to drink his second helping more slowly. Jamie was already sipping so slowly that I suspected he thought he'd be taken home to bed when his cup was empty.

"Take your time," Mother told me. "Rose Noire and your father are saving seats for all of us."

"Unfortunately, no one from Henry's department will be here tonight," Minerva said.

"Are they still trying to locate Jerome Lightfoot?"

"And not having much luck," Minerva said. "It's beginning to look as if after killing poor Mr. Vess he went straight home, packed his suitcases and took off. They've got a bulletin out on his car."

"I hope they catch him soon," I said. "Actually, I hope some other county catches him soon."

"I confess, I agree." Minerva shook her head. "I'd purely love to hear that he's been spotted a good long ways from here and locked up in someone else's jail. I had words with that man, more than once — if I'd known what kind of man he is! A cold-blooded killer!"

"Actually, I'm not sure cold-blooded could ever describe Mr. Lightfoot," one of the other Baptist ladies said. "I've never seen him when he wasn't in a temper over something."

"A hot-tempered killer, then," Minerva said. "And running around loose, and him knowing full well that I'm one of the people who's been trying to get him fired. Makes me feel all funny."

"Sit down, Minerva, dear," Mother said. "And have some tea."

"I can't blame you one bit," the Baptist lady said.

"I don't see how any of us will sleep tonight," exclaimed an Episcopalian.

Most of the church ladies chimed in either with the rumors they'd heard or to say how anxious they were. But by some unspoken agreement they all deferred to Minerva's superior cause for alarm — after all, she was not only a known enemy of the fleeing killer but her husband was even now risking life and limb to bring the fugitive to justice. Several of them vied to see who could refresh her tea.

"I'm sure we'll all be praying for a speedy

end to this terrible situation," Robyn said. She clasped Minerva's hands. "And for the safety of our brave law enforcement officers, and for the soul of poor Mr. Vess."

"And for Mr. Lightfoot, too," put in Reverend Wilson, craning around from behind the table, where he was filling cups of cider. "For 'I say to you, that likewise joy shall be in heaven over one sinner that repents, more than over ninety and nine just persons, which need no repentance.' There is still hope for Mr. Lightfoot."

There were murmurs of "amen," from the assembled tea ladies and Minerva lifted her chin and looked comforted.

"Although I hope no one will object if I hope Mr. Lightfoot starts his repenting very soon, and from the inside of a jail cell," I added.

"Lord, yes," Minerva said.

"I look forward to the day when he is safely locked up," Reverend Wilson said. "And I can begin to help him wrestle with the heavy burden of sin he must be carrying."

"I just hope Henry finds him before Christmas Day." Minerva looked anxious. "I remember one terrible year back in Baltimore, not too long after we were married, when he was working twenty hours a day trying to catch a serial arsonist and didn't have time to open our presents until three days after Christmas. And he's not a young man anymore."

"Oh, that reminds me, dear," Mother said. "Before I forget."

She glided over to the tea table, reached underneath, and pulled out a gaily wrapped package.

"This is for you, Meg dear."

I suppressed the urge to ask her why she felt it necessary to give me the present now, when I would either have to run out to the car to stow it or lug it with me during the entire play.

"Thanks," I said instead. I couldn't help noticing that she was displaying none of the delight she normally took in presents, even when they were intended for other people. In fact, she had looked relieved the second it left her hands. "Who's it from?"

"Cousin Sylvia." From her grave tone of voice, she obviously knew how I felt about getting a parcel from Sylvia. For that matter, how everyone felt. We both stared at the parcel for a few moments in silence.

"What's wrong?" Robyn asked.

"Cousin Sylvia is an avid knitter," I said.

"I love hand-knitted presents," Robyn said. "Lucky you!"

"Sylvia's taste is . . . unusual," Mother murmured.

"She has no taste," I said. "And her color choices are so peculiar that I really think someone should find a way to test her for color blindness."

"She tries so hard," Mother said.

"Mostly she does bulky Christmas sweaters," I said. "With Santas or reindeer or Christmas trees or bells. Only she does her own designs, so everything just looks like multicolored amoebas. Or psychedelic Rorschach tests."

"Still — one could make allowances," Mother said. "If only she'd use natural fibers. Wool. Cotton."

"I don't think it's possible to dye natural fibers in colors garish enough to please Sylvia," I said.

"Now you've roused my curiosity," Robyn said. "You must come and show me this sweater after Christmas."

"I'll show it to you now." I began picking at the tape at one end of the soft, bulky parcel.

"You can't open that now," Mother said.

"Why not?" I asked. "She won't be here to see me open it on Christmas Day. Even if she were, I can tape it up again."

"Well, it would be nice to see what we're

368

all in for this year," Mother said. "Once she comes up with a pattern she likes, she usually does it up in different color combinations for everyone," she added to Robyn.

"I'm just surprised she gave me a present at all," I said. "I thought she wasn't speaking to me. She found out I'd given away some of the sweaters she's made for me and Michael over the years."

"You should never have donated them to the church rummage sale," Mother said.

"She knitted those sweaters you donated to the rummage sale?" Robyn exclaimed. "Oh, my." She regarded the parcel with alarm.

"I knew better than to donate them anywhere else," I said. "I know she haunts every thrift shop for miles around. I just didn't think she'd come to the Trinity rummage sale."

"Next time just mail them to Cousin Alicia in California," Mother said. "That's what I do. She has found someplace that's happy to have them. Possibly some organization that helps the visually impaired. And then — Oh, my!"

I had finally succeeded in removing the paper from the sweater and held it up. Mother and I stared at it, speechless.

"Actually, this one is rather nice," Robyn said.

It wasn't Sylvia's usual bulky horror. It was a soft, boatneck sweater, all black except for the neckline, hemline, and the ends of the sleeves, which shaded into black flecked with a slight hint of metallic gold. I held it against my body and measured. I'd have to try it on to be sure, but it looked as if it would fit me perfectly. And look good on me. Perhaps Mother had brought the wrong parcel. I checked the tag: TO MEG FROM SYLVIA.

"It's beautiful," I said.

"Of course, given Sylvia's color sense, she probably thinks it's hideous," Mother said.

"Exactly," I said. "She really must hate me. Unless she's suddenly had a complete change of taste since last year. And I think it's wool."

"Wool-cotton blend, if I'm not mistaken." Mother was fingering the sweater with appreciation. "Very nice. And no, your brother opened his early, too. I'd say his is worse than usual. I believe it's meant to be Santa petting Rudolph and the rest of the reindeer — although if so, you'd think she'd have used red and brown instead of orange and purple. Rob thinks it's supposed to be a fruit basket being savaged by mutant hyenas.

If that turns out to be a little small for you, let me try it on."

"Hands off!" I pretended to swat her fingers. "I'm the one who insulted Sylvia. I should bear the burden of her displeasure."

"I still have the last sweater or two she sent me and your father," Mother said. "I haven't mailed them to Alicia yet. I could donate them nearby."

"Good idea," I said. "Offend her as soon as possible, before she starts on your gift for next year. Why not donate them to the rummage sale we'll be having with Mrs. Thornefield's things?"

"Estate sale," Mother corrected. "And yes, that's a lovely idea. We need to schedule it soon. Though not until after I've had Sotheby's and Christie's in to look at a few of her things that might bring more at auction."

"Not the furniture, I assume," I said.

"Of course the furniture," Mother said. "Mrs. Thornefield had excellent taste. Sheraton, Chippendale, Hepplewhite."

"Then where did all those old horrors in the basement come from?" I asked. "I can't see anything but big, heavy stuff that I wouldn't give houseroom to."

"Big, heavy stuff?" Mother suddenly looked anxious. "That doesn't sound like Mrs. Thornefield's things."

"They probably put the best stuff at the far end of the basement," Robyn said. "Away from the furnace, not to mention prying eyes. The big stuff's probably church castoffs."

"And there are tons of boxes," I said. "I suppose they might have boxed up anything really fragile."

"We could go over there now," Mother said. "Just to check it out."

"The play's starting in fifteen minutes," I said, glancing at my watch. "And I should put in appearance at the cast party. Let's just get there early on Boxing Day. We told everyone to come at noon, right? We can get there a few hours early."

"Why not tomorrow?" Mother asked.

"Tomorrow's Christmas Eve," I protested. "We all have wrapping and cooking to do."

"It won't take long."

"You haven't seen the basement lately. Even if my shoulder were back to normal, there's no way the two of us could manage all the boxes."

"I can round up several of your more athletic cousins to help us do any shifting around we need."

"As long as we're finished in time for the live Nativity pageant and the carol sing-along," I said.

"Thank you, dear."

"Probably time we all took our seats," Robyn suggested. As we'd been discussing the sweater the incoming crowds had swelled, and now the lights in the foyer blinked to signal that it was time for us to enter the auditorium.

Riddick, who had been hovering nearby for the last several minutes, cleared his throat and stepped forward.

"Is it okay if — I mean, I'm happy to stay on if I'm needed but . . ." He let his words trail off and touched one side of his head gently, as if to remind us of his migraines.

"Go home, then," Robyn said. And then, as if startled by how brusque her words had sounded, she stepped forward and patted his shoulder. "You really don't need to hang around if you don't feel up to it. Or if there's something else you'd rather be doing. Go home and take care of yourself."

He smiled wanly. Then he turned and began walking slowly toward one of the side exits. I noticed that the farther he got from us, the faster his pace became. Clearly there was nothing wrong with his legs.

"Did I sound too impatient?" Robyn asked Mother and me in an undertone. "I confess, I feel impatient. He's been complaining all day. What is one supposed to do with people who insist on hanging around and whining when you've told them multiple times it's perfectly fine for them to leave?"

"Just what you did now," I said. "Tell them it's okay to go."

"Subtlety is lost on Riddick," Mother added.

I discarded Sylvia's wrapping paper in a nearby trash can and carefully stowed my beautiful new sweater in the tote I always carried whenever I went anywhere with the boys. I'd trained myself to call it a tote rather than a diaper bag because I'd long ago realized that even when the boys no longer needed diapers they'd still need the million and one other things I carried in the bag.

"Don't forget to thank Sylvia," Mother said.

"Are you sure I should?" I asked. "What if I thank her and get the mutant purple reindeer next year?"

"So true." Mother frowned.

"I know," I said. "I'll tell her that I like the sweater so much because there are only so many times you can wear a Christmas-themed sweater — or for that matter any brightly colored sweater — but a nice neutral black sweater works fabulously any time."

"Let's hope she takes the hint," Mother said. "Why don't you tell her I said that?"

"Happy to," I said. "Josh? Jamie? Finish off your cider so we can go watch Daddy's play."

CHAPTER 37

Rose Noire, Dad, and Michael's mother were saving places for us in the front row, so even though Mother, the boys, and I slipped in only a few minutes from curtain time we had good seats. The boys were awed at the number of people who'd come to see their daddy, and we gave in and let them stand on their seats for a few minutes, gazing in wonder at the several hundred audience members. More than a few of the audience had come in costume — some in Victorian garb and others in whatever they'd worn for Halloween. The hall was filled with robots, pirates, vampires, ballerinas, werewolves, mafiosos, cowboys, cartoon superheroes, six-foot cats and rabbits, and innumerable Goths and fairies. The audience sparkled almost as much as the hall, which was decorated not only with the usual evergreen and tinsel but also with tiny multicolored LED lights that pulsed in patterns to the Celtic holiday music that was being piped through the hall's speakers. Clearly the tech crews were having fun tonight.

About the time we got the boys settled down and facing forward again, the lights dimmed and Michael strode out onto the stage, wearing his Victorian costume — a top hat, a black frock coat, a red cravat, and a bright red plaid waistcoat. The audience burst into applause, and the boys jumped up on their chairs again and shouted "Daddy! Daddy!" while applauding wildly. Michael spotted them, and strode to the front of the stage to bow to them. Then he pointed at each one in turn with his forefinger and fixed them with a stern look until they both sat down and assumed expectant expressions. The audience laughed and applauded, and I could hear a few people saying things like "Aren't they adorable!" Well yes — most of the time.

Michael set down his top hat on a nearby prop chair, stepped to the podium, and began.

"Stave One," he announced. "Marley's Ghost. Marley was dead, to begin with."

Josh settled down immediately and stared at Michael as if intent on every word. Jamie spent the first five minutes wiggling and craning his neck around, so he could catch a glimpse of all the people staring at his daddy. Then, after another few minutes of scanning the rafters intently — no doubt in hopes of a cameo appearance by another snake — he settled down with his head against my side and went quietly to sleep. Josh remained rapt, with his mouth hanging open. In fact, occasionally I saw his lips moving, and I realized he was mouthing the words along with Michael.

I was absorbed myself, at least at first. No matter how many times I saw him rehearsing, I was still surprised at how much better it seemed when he took the stage. Was it the lights and the theater setting? Or did he take the energy most people would fret away in stage fright and channel it into his performance? I marveled at how different he made his voice for each character, at how I almost could see what he was describing come alive.

And then he came to the part of the story where Scrooge goes home to his gloomy lodgings and, after the shock of briefly seeing Marley's face where the door knocker should have been, gives way to an uncharacteristic fit of nerves and searches his rooms.

"Nobody under the bed; nobody in the closet; nobody in his dressing gown, which was hanging up in a suspicious attitude against the wall."

There were chuckles at that, and I remembered my own brief moment of fright when I'd been searching the Trinity church basement and had been startled by the coat tree, with its own suspicious attitude.

Thinking of the coat tree reminded me of the whole mass of clutter currently infesting Trinity — in the furnace room, the classrooms, the storage closets, and the office that would soon cease to be mine. Strangely, the clutter no longer oppressed me, perhaps because I knew it would be leaving soon. As Michael acted out the confrontation between Scrooge and Marley's ghost, part of my mind was following him, and the other half was happily making lists. Things we'd need for the church clean-out. Things Michael and I could donate to swell the estate sale. Places where we should publicize the sale.

I felt wonderfully content. I had my family all around me. The boys seemed happy. And I was simultaneously doing two of my favorite things: watching Michael perform and making mental plans for organizing a project.

I glanced over at Mother, who was sitting proudly upright in her Victorian finery and following the performance with the keen appreciation she bestowed on anything belonging to a more genteel bygone era. But she didn't look as content as I felt. Clearly she was still concerned about Mrs. Thornefield's estate. I hoped it turned out that some of the larger boxes held the furniture Mother remembered so fondly.

And if they didn't — well, I remembered hearing that Mrs. Thornefield's house had been rather run-down by the time it had come into Trinity's hands. What if she hadn't been quite as well off as she'd led everyone to believe? What if she'd had a cash-flow problem and had solved it by selling a few of her nicest pieces?

Mother would be so disappointed. Maybe I should try to postpone our box-opening visit until after Christmas?

No. It would only prey on her mind. If the Sheraton and Hepplewhite furniture had been sold, best find out as soon as possible.

Jamie woke up after half an hour's nap, and from that point both boys remained wide awake to the end, following Michael's every word, and laughing when the audience did, though I suspected they were laughing not because they understood the funny lines but out of delight, because so many people were laughing at Daddy's jokes.

Michael took ten curtain calls. Afterward we took the boys backstage to see everyone congratulating Daddy in his dressing room. They were incredibly impressed.

And also starting to show signs of impending crash and burn, in spite of the preemptive extra napping earlier in the day.

"Rose Noire and I are going to take them home," I told Michael. "Before they ruin everyone's impression of them as little angels."

Michael's face fell.

"You mean you're not coming to the cast party?" Dad asked. "Your mother and I will be there."

"Your father will," Mother said. "I am worn out and planning to go home to bed."

"Besides," I said. "With a cast of one, how big can it be?"

"Okay, it's also the unofficial departmental Christmas party," Michael said. "And all of my family are invited! And it doesn't start till midnight, after we finish cleaning up the theater, so you could run the boys home and come back for it — if that's okay with Rose Noire."

She had no objection, so after making our good-byes to everyone, we led the boys out to the parking lot. We had to carry them the second half of the way.

"Let's just put them in my car," Rose Noire said. "I'm giving Rob a ride home — he can help me carry them in and you can head to the cast party a little sooner."

By the time we strapped them into their car seats, both boys were fast asleep. So I applied my best good night kisses to their unconscious foreheads and waved as Rose Noire and Rob drove off.

"Does this mean you're coming to the cast party after all?" I turned to see Robyn picking her way across one of the parking lot's many patches of ice. "It sounds like fun."

"I'll be a bit late," I said. "I have to pick up a few things at the grocery store. Don't mention that to Mother if she changes her mind and decides to come," I added.

"Because she would think planning for the rummage sale should trump mere groceries?" Robyn said, with a laugh.

"Something like that," I said. "You have no idea."

"Actually, I do." She looked serious for a moment. "Your mother is a force of nature. I'm just glad she's usually on my side. Call me when you and your mother are coming over tomorrow to inspect the boxes. Matt's back from North Carolina. He and I can help."

My errand at the grocery store didn't take long. I was picking up supplies for tomorrow night's secret Christmas dinner. Cans of refrigerator rolls. Cranberries. Cranapple juice for the boys to drink — we always served it on festive occasions so they would feel included when we lifted glasses of red wine for toasts. I pondered getting some ice cream, a popular favorite with the boys and Michael. But I wasn't sure there would be room in the tiny freezer compartment of the basement apartment's ancient toy-sized refrigerator for both the ice cream and an ice cube tray.

The store was surprisingly crowded for such a late hour. Some of the people were piling their baskets high with the makings of their own Christmas dinners — turkeys, geese, ham, ribs, pork roasts, potatoes and sweet potatoes, green beans, cranberries, pies, premade pie shells, cans of pumpkin, bags of flour and sugar — looking at other people's carts was giving me an appetite. And just walking down the spice aisles and seeing people filling their carts with cinnamon, cloves, allspice, nutmeg, and other spices made me happy.

In the housewares aisle, I convinced a

young, recently married Shiffley that no, a fancy electric mixer would *not* be the perfect present for his wife and suggested he contact Rose Noire, who could put together a deluxe basket of luxurious foods and wonderfully scented sachets, lotions, and potpourris. And then I ended up giving her card to several other present-seeking husbands and boyfriends who had been eavesdropping on our conversation. Tomorrow, I knew, would be one of her busiest days of the year, as the growing number of men who waited till the last minute to start looking for presents for their wives and girlfriends descended on her en masse, all begging for special gift baskets. A good thing she started making up the special baskets before Thanksgiving, though this year business had been going so well that several times in the last month she'd enlisted the rest of the household, even the boys, for several intense evenings of cutting up and wrapping soap, mixing and bagging potpourri, using rubber stamps to create labels, and doing all the other small tasks needed to get her supplies back to a good level.

All in all, I was in a good mood when I left the market. When I got to my car, I put the few things that were going home in the trunk, and the two bags of items going to the basement apartment on the front passenger seat. Probably a good idea to deliver them before I went home, lest one of the mothers come across the cranberries and ask what they were for.

My route to the apartment led near Trinity, and on sudden impulse, I passed the turn that would have been my most direct route to the basement apartment and took a slight detour. I realized that Mother had been on my mind. And I found myself suddenly thinking that perhaps it had been a little too easy to convince Mother to postpone her inspection of the estate sale hoard until tomorrow. And that her decision to go home and rest rather than attend the cast party was slightly suspect. And Mother was on the vestry — wasn't it possible, even probable, that Mother was in possession of one of those million spare keys Robyn had mentioned? And that in spite of Trinity being a deserted recent crime scene, she might decide to drop in to check on Mrs. Thornefield's legacy?

CHAPTER 38

Sure enough, Mother's gray sedan was in the parking lot. Toward the left side, as close as you could get to the basement door. I didn't see any lights on in the church, but I caught a few flickers of light through the basement windows, as if someone was walking around with a flashlight.

I parked my car next to hers. I put the groceries destined for the apartment on the floor and threw a couple of things on top of them, in case she came out and peeked inside before I found her. Then I headed for the stairwell that led to the basement door. The parking lot was empty except for our two cars, which would have been unheard of, except that there was nothing scheduled here tonight — I'd relocated everything that was supposed to happen here today to other venues, and hadn't rearranged anything after the chief finally released the crime scene. The parking lot would be full enough tomorrow. All the parking lots. But to-night . . .

The basement door was new — no doubt Randall had arranged to replace the one the firefighters had broken down to get to the fire. But to my relief my key still worked. I unlocked the door, holding my key ring tightly so nothing clinked, and turning the lock as quietly as possible.

The hall was dark, but there was enough moonlight streaming in the windows for me to see in the hall. Should I go back and get my flashlight? No, once I'd surprised Mother, we could turn on the lights. I had no idea why she was creeping around with a flashlight. Surely as a member of the vestry she had more right than most to be here.

I found her standing in the furnace room with her hands on her hips — well, the hand that wasn't holding the flashlight — glaring at some of the hulking furniture stored there.

"You see?" I said. "Seriously ugly furniture."

She started slightly.

"Hello, dear," she said. "I am perturbed. These are not Mrs. Thornefield's things."

"Must be some of the stuff from the church attic, then."

"No." She shook her head with quick

impatience. "I helped clean out the attic. Remember — just after the dear rector arrived."

"I remember," I said. "I was just thinking the other night how much better the basement looked, even with all Mrs. Thornefield's stuff."

"The guild inspected everything in the attic, the closets, and the basement," Mother went on. "We put all the things the church really needed in neatly labeled plastic bins, and we hauled out bags and bags of trash and recycling, and we boxed up everything that might possibly sell at the rummage sale and had it hauled down here, to the basement. None of this hideous old furniture was here then."

"How can you be sure it's not Mrs. Thornefield's? Even if it wasn't in her living room, maybe she had it in her attic?"

"Mrs. Thornefield enlisted my help," Mother said. She was opening up a box, using a small jeweled metal nail file to slice open the packing tape. "In fact, the guild's help. She didn't entirely trust our old rector. Not his character, of course; the dear man was above reproach. But even those of us who were fondest of him realized that dear Dr. Womble wasn't a very practical person. Mrs. Thornefield was afraid he'd just give her things to the poor, not realizing how valuable they were. So one day she invited the officers of the guild to tea, and she gave us a full tour. Including her basement and attic. There wasn't any ugly old furniture in her attic — only a few seasonal items and a number of banker's boxes containing all her financial records. She wanted us to know where those were. And she showed us her basement so we'd be aware of what a nice wine collection she had. Everything in her house was perfectly organized, spotlessly clean, and in impeccable taste. Nothing like this!"

"How long was that before she died?" I asked. "Maybe she downsized a bit. Sold some of the nicer furniture. To make sure the church got its full value." Or to live on, if I was right about her having financial reverses.

"Only a few months. Look at this . . . this . . . rubbish!" She pulled a few items out of the box she'd been opening up and shook them at me, sending the flashlight beam darting wildly. In her left hand, along with the flashlight, she held a small bronze-colored statue of a scantily clad nymph. In her right she held a superlatively ugly china lamp.

"Maybe someone else donated a few

boxes of junk that Robyn — or more likely the old rector — forgot to mention?"

Mother focused the flashlight beam on a label on one side of the box, which read THORNEFIELD ESTATE. BOX 14.

"I've opened up six boxes whose labels claim they are from the Thornefield estate," she said. "And so far I haven't found a single thing Mrs. Thornefield would have allowed in her trash can!"

She strode over to another box and began slicing at the packing tape with her nail file. Surely she wasn't planning to inspect every box in the basement?

"Let's work on that tomorrow," I said. "Preferably once we've already moved the boxes — we're only going to have to tape those up again to move them."

"I can't rest till we get to the bottom of this," she said. But she did stop hacking at the box she was trying to open. "I think someone has stolen Mrs. Thornefield's legacy."

"We can't possibly get to the bottom of it tonight," I said. "And if someone did steal anything, you're making it harder for the chief to figure out what happened. We need to leave those boxes sealed, so the guys from the Shiffley Moving Company can tell us if those boxes are packed and sealed the way they would have done it. That one you were working on — it looks to me as if it could have been opened up and then resealed."

Mother frowned as she looked down at the box.

"How can you tell, dear?"

"The tape that's closed up the top doesn't quite match the tape on the bottom," I said. "It's a little more opaque. And there's a little area right by the tape where it looks as if someone peeled off some tape, and the top layer of the cardboard with it."

Mother bent down to inspect the label more closely.

"You're right, dear. I wonder why I didn't spot that."

"You have to hold the flashlight at just the right angle," I said. "You'd probably have noticed it immediately if you'd turned on the lights to do this." I walked over to the wall and flipped the light switches.

Nothing happened.

I walked out into the hall and flipped a switch out there. Still nothing.

"The lights aren't working, dear," Mother said. "I assume it's something to do with the fire. Or with it being a crime scene."

I thought for a moment, then shook my head.

"The lights were working fine right after

the fire," I said. "And I'm pretty sure they were on when I was here this afternoon, talking to the chief and Robyn and the fire chief."

"Then perhaps there was some damage that didn't come to light until now," Mother said.

"If there is, that could be dangerous," I was pulling out my cell phone. "It could be a fire hazard — we should call the fire department. And dammit, I need to cancel all the events we have scheduled here until we're sure the building is safe and —"

"Drop the cell phone."

Mother and I both whirled to find Riddick Hedges standing in the doorway to the furnace room. In his left hand he held a flashlight so large it dwarfed Mother's little pocket light. In his right hand he held a gun.

CHAPTER 39

"Riddick!" Mother exclaimed. "Just the person we need. There appears to be something wrong with the power. Do you think you can do anything?"

Riddick looked at her for a few moments in disbelief. Actually, I did, too.

"Yes, the power is out because I cut the wires," Riddick said finally. "Now you" — he focused his flashlight beam on me — "I said drop that phone."

I leaned over, put the phone on one of the boxes, and then leaned back and tried to look as if the phone were unreachably far from me instead of a good lunge away.

"Not good enough," he said. "Put it on the ground and kick it over to me."

Reluctantly, I followed his orders. To my chagrin, he managed to bend over and pick it up while still keeping the gun, the flashlight, and his eyes aimed at us. I wouldn't have thought him that agile. I noted that he put my phone in his right pants pocket.

"Riddick, dear," Mother said. "There's really no need for this."

"Don't 'dear' me, you bossy old cow," Riddick said. "You and the witches of St. Clotilda's have had a lot of fun laughing at me all these years, haven't you? 'Poor Riddick — he tries so hard, but he just doesn't understand anything.' "

I had to admit, his imitation of Mother was spot-on.

"I have always tried to be respectful and supportive of you," Mother said. "In fact —"

"Shut up," he said. "There's some duct tape over on top of those boxes. Get it, and start taping up your ankles."

Mother and I looked at each other. She raised one eyebrow — the one on the side away from Riddick.

I realized she was asking me what to do. And looking — nervous. Maybe even scared. I wasn't sure I could remember seeing Mother scared. Or having her ask me for help.

"Sometime this century, ladies," Riddick barked.

Probably not the time for an existential crisis.

"Let's look for the duct tape," I said. And

394

for anything that we could use as a weapon.

If only Mother wasn't here, I thought, as I scanned the nearby floor and the tops of the boxes. I couldn't help thinking that if I were alone, I'd have a much better chance of getting the drop on Riddick. Or if I tried and failed, at least I'd only be failing myself. Mother's slender figure looked alarmingly frail at the moment. And why on earth would anyone over sixty wear boots with dainty little high heels at any time, much less with a foot of snow on the ground? Any escape plan that called for running fast was obviously not going to work.

Mother was playing her tiny flashlight over the top of the boxes. At one point the beam spilled over and illuminated the area around Riddick's feet, just for a second. There was something by his right leg. It looked a lot like the bright red plastic gas can we kept in the garage. Evidently Riddick had come back to have another go at burning up the junk in the basement. The stuff that almost certainly had never belonged to Mrs. Thornefield. I'd bet Riddick had hauled all her valuable things away, and maybe even sold most of them already.

Mother was eyeing her little nail file, but since it was only about five inches long and already warped from hacking through box tape, I didn't think it would do us much good. I was a lot more interested in the tacky bronze nymph, which had a lot of nice sharp edges. But I'd have to get much closer to Riddick to be able to use it.

"What's taking so long?" Riddick asked.

"There is no duct tape here," Mother said.

"There has to be," Riddick snapped.

"What, did you leave it down here when you killed Mr. Vess?" I asked.

"Keep looking," Riddick said.

Fine with me. The longer we could stall Riddick, the better. Surely sooner or later Michael would start worrying that I hadn't shown up at the cast party. Or Dad would wonder what was taking Mother so long. Or one of the deputies would swing by the parking lot, spot our cars, and come to check things out. I wasn't sure why Riddick was so intent on binding us — if I were a cold-blooded killer, I'd have just shot my prisoners and have done with it. Maybe he was a little squeamish about actually shooting us. Or maybe he didn't want to risk the noise. For whatever reason, he obviously preferred to tie us up and let the fire do his dirty work. Well, that was good for us. We needed time. Time, and a distraction.

"Did Vess actually figure out what you were up to?" I asked aloud. "Or were you just afraid he might if he kept poking?"

"Vess was a meddling busybody," Riddick said. "Don't try to pretend you're sad about his death."

"Any man's death diminishes me," Mother quoted. "Oh, look! I found the roll of tape."

She sounded so pleased that I couldn't help shooting her an exasperated look. Did she really not get what was going to happen once Riddick had the tape?

"But I don't think it's going to be very useful," Mother went on. She held up the roll and pulled at the end of the tape. About four inches of tape came away, followed by the brown paper strip that marked the end of the roll.

"That can't be my roll." Riddick sounded cross. "Keep looking."

He followed his own advice, dropping the flashlight beam to scan the floor, starting at his own feet and gradually moving outward.

And I realized that if he was pointing the flashlight at the floor, he couldn't see what we were doing. I reached out, very slowly, and grabbed the ugly china lamp. I wasn't close enough to him to whack him, and it was such an odd shape that I didn't like my odds of throwing it at him accurately but maybe —

I tossed the lamp as far to my right as I

could. It landed with a crash near the furnace.

"Who's there?"

As I hoped, Riddick whirled and pointed gun and flashlight in the direction of the crash. I launched myself toward him, taking a few steps and then bringing him down with a flying tackle. I realized too late that I should have taken my arm out of the sling before attacking. We landed hard on the concrete floor, and unfortunately most of my weight landed on my bad arm. I managed not to scream — I kept it down to a loud yelp. I heard something metal skitter across the floor. I hoped it was the gun. Yes, it must be the gun, because I could see the flashlight beam darting about wildly as Riddick started whacking me with it. I raised my good right arm to keep him from hitting my head, and was trying to get my left arm into play so I could hit him back when —

Thunk! Riddick suddenly went limp, and I heard a small metallic tinkling noise on the floor near me.

"Take that, you rude man!" Mother exclaimed.

I grabbed the flashlight from Riddick's now limp hand, scooted out of reach, and turned the beam on him. Mother had hit him with the bronze nymph. The tinkling noise had been one of the statue's slender, graceful arms breaking off on contact with Riddick's skull.

His eyes were closed and I saw a small trickle of blood making its way down his forehead.

I scrambled over to the gun, shifted the flashlight into my left hand, and took firm hold of the weapon.

My left arm wasn't liking this at all, so I walked back and handed the flashlight to Mother.

"Thank you, dear," she said. "If you want to tie him up, I have a full roll of packing tape in my purse."

She kept the flashlight trained on Riddick and the gun at the ready — pointed at the ceiling, thank goodness, not at Riddick and me. I fetched the tape and tied him up. It took rather longer than usual, working with only one good arm. I was relieved that he didn't wake up while I was doing it, but equally relieved to hear him groan slightly as I was finishing off his ankles. I checked his pulse. It was steady, and I saw his eyelids flutter.

I put as much distance as possible between me and him and sat down heavily on a box.

"Here, dear." Mother handed me the gun and the flashlight. "You just rest. I'll go out in the hall where the cell phone reception's better and call Chief Burke."

I sat, watching Riddick regain consciousness and begin to struggle against the tape. I put the flashlight on the box beside me and the gun in my jacket pocket. My left shoulder was killing me, and I wouldn't have the strength to lift the gun if Riddick wriggled out of the tape.

I wasn't sure if I was relieved or annoyed at hearing the dainty but firm tap-tap-tap of Mother's boot heels as she walked out into the hall.

"Hello, Debbie Ann? Meg and I have caught the *real* killer."

CHAPTER 40

"I can't believe it! Every church in Caerphilly is back to normal! We can all have our Christmas Eve services as planned! And it's all thanks to you and your mother!"

Robyn was standing in the doorway of Trinity, welcoming the congregation to the ten o'clock service. Maybe the churches were back to normal, but I still hadn't recovered from the previous night's excitement.

Robyn looked as if only the vivid presence of my bright red velvet sling was keeping her from hugging me. I'd chosen the color for that very reason. She settled for patting my undamaged right arm repeatedly.

"Mostly back to normal," I said. "Rumor has it that the Baptist church isn't quite as fresh smelling as they'd like."

"They'll be fine," Robyn said. "Father Donnelly and I gave them some incense yesterday, and just in case they can't quite bring themselves to use it, Randall Shiffley dropped off a couple of cans of pine- and spruce-scented air freshener this morning. Go have a seat down front — you want to get a good view of your boys."

I followed her orders. Mother and Michael's mother were already there in Mother's usual third-row pew, saving me a seat by piling their coats and cameras between them.

I'd gotten about six hours of sleep, thanks in part to the chief's suggestion that I go home after having my shoulder looked at in the ER, and give him my full statement today, after church. Still, never had I so appreciated Robyn's penchant for brief and pithy sermons. Even the parents who hadn't been up late probably felt the same, since we were all keenly aware of the occasional giggles, sneezes, whispers, and sounds of minor combat emanating from the doorways on either side of the church where the children were waiting for their entrances.

Finally the moment came. The organist began softly playing the opening bars of "O Little Town of Bethlehem" and Michael stepped to the podium to begin reading from the book of Luke.

" 'In those days Caesar Augustus issued a decree that a census should be taken of the entire Roman world.' "

A sixth-grader in a toga stepped out and held up a scroll made from two empty paper towel rolls, a long sheet of paper, and about a ton of gold glitter. He'd have looked more authentic if his mother hadn't made him wear a turtleneck under the toga but the mother in me approved of her caution.

" 'So Joseph also went up from the town of Nazareth in Galilee to Judea, to Bethlehem the town of David . . .' "

As Michael continued to narrate and the organist played softly, Mary and Joseph, seventh-graders chosen for good behavior, entered from the right and headed for the manger. Mary was leading, rather than riding, a donkey whose sneaker-clad rear feet had an alarming tendency to step on the heels of the snow boots his front feet were wearing. Mary abandoned the donkey once she reached the manger, which was right in front of the altar. As soon as the donkey came to a halt, its stomach began to writhe alarmingly, until Joseph kicked both sets of feet several times and stage-whispered "Cut it out, you idiots!"

While her husband was disciplining the donkey, Mary reached under the manger and matter-of-factly pulled out the doll that represented the infant Jesus and plunked him down in the straw. But then she remembered her character and assumed a beatific expression as she gazed down at the doll.

On this cue, all the animals filed in. In addition to the boys in their dinosaur costumes, the denizens of the stables included a brightly colored parrot, an elephant, a Wookiee, and Winnie-the-Pooh. They all took turns peering down at baby Jesus while the choir led us through all six verses of "Friendly Beasts," after which the Wookiee chivvied the rest of the creatures to the right side of the stage, where they all took their seats on hay bales placed there for their comfort.

" 'And there were shepherds living out in the fields nearby, keeping watch over their flocks at night.' "

Several comparatively tall boys and girls dressed as shepherds appeared at the far right, herding twenty smaller children dressed as sheep. The sheep milled about restlessly, being shushed occasionally by their keepers or whacked with crooks, while the choir and the congregation sang "While Shepherds Watched Their Flocks by Night" — thank goodness only the first verse this time. Then the shepherds herded their charges past the manger and got them settled down on the left side of the stage on more hay bales, except for a couple of small boy sheep who insisted on sitting with my two little dinosaurs.

Michael switched over to the book of Matthew.

" 'Now after Jesus was born in Bethlehem of Judea in the days of Herod the king, behold, wise men from the east came to Jerusalem.' "

The three children chosen to be wise men — or, in this case, two wise men and one wise woman — filed out from the left, carefully holding boxes wrapped in gold paper, presumably containing the gold, frankincense, and myrrh, while we all sang the first verse of "We Three Kings." I was relieved to see that there weren't any children in camel suits — especially since the donkey still erupted from time to time with stomach-writhing and alarming sounds of internal conflict and had to be suppressed by Joseph.

" 'Then, opening their treasures, they offered him gifts, gold and frankincense and myrrh.' " The wise persons all popped the tops of their boxes and showed the contents to Mary, who nodded with approval. " 'And being warned in a dream not to return to Herod, they departed to their own country by another way.' " At this, the wise men looked anxiously back the way they'd come, and then set down their boxes at the foot of the manger and tiptoed off in the other direction.

Then the choir started us off with "Joy to the World" and at the end of the song, the wise men came back. All the participants took a bow while we applauded, and then all the parents and grandparents put away their cell phones and cameras and the children scampered out to join their families in the pews for the rest of the service.

A good thing we weren't as tightly scheduled as we had been over the last few days, because after the service was over, everyone milled around for at least half an hour, praising all the pageant participants and sharing the latest gossip and generally reveling in the fact that Trinity was ours, not just for the moment, for the whole rest of the day and all day tomorrow. Doubtless all the other churches were feeling a similar sense of relief.

When everyone finally began drifting away, Michael took his mother and our two dinosaurs for lunch at Mother and Dad's while I headed over to the police station for my interview with the chief.

I took the long way around, in part so I could drive by as many churches as possible. In fact, I cruised through the parking lots of several. The choir was in full and glorious voice at New Life Baptist Church. The parking lot at St. Byblig's was full, and there were cars parked up and down the road so far in both directions that a couple of parishioners were using their vans to haul latecomers to the door. An early service had just ended at the Presbyterian church and even though it was still below freezing, many of the congregation were lingering in small groups in the parking lot. From the clouds of breath steam rising from most of the groups they were all talking a mile a minute. I exchanged waves with Randall and at least a dozen other Shiffleys. On the lawn of the Methodist church, several people were laughing happily as they hauled away the last few inanimate Nativity figures and shoveled the area, in preparation for this afternoon's live Nativity.

By the time I reached the police station, I was elated from the sight of so many of my friends and neighbors enjoying their Christmas rituals untroubled by pranks. I was looking forward to my interview — I also had a lot of questions, and provided the chief was in a good mood and I was tactful about how I asked, I stood a good chance of getting answers to most of them.

I got a few of my answers before I even

went in. As I parked in the visitors' section of the station lot, I saw a Goochland County Sheriff's Department car pull up by the front door. Horace and Vern Shiffley appeared to be watching this new arrival with interest so I went over to wish them good morning and see what I could see.

"Good news," Vern said. "Our friends up in Goochland County have apprehended Jerome Lightfoot."

"But is he still a wanted man?" I asked. "Now that we're pretty sure he isn't the killer, I mean."

"Maybe he's not the killer," Vern said. "But he probably isn't Jerome Lightfoot, either. He had several complete sets of identity papers with him, and they're probably all false. But we sent in his fingerprints, so we should find out who he really is pretty soon. I'm betting the New Life Baptist Church won't be the only place charging him with fraud."

"Speaking of fingerprints," I added. "If he's not the killer, how did his prints get on the murder weapon?"

"He threw it at someone," Horace said. "During one of his tantrums when the choir was rehearsing at Trinity. According to some of the ladies from the Altar Guild, at one point he started heaving anything he could find at people — not just the candlesticks but hymnals and flower vases and seat cushions. The ladies packed up everything that wasn't nailed down and shoved it all in the sacristy for safekeeping. And according to them, Riddick was making himself helpful for a change."

"So when he surprised Vess in the basement —" Vern began.

"Or arranged to meet him in the basement —" Horace put in.

"He brought along the candlestick," Vern finished. "Knowing he could use it to frame Lightfoot. One of the ladies mentioned that she couldn't find it Sunday morning to polish it, but she figured it had just been put away in the wrong place. Riddick had probably hidden it someplace to use when he did away with Vess."

"Which is going to make it a lot easier to prove premeditation," Horace added.

"You here to see the chief?" Vern asked.

I nodded.

"Wait here until they take Lightfoot through the lobby," Horace said.

"Or whatever his name is," Vern grumbled.

Given what the so-called Lightfoot had done to my shoulder, I thought this was good advice. I spotted several other familiar figures also watching Lightfoot's entrance.

"What's Caleb doing down here?" I asked.

"Just got his anklet taken off," Vern said. "County attorney's offering him and Ronnie probation, provided they make financial restitution and do about a zillion hours of community service."

"Good," I said. "Is that Duane Shiffley with him?"

"It is," Vern said. "Seems Duane is dead set against seeing any more young Shiffleys following in his unfortunate footsteps. Going to stick to Caleb like a burr to a hound dog until he's sure the kid has done all his community service and seen the error of his ways. If Caleb wants to go to the devil he'll have to do it over Duane's dead body. Probably safe to go in now."

I took Vern's advice, wishing Caleb and Duane a merry Christmas as I passed. The chief was standing in the lobby, gazing down the hallway that led to the jail, with a satisfied expression on his face.

"Good morning, Meg," he said. "And merry Christmas. I won't take too much of your time — I know you have a lot on your plate."

And it didn't take much time, probably because he'd already taken a very detailed statement from Mother last night. I went through my story, and he took a few notes, but that was it. And he was obviously in such a genial mood that I didn't hesitate to ask a few questions of my own.

"So was Mother right?" I asked. "Had Riddick stolen all of Mrs. Thornefield's nice things?"

"Stolen just about everything," the chief said. "And started selling everything off. Fortunately he was keeping good records, so we shouldn't have too much trouble recovering either the items from the buyers or the purchase price from Riddick's bank account, whichever Trinity prefers. And the items he hadn't yet sold were all packed up — apparently he was planning to take it all with him."

"Even the furniture?"

"He had it all loaded in a stolen truck," the chief said. "Quincy Shiffley's truck, in fact. Once we've inventoried it, the Shiffley Moving Company can bring it out to your barn to get ready for that auction."

"What about the stuff in the church basement?" I asked. "Did he steal that, too?"

"No, he bought it all at various junk shops, estate sales and yard sales over the past six months, since Mrs. Thornefield passed away," the chief said. "He knew everyone would get suspicious if there wasn't a house full of furniture and boxes down in the basement. I suppose it never occurred to him that anyone would be that familiar with the contents of Mrs. Thornefield's house."

"He should have known Mother better by now," I said.

"And it's a good thing you knew your mother well enough to suspect she couldn't rest without inspecting the basement," the chief said.

"And did Mr. Vess suspect what was going on?" I asked. "Or was he just unlucky enough to be snooping in the church when Riddick was making his final haul? Or will we ever know?"

"We have a pretty good idea," the chief said. "We've recovered two files Riddick apparently stole from Mr. Vess. The one on the Thornefield estate and one on Riddick himself. Apparently, Vess had been suspicious of Riddick for years."

"But he was suspicious of everybody," I said. "How was anyone supposed to know he was right about Riddick?"

"Precisely! The boy who cried wolf!" The chief leaned back in his chair and clasped his hands behind his head. I recognized the welcome signs that he was in a good mood and felt like sharing the details of his case. "And unfortunately Mr. Vess was rather fixated on the notion that Riddick was stealing money. All Riddick had to do was keep the cash and bank accounts clean and he could steal the church blind without Vess being any the wiser."

"But if Vess had suspected Riddick for years — do you mean this was going on even before Mrs. Thornefield's estate?"

"It's been going on nearly twenty years," the chief said. "Though on a much, much smaller scale," he added, seeing my shocked expression. "Apparently early in their working relationship, Dr. Womble, the previous rector, recognized that Riddick might be finding it difficult to manage on the relatively modest salary the church was paying him. So the good doctor encouraged Riddick to take any little items he might find useful from the rummage sale donations."

" 'Little items'?" I said. "Like that silver Tiffany tea service Mother was burbling about before church this morning?"

"It began with little items," the chief said. "But it wasn't long before Riddick realized the true value of the items donated by more affluent parishioners. That's when he began his practice of replacing valuable objects with cheap counterparts purchased in thrift shops. He also started pretending to sell some of the donated items to antique stores and thrift shops — supposedly for larger sums than they'd bring at the rummage sale. But of course he was selling his thrift shop purchases, not the donations."

"He's lucky no one ever recognized any of his thrift shop junk."

"It's not luck," the chief said. "He stuck to thrift shops at least three hours' drive away."

I shook my head in amazement.

"Riddick, of all people," I said. "And for twenty years?"

"He was only doing it on the large scale for the last six or seven years," the chief said. "Until your mother came along. She's the reason he was leaving Trinity."

"Mother? I thought it was Robyn."

"Robyn annoyed him," the chief said. "All that emphasis on efficiency and decluttering was going to make it harder to run his racket. But his problems really began when your mother was elected to the vestry. Riddick could tell everyone else on the vestry that a thrift shop had offered a few hundred dollars for some old threadbare rugs and they'd say 'Great!' Your mother would want to see the rugs first. She'd almost shut him down even before Robyn arrived."

"Good for Mother!" I exclaimed. "But I guess he couldn't resist going for one more big score with Mrs. Thornefield's estate."

"Yes," the chief said. "He was hoping to use the disruption arising from the change in rectors to cover his tracks. At first, the pranks alarmed him. Having dozens of inquisitive Baptists swarming all over the church must have made him nervous. But he soon realized that if he kept the pranks going, he could exploit them to help him pull off his final theft. And to get rid of Mr. Vess, whose suspicions were finally becoming inconvenient."

"Don't tell me — after hearing Mother go on about the valuable furniture for the last three or four months, Vess finally took a look at the junk in the basement and figured out what was up?"

"No." The chief was wearing what could only be called a Cheshire Cat grin. "Riddick was planning to move to the greater Los Angeles area, and he was looking for someplace to stash his loot. In late October, he made the mistake of using his office phone to call a storage locker company in Van Nuys. Apparently Vess reads every line of the church phone bill, and when he saw a ninety-cent long-distance charge that didn't seem legit, he couldn't rest till he got an explanation. He'd been bugging everyone about it. What if he called the storage place and they gave him Riddick's name? So Vess had to go."

"Good grief," I said. "I remember all that fuss about the ninety-cent phone call. Our budget's tight, but not that tight."

"Won't be tight at all when we recover what Riddick embezzled," the chief said. "It'll be at least a million."

"A million *dollars*?" My jaw fell.

"At least."

"Well, that answers another question," I said, when I finally got my voice back. "I was still having a hard time believing anyone would commit a murder over a bunch of old furniture, but a million dollars?"

"Definitely ample motive," the chief said. "And if Riddick has any money left after Trinity has taken back what he stole, Quincy Shiffley will probably sue him for mental anguish. He's still convinced some of his ducks are missing."

"So Riddick definitely stole the ducks?"

"Using Quincy Shiffley's truck," the chief said, nodding. "Horace found ample forensic evidence to prove that. We may never know if Riddick committed the duck prank just to cause mischief — because he could see how much the first two pranks and the resulting church-swapping upset Mr. Vess — or if he already had murder in mind. I'm pretty sure he used the ducks in the hope of casting suspicion on Mr. Vess."

"Since Mr. Vess had better access to the ducks than anyone else in the county," I said, nodding.

"And Riddick lit the campfire near Temple Beth-El to make sure all eyes were there and not on Trinity Episcopal," the chief went on. "And he seems to be a belt-and-suspenders kind of crook, so I expect we'll find he planted those beer bottles with the boys' fingerprints on them just in case we didn't believe that Mr. Vess had somehow incinerated himself while trying to fill the Trinity basement with stolen rabbits. So Ronnie and Caleb will have to deal with whatever punishment their parents impose for underage drinking, but I'm convinced they're innocent of the duck and rabbit thefts."

"Good," I said. "I thought they sounded sincere. On another topic — not that I want to pry into New Life Baptist's business, but what's the story on Jerome Lightfoot? Is it just me, or was it a little weird for someone to go to all that trouble just to get a job as a church choir director? Even for such a distinguished choir as yours," I added hastily.

"Indeed," the chief said. "Apparently, to

judge from the last three churches at which he worked — two of them under different pseudonyms — his modus operandi is to use his position as choir director to worm his way into the confidence of key church financial officials and then arrange to have the blame fall on them when he absconds with as much church money as he can manage. His previous flights have all taken place either at Christmas or Easter, when he could add substantial cash sums from the collection plate to what he was pillaging from the church bank accounts. I rather doubt he could have pulled it off here in Caerphilly — our treasurer was gratified to have his daughter chosen as a soloist over two arguably more worthy vocalists, but he's not that gullible. Still, you never know."

"And even if he was planning to try this Christmas, I bet all the church-swapping threw a monkey wrench in his plans," I said. "That could account for what a nasty temper he was in every time I saw him over in Trinity."

"His temper was rather nasty at the best of times," the chief said. "But yes, I recall Minerva mentioning that he was behaving badly, even for him. She put it down to tension over the important concert, but perhaps he was merely vexed that he'd have to put up with us till Easter to get another big cash haul. And since poor Mr. Vess was killed after starting an inquiry into Lightfoot's background and Lightfoot took flight so soon after the murder — well, it's a lucky thing you and your mother managed to apprehend the real killer."

We fell silent. I didn't know what the chief was thinking, but I was musing over the fact that however annoying Barliman Vess had been, he had probably helped save Trinity from a good many real financial problems. He'd caught on to Riddick's plot in the end. He'd probably been the first to suspect Lightfoot. He'd still be around to vex us all if he'd trusted Robyn or his fellow vestry members enough to confide in them. We'd be choosing his replacement on the vestry soon, and we'd better find someone else with his unique combination of financial savvy and suspicious nature. I pulled out my notebook and wrote a reminder to think of some good candidates before Mother tried to draft me.

"Well, I won't keep you any longer," the chief said, standing up to signal that our interview was over. "Thanks to you, we're having our full schedule of Christmas Eve activities over at the New Life Baptist Church. Minerva said if you don't have a chance to get home for lunch, you're welcome to drop by for the potluck at noon."

"I'll keep it in mind if anything interrupts me on my way out of town."

CHAPTER 41

But nothing interrupted me on the way out of town. Mother had saved me a plate, and I arrived in time to help Michael's mother and the boys make Christmas cookies. Michael disappeared — ostensibly to do some last-minute Christmas shopping, though I knew he was actually going over to start cooking our private dinner, especially the turkey, which was larger than expected and would take forever.

"But what happens when you need to leave for the live Nativity and the carol singing?" I asked. "You can't just leave the turkey cooking in an empty house."

"I've hired a sitter," he said.

"For the turkey?"

"One of my students who isn't going home for the holidays will be sitting in the apartment, studying and basting the turkey at half-hour intervals while I'm gone. And no, we don't have to invite him to share the bird he's basting. He'll be at your mother's tomorrow with the rest of the hordes."

When Michael came back from cooking we informed the boys that we were doing something special for dinner after the carol sing. We swore them to secrecy, of course, though I was relying less on their discretion than on the fact that they wouldn't be out of our sight until we took off for the apartment. And if they did babble about the "something special," I planned to say that we were going to take them driving around to see Christmas lights until they dozed off in their car seats.

Around three we all bundled up to go back into town for the live Nativity.

Randall had arranged for a crew to deliver dozens of hay bales to the newly shoveled town square and arrange them in loose rows facing the Methodist church, which was slightly elevated above the square, giving us a good view of the empty stable. Once everyone was seated and just as we were all getting restless and a little cold and wondering when the show would start, we heard baas and bleats and short, sharp barks. We craned our necks to see a flock of sheep coming around the corner into the blocked-off street in front of us. It was Seth Early in a rough homespun shepherd's robe leading at least fifty of his enormous Lincoln sheep, accompanied by half a dozen Methodists, similarly dressed, and Lad, Seth's Border Collie, who did such a good job keeping the flock together and in motion that the humans with their crooks were clearly just for decoration.

Following in the wake of the sheep were the other animals. A dozen cows, complete with old-fashioned bells, marched sedately behind two milkmaids in biblical costume. The half dozen lively goats each had its own keeper and still caused more trouble than all the cows and sheep put together.

I waved to my friend Betsy, who was leading several American Mammoth Jackstock donkeys, including one named Jim-Bob who had helped save my life during the summer. The final donkey pulled a rough wooden cart driven by Rose Noire and piled high with wooden cages containing ducks, geese, and chickens.

Next came the llamas, led by a tall shepherd I recognized as my brother Rob. Another donkey pulled yet another wooden cart, this one driven by Dad and bearing my grandfather, who was holding the leashes of his three wolves. He was right — the Arctic Wolf was particularly striking.

Caroline Willner followed, riding a small

elephant that lived at her wildlife sanctuary. She was followed by more costumed men driving a pair of large pigs, a woman leading a very temperamental zebra, and a small flock of ostriches and emus.

It all made for a very unusual manger scene by the time they finally got all the animals gathered around the stable — except for the wolves, which Grandfather kept a little way down the slope toward the street, since the way they were straining at their leashes indicated that they were far too interested in the other animals.

After all that, the appearance of the holy family and the assorted angels, shepherds, and wise men was almost an anticlimax — well, except for the fact that the three wise men arrived leading two camels with magnificent bejeweled trappings. In spite of the many anachronisms, the pageant was a smashing success.

When it was over and the animals were being led off, we all turned around to face the enormous Christmas tree in the center of the square — which meant that anyone who had a back-row seat for the living Nativity now had a front row seat for the caroling — and after Randall ceremoniously plugged in the tree lights, Minerva Burke led us all in a half hour of Christmas carols before wishing us a merry Christmas and telling us to go home and start celebrating with our families.

Michael ducked out a little early with the boys. I stayed behind to make our excuses — no, we weren't coming over to Mother and Dad's for the evening — the boys were a little tired, and we had presents to assemble before we fell into bed ourselves.

"But we'll see you bright and early on Christmas Day!" I said. Probably too early; all the grandparents were determined to be there when the boys woke up and saw their presents. I'd already made sure Mother and Dad could find their keys to the house so I wouldn't have to let them in.

I took a circuitous route when I left the town square and kept my eye on my rearview mirror. Not that I really expected anyone to be following me for sinister reasons, but I couldn't help worrying about being spotted by some well-meaning friend or relative who might try to catch up with me to congratulate me on my lucky escape or want to hear the details.

I finally turned into the familiar quiet, tree-lined street and then through the familiar gateway in front of the house that Michael's friend Charlie now owned. An eight-foot fence that in summer would be covered with climbing roses and honey-suckle vines instead of snow and ice con-cealed a surprisingly large parking lot, a legacy from when the house had been chopped into eight or ten cramped apart-ments. By the time Michael had come to Caerphilly, a prosperous faculty member had turned the building back into a single-family dwelling, except for the basement apartment.

The twinmobile, our van, was already there. I hurried down the narrow brick steps along one side of the house to knock on the low door, whose bright red surface was half hidden by an enormous green wreath fes-tooned not only with a red bow but also a half-price sticker from the Caerphilly Mar-ket. I could hear carols playing inside — a very nice choral version of "Adeste Fidelis." Josh opened the door on my first knock — clearly he'd been keeping watch.

"Mommy!" he exclaimed. "Come see playhouse!"

It did seem almost toylike compared with our current house. The ceilings were only seven feet tall so that Michael, at six four, had to duck when he went under an over-head light fixture. It was basically one not-very-large room with alcoves for the kitchen and bath and closet. In our time the kitchen had consisted of a microwave, a toaster oven, and a hotplate on top of a mini refrigerator, and we'd done dishes in the bathroom sink. Now it was fitted out with the smallest stove and kitchen sink I'd ever seen, and a slightly larger and newer mini fridge. Of course, the expanded kitchen took up a few more square feet of what was already a pretty minuscule living space, but it was definitely an improvement.

Charlie had replaced the hideous sofa bed I remembered with a nice new futon sofa. But the bathroom was still separated from the rest of the apartment by the same curtain made of a vintage sixties Indian-print cotton bedspread.

Still, it was cozy. And filled with the most delicious smells — turkey and gingerbread and pumpkin pie. And decorated just as extravagantly as our house was, though clearly by different hands. The bathroom curtain had been drawn aside to reveal a skinny six-foot spruce tree occupying the shower stall — one of the few spaces large enough to hold it. The tree, the rest of the bathroom, and the whole apartment were decorated with red and gold paper chains, lopsided stars cut out of gold paper, and garlands of evergreen held together with Scotch tape, from which I deduced that Michael and the boys had picked the vegetation themselves. A papier-mâché Santa and nine papier-mâché reindeer hung from the ceiling. The power cord to Rudolph's flashing red nose was wrapped in tinsel and taped across the ceiling and down one wall until it could reach a vacant outlet. And taped to all the walls were Christmas posters painted by the boys. Wise men riding on beasts that looked a lot more like llamas than camels. Mary and Joseph bending tenderly over a baby Jesus who seemed to be occupying a car seat rather than a manger. Santa Claus, Mrs. Claus, and the elves surrounded by a three-foot-high avalanche of presents — including what I suspected was a giant hamster cage. A giant Christmas tree almost hidden by the wrapped presents piled around it. A mantel from which hung a line of stockings large enough for giants.

"Did you guys do all this?" I asked. "It's beautiful!"

Josh beamed. Jamie, overcome with praise, buried his head in the sofa cushions with his rump sticking up, ostrichlike.

Just then I spotted a completely unexpected sight.

"Did Charlie actually add a fireplace?" I exclaimed.

"Couple years ago," Michael said. "He

added one onto the side of his living room, which is right upstairs from here, and decided it wouldn't take too much more to add one down here."

"We can make s'mores now," Jamie suggested.

"After dinner," Michael said.

"Can we hang stockings here, too?" Josh asked.

"No, we've already got stockings at home."

"But Santa could come here, too," Josh protested.

"Mommy, listen," Jamie said. "It's our Baptists." He scrambled over to the end table where the soft strains of a choir singing "O Little Town of Bethlehem" were coming from a portable speaker hooked to Michael's iPod. Suddenly "Adeste Fidelis" blasted forth at such incredible volume that we all flinched and Michael hurried to turn the volume down.

"Sorry, Daddy," Jamie said.

"It's okay," he said. "He's learned how to operate the iPod," he added to me.

"I'm impressed," I said. "And that does sound like the New Life Baptist choir."

"It is," Michael said. "I got a couple of sound techs from the drama department to record the Saturday night concert. They've cleaned up the files, and now you can buy a copy of the concert on the church Web site for a small donation to their cleanup fund."

"Fabulous," I said.

Since the kitchen really was too small for more than one person, the boys and I sang along with the Baptists while Michael finished the dinner preparations. Finally a timer went off, and he ran upstairs with potholders, then returned carrying an enormous roasting pan.

"Turkey's ready," he said as he lifted the lid, filling the entire apartment with the mouthwatering scent of the turkey. "I actually had to borrow Charlie's oven upstairs to cook it in — I'd forgotten how tiny this kitchen is. But for the rolls of refrigerator biscuits — this oven should work fine."

"Mommy, want gwandbewwy sauce," Jamie said.

"Grandberry?" I echoed. "Oh, cranberry sauce. Right. Do you want me to start on the biscuits or —"

Someone knocked on the door.

"Don't answer it," Michael and I said in unison. But Josh, vastly proud of his doorman's job, was already opening the door.

"Gampa!" he exclaimed. "Come eat turkey?"

"If I'm invited." Dad looked plaintive.

Michael and I exchanged looks. He raised

an eyebrow. Well, it wasn't as if we'd been trying to avoid Dad. I nodded.

"You're allowed to stay on one condition," Michael said. "Tell us how you figured out we were here."

"I deduced it." Dad sounded very proud of himself. "This morning at church I was talking to Clyde Flugleman from the turkey farm, and found out Michael had bought a bird, so I knew you were planning something. And then after services, I stopped for gas at Osgood Shiffley's station and overheard him giving directions to a young man who was having trouble finding this address. And when he said he was turkey sitting for his professor — well, I figured it out immediately. But don't worry — your secret's safe with me."

"So much for keeping secrets in a small town," I murmured.

"Have a seat," Michael said.

"I brought some rolls." Dad held up a bag from the Caerphilly Bakery that was large enough to contain a year's supply of bread. "Margie at the bakery made them fresh this morning." He held the bag open slightly and we all sniffed eagerly at the warm, yeasty smell.

"Much better than refrigerator biscuits," I said. "Michael, do we have any wine?"

"Oops," Michael said. "I meant to get some."

"I can go." Dad stood up. "It won't take —"

"No, sit," Michael said. "I can borrow some from Charlie and replace it later."

"Is there anything you want me to do, then?" Dad asked.

"Story," Jamie demanded. He handed Dad the pile of Christmas children's books Michael had brought along to entertain the boys.

Another knock at the door. This time Josh opened it to let in Rob.

"Hey," Rob said. "Any chance of a bite of turkey? I brought a contribution."

He held up a container of ice cream in one hand, and in the other another large bag from the Caerphilly Bakery. From the odor of fresh-baked chocolate that had followed him into the room I suspected the parcel contained either brownies or chocolate chip cookies.

"How did you find us?" I asked. "Not that you're not welcome."

"I knew from the way Dad was acting that he was up to something," Rob said. "So I followed him to the bakery. And then when he left, I went in and Margie told me all about it."

"Oh, dear," Dad said. "It never occurred to me that Margie would spill the beans."

Rob shrugged.

"I'll take those." I relieved him of his parcels. Yes, I was right — brownies *and* chocolate chip cookies. Rob made a beeline for the fire.

"Before you get too comfortable, go upstairs and get a couple more chairs," Michael said, handing Rob a key ring.

"Can do." He bounded out, forgetting to close the door behind him.

" 'Twas the night before Christmas,' " Dad began. " 'When all through the house.' "

"I'm not sure I can fit the ice cream in the freezer," I said.

"Stick it outside the door," Michael said. "It won't melt out there. And while you're at it, shut the door, will you?"

" 'Not a creature was stirring —' "

I stashed the ice cream outside and was turning to come back in when —

"Hello?"

I looked up to see Rose Noire carefully coming down the narrow stairway with a huge covered bowl in her hands.

"Now I know you didn't come for the turkey," I said. Roast turkey was only one of many reasons I couldn't imagine becoming a vegetarian, but Rose Noire never even seemed tempted.

"Heavens, no!" Rose Noire shuddered slightly. "But I am fond of mashed potatoes and cranberry sauce and pumpkin pie. I brought a big salad."

"How in the world did you find us?" I asked.

"That nice Mr. Gardner who lives upstairs bought half a dozen special gift baskets to take to his mother and aunt and sisters," she said. "And when I delivered them yesterday morning, he was down here tidying up a bit, and he told me how sweet it was that his friend was borrowing his old bachelor apartment to have a quiet little Christmas dinner with his wife and twin sons. I knew it had to be you. He probably didn't know we were related. And I wasn't going to barge in until I realized from the hints he was dropping that your father knew and was planning to come."

"He was dropping hints?" I winced. "We'll have the whole family here before long."

"I doubt if any of the others know about Mr. Gardner," she said.

"Well, come in," I said. "We'll have to send Rob back upstairs for more chairs."

We'd gotten everyone seated, Dad's reading was keeping the boys entertained, the

434

rolls were warming in the oven, and Michael was beginning to carve the turkey before the next knock came. This time I answered.

"Horace," I said. "Welcome. Did you follow Dad or Rob or Rose Noire?"

"Actually, I figured from some hints your dad dropped that you guys were up to something," Horace said. "So I put the word out over the department radio and one of the other deputies spotted all your cars here."

"I was not dropping hints!" Dad protested.

"Did you bring anything?" Jamie asked.

"Jamie!" I said. "That's no way to greet a guest."

"Actually, I brought your grandfather and Caroline and Mrs. Waterston, if that's okay," Horace said. "Seems they all have a hankering for an old-fashioned Christmas dinner."

The apartment seemed to get even smaller as they all trooped in.

"Lovely idea," Michael's mother said, handing me a bottle of red wine. "A nice quiet little immediate family event before tomorrow's madhouse."

"Merry Christmas!" Grandfather stepped into the room, holding a second bottle. "Are we in time for dinner?"

"Monty, you old goat!" As she entered, Caroline pretended to swat him with one of the bottles of white wine she was carrying. "You haven't even been asked to stay yet."

"Well, we will be, won't we?" He frowned at me. "You are serving normal food, aren't you? None of this fancy slop."

"Shush!" Caroline hissed.

"Someone go bring the dogs in before they get cold," Michael's mother said. "And the ducks."

"Ducks?" Michael and I spoke in unison, and not without alarm.

Dad and Rob went out and returned. Dad was leading Spike and Tinkerbell, while Rob was carrying a cage containing two ducks.

"Ducks are social animals," Michael's mother said. "Your grandfather thought Ducky Lucky could use a friend."

"Don't worry," Grandfather said. "They're both going back to the zoo with us tonight."

"Now we just need hamsters," Jamie said.

"Guinea pigs," Josh contradicted.

"Okay," Jamie said. "Hamsters *and* guinea pigs."

"I suppose we should be glad they didn't bring the llamas," I muttered.

"Not yet, anyway," Michael said.

"Have a seat, everyone, if you can find one," I said aloud. "Rob, more chairs."

"I'll keep slicing," Michael said.

"Put these on ice," Caroline said, handing me her wine bottles. "Monty, Dahlia, give her the red wine. We should open one to let it breathe a little before dinner."

We kept Rob busy ferrying chairs, dishes, glasses, and silverware down from Charlie's kitchen. He even found a card table upstairs, and a tablecloth large enough to cover both it and the small parson's table that had served Michael and me as both dining table and desk. At last we were all seated, a little tightly packed, but most of us had at least enough space to set down our glasses, if not our plates. The ducks were perched on the coffee table, where they could see the meal — I hoped they either didn't notice we were eating turkey or weren't sentimental about their distant cousins. We'd put food and water down for the dogs, but both preferred to curl up under the table, hoping for handouts. They probably wouldn't be disappointed.

Michael had brought a lot of candles — the LED faux candles we'd taken to using since the boys began walking and grabbing things — and when we finished scattering them all around the room their flickering and the dancing flames of the fire made our makeshift dining table look pretty nice after all.

"Who wants to say grace?" Michael asked.

"God bless us, every one!" Jamie shouted.

"I think that covers the situation," Grandfather said. "I'll take some turkey."

"Gwandbewwy sauce," Jamie said, holding out his plate.

Everyone was so busy passing dishes and waving plates that I was the only one who noticed that someone else had knocked on the door. Rather softly. I was closest, so I went over and opened the door.

Mother. Carrying a small dish.

"Hello, dear," she said.

"Mother," I said. "What a surprise."

Behind me all conversation came to a stop.

"Gamma!" Jamie exclaimed.

"Gamma want turkey?" Josh asked.

"Such a nice idea," Mother said. "Tomorrow's dinners will be so big and formal. A nice little intimate gathering tonight is just the thing."

"A lot less intimate than they were planning," Grandfather said. "With all of us barging in."

"Monty!" Caroline said, swatting him for real.

"I assume Meg and Michael were keeping their plans close to the vest to avoid having too big a crowd," Mother said. "And no doubt would have invited all of us had the unfortunate events of the last day or two not distracted them from getting everything ready as they planned."

Did she really believe that, or was she just giving us a graceful out?

"We should have realized that if we'd reached out, all of you would have been happy to pitch in," I said loud. "As you have without even being asked. Just one question, Mother: How did *you* find out where and when we were having this?"

"I have my methods, dear." She smiled very sweetly, and I knew it was no use. She'd never tell.

"Rob, fetch another chair," I said.

"Roger," he said, and raced out.

"I was planning to surprise you with a small, plain turkey at my dinner," she said. "Will you still want to eat turkey tomorrow?"

"I can always eat turkey," I said.

"I could eat a whole turkey, Gamma," Josh said.

"Me, too," Jamie added.

"I brought tomato aspic," Mother said handing me the bowl. "I know it's always been one of your favorites."

As I nudged dishes aside to find a place

for the aspic, Mother stood for a few moments, surveying the apartment. Back when Michael and I had been living there, she had disapproved of it so strongly that she'd showered us with paint and fabric samples and so many decorating books that we'd taken to using stacks of them for our end table and coffee table. I never had managed to convince her that no amount of decorating would make the place any bigger. She reached out toward one of the boys' posters — one that was particularly crooked — and I had to bite my tongue to keep from telling her to leave it alone; I liked it that way.

But she only smoothed down the tape to make sure it was securely fastened and nodded with approval before sitting down at what had been Rob's place. Rob raced back in with another folding chair and found a place to put it where he could set his plate atop the duck cage.

"My, this is nice." Mother surveyed the table with an equally approving eye. "Perhaps I should go retro next year. A very traditional holiday dinner."

I saw Michael's mother frown slightly, and her face took on a familiar competitive look. Dare I hope that next year would see a duel over who could serve not only the most elaborate but the most traditional dinner?

"Merry Christmas, everyone!" Mother said.

She lifted her wineglass — well, it had been Rob's wineglass, but it was hers now. We all followed suit, even the boys, who were drinking cranberry juice in their stemmed glasses.

"Merry Christmas to all," Josh exclaimed.

"And to all a good night," Jamie finished.

ABOUT THE AUTHOR

Donna Andrews is a winner of the Agatha, Anthony, and Barry Awards, a *Romantic Times* Award for best first novel, and three Lefty and two Toby Bromberg awards for funniest mystery. She is a member of MWA, Sisters in Crime, and the Private Investigators and Security Association. Andrews lives in Reston, Virginia.